"Tell me what's going on,"
Katherine demanded.

"All right." Nick looked at her, wondering where he could begin. Finally he settled for the simplest approach. "There's a treasure hidden in the valley, and its location is somehow linked to the writings you're here to translate."

Her eyes widened. "This is all some stupid treasure hunt?" She stood to face him angrily. "I asked you if you were after the gold and silver in the caves, and you said you weren't. And I believed you! Now you're telling me that you dragged me down here to play some stupid *game*!"

"Will you let me explain?"

Katherine cocked her head challengingly. "Will it be the truth?"

"I've never lied to you," Nick said softly, but he knew it wasn't true. He *had* lied, by not telling her things—things like the way he really felt about her.

Dear Reader,

Once again, Silhouette Intimate Moments has something new in store for you. This month we both begin a series that will carry you into the future *and* bring you a book by one of your favorite authors that, for some of you at least, will awaken memories of past pleasures.

Let's start with the new: Lucy Hamilton's Dodd Memorial Hospital Trilogy. Set in a fictional Los Angeles hospital, these three books are all connected by their setting and their cast of characters, but each one also stands alone as a completely satisfying romance in its own right. And who better to tackle such a project than Lucy Hamilton, a former medical librarian who just happens to be married to a doctor? We think these books will excite you so much that once you check into Dodd Memorial, you may not want to check out!

And what about that favorite author we mentioned? Of course she's none other than Nora Roberts. And the book? It's *Irish Rose*, and if that title sounds familiar to some of you, it's because Nora's very first Silhouette Romance was a heartwarming story called *Irish Thoroughbred*. For those of you who recall that first book, this one should provide a welcome trip down memory lane. And for those of you who met Nora through her later works, we think this book will show you why she charmed so many readers right from the start.

Don't miss our other offerings this month, either, because once again we're introducing some new authors you'll be hearing more from in the future. And, as always, keep your eye on the months ahead, when authors like Parris Afton Bonds, Emilie Richards and Linda Howard will be coming your way.

Leslie J. Wainger
Senior Editor
Silhouette Intimate Moments

Mary Anne Wilson
Hot-Blooded

Silhouette Intimate Moments

Published by Silhouette Books New York

America's Publisher of Contemporary Romance

SILHOUETTE BOOKS
300 East 42nd St., New York, N.Y. 10017

Copyright © 1988 by Mary Anne Wilson

ISBN: 0-373-07230-9

First Silhouette Books printing March 1988

America's Publisher of Contemporary Romance

Printed in the U.S.A.

MARY ANNE WILSON

fell in love with reading at ten years of age when she discovered *Pride and Prejudice*. A year later she knew she had to be a writer when she found herself writing a new ending for *A Tale of Two Cities*. A true romantic, she had Sydney Carton rescued, and he lived happily ever after.

Though she's a native of Canada, she now lives in California with her husband, children, a six-toed black cat who believes he's Hungarian and five timid Dobermans, who welcome any and all strangers. And she's writing happy endings for her own books.

For Tom, who told me I could.
For Anita, who never let me give up.

Prologue

June—the Upper Amazon region of Brazil

A world of pain surrounded Nicholas Dantry. His shoulders and back muscles contracted spasmodically, and his arms knotted, the tendons standing out like heavy cords. His bloodied hands clutched a gnarled root that grew out of the valley wall, the full weight of his two hundred pounds supported by numbed fingers and wrists that felt ready to dislocate.

Nick tried to think, to figure out how long it had been since he'd lost his footing and plunged off the overgrown jungle trail that cut down into the valley, but time eluded him. It had no validity here. A second seemed like an eternity—an eternity like a second. He tried to breathe, to make his lungs take in a full ration of the heavy air. The tangle of roots and vines that kept him from plummeting into the jungle bottomland more than a hundred feet below seemed horribly flimsy.

Nick closed his eyes tightly for protection against the red glare of the Brazilian sun that cut through the high canopy of overhead branches. The brilliant light brought unbearable heat and humidity, and caused perspiration that stung as it trickled from his thick black hair down his face and across a throbbing abrasion on his left cheek.

His numbed legs lacked the ability to find toeholds, and his injured hands, his only support, throbbed in time with the thundering echo of each heartbeat. Nick knew he could endure the pain, but the insidious weakness began to frighten him.

Willing his hands to keep their grip on the fragile lifeline, Nick called into the untamed emptiness above. Over and over again, his screams echoed in the hot air until his voice became a hoarse croak and his fingers began to slip. Nick twisted, frantically tightening his hold on the fibrous vines, and his breathing became shallow and insufficient.

He'd thought about death before, several times, but in the abstract, in the deep of night long after he'd survived danger. But now death stood in front of him, biding its time. It had become a real enemy. And it had chosen to come for him in this savage land. There would be no flaming exit, no spectacular end. Just a simple slip of his hands, then the fall into oblivion. Because of that, he raged against it, against the very idea of giving up his existence.

No, he wouldn't accept this. It had to be a dream. Something would happen; something would change.

So Nick clung to the vines and waited. But nothing happened—no deliverance, no answers, no miracles. He was definitely wide awake, he knew, and weakness seeped into his soul as pain and fear finally came. Tears mingled with the dripping perspiration on his face.

Nick hadn't cried since childhood. Strangely, he remembered the very day.

"Nicholas, Nicholas." A voice echoed from his past, his mother talking softly to him at his eighth birthday party when he'd fallen from his new bike and tried to hide his tears. *"Boys can cry. Sometimes it helps the little hurts to go away."*

"What about the big hurts?" he wanted to ask the memory, the mother who hadn't been there for his next birthday. "What about dying?"

He shuddered; the boy and the man merged and at that moment, deep inside, he realized he couldn't hide from death this time.

Suddenly there was a flash against his closed eyelids, and he forced them to open a slit, squinting upward at a distorted shadow. *I'm delirious.* He chuckled with faint hysteria, and his fingers started to slip.

A figment of my imagination, he reasoned, despite the swift movement of a blurry figure over him. Then a hand closed over his hand, a rope was looped around his wrist, and he was pulled upward.

The relieved laughter that filled his being came out in a sob. All that mattered was that he'd done it. He'd beaten the odds again. He wouldn't die today.

Chapter 1

One year later...

The man is crazy."

Kate Harding made her pronouncement slowly, allowing each syllable half a second on her tongue while she stared out the window of the book-lined study. With her back to her father, who was working at his large cherry-wood desk, she took a deep breath. "Nicholas Dantry is definitely crazy."

Jon Harding kept his eyes on the open ledger in front of him and asked, "What was that, Kate?"

"Nothing, Dad." She sighed as she crossed her arms over her breasts, mussing the ivory silk of her blouse. She shifted, the nap of the worn Oriental carpet soft under her stocking feet. "I was thinking out loud about the meeting tonight." Her naturally husky voice held an edge of perplexity. "I've been trying to figure out what sort of business proposition a man like Nicholas Dantry could have for me."

"A man like what?" Jon asked a bit absentmindedly.

"A crazy man who risks his life for fun, on a whim. He's got everything, but he doesn't care if he dies," she murmured.

"Oh, I suspect he cares," Jon countered. "Sometimes the very thing we fear the most is the thing we constantly run after and challenge."

"Maybe." Her golden eyes scanned the campus of Drake College through the windows of the old white bungalow. The gentle softness of twilight shrouded the old brick buildings and the grassy expanse of the quadrangle with a certain shadowy grandeur. "Strange that he would call me. I had no idea he knew I exist, much less that I do free-lance work."

"It sounds intriguing to me," Jon said, making notations in the margin of the ledger.

"It's intriguing, all right." Kate caught at a strand of the hair that tumbled freely in an auburn cloud around her shoulders and partway down her back. She began to twist a lock around one slender finger—a nervous habit carried over from childhood. In silence she watched bare wisps of fog drift inland from the northern California coast twenty miles away to halo the security lights as they flashed to life. She finally spoke up. "I wonder why I agreed to the meeting at all."

"Natural curiosity," Jon suggested as he sat back in the swivel chair and closed the leather-bound book. "An inborn need to know everything there is to know about anything. A trait you get from my side of the family."

"Curiosity?" she asked as she turned to find her father smiling at her. "From your family?"

He nodded and ran his fingers carelessly through the thick thatch of pure white hair that framed his thin face. "Yes. From the Hardings."

"It was Mother's great-uncle James who was a private detective," she countered.

Jon waved a hand in dismissal. "My family was much too proper to go into anything as crass as peeping through people's windows to make a living." He lifted a brow. "Some might call us stuffy, but the Hardings have always had true intellectual curiosity...the kind that makes you look for answers in books. And you're a Harding."

Kate wasn't at all sure that she liked being called stuffy. Maybe she could accept traditional or normal or rational. "True intellectual curiosity. A nice phrase."

"You have it, that and a real gift for languages."

"And just how would a man like Nicholas Dantry know about my 'gift'?"

Jon quirked one brow. "Maybe from someone you've done work for at one time or another. You've got a growing reputation, and the field of linguistics isn't exactly huge."

"He certainly insisted on this meeting. 'I can't wait until Monday,' he said. 'Time is of the essence.' He all but cut me off when I tried to make the meeting for next week."

Jon stood and stretched to ease his cramped muscles. "The man's in a rush. So this must be very important to him...one way or another. Of course, our idea of important and his might be two different things." He glanced at the wall clock that hung next to the sliding doors. "In about two hours you'll find out if he needs you to translate French menus or German business papers."

Kate leaned back, half sitting on the window ledge behind her, her arms still crossed. "French menus?" she asked with one finely drawn brow lifted expressively, a gesture that perfectly mimicked her father's of a moment ago. "Well, you're right. I'll find out soon enough. It's intriguing, but I doubt that I'd take on any job he has, anyway."

Her father watched Kate intently. "Why? You're looking for extra work, aren't you?"

"Of course I am. But I really want to start on my doctorate next year. I've wasted enough time."

"Exactly." Jon nodded. "You've got your life all planned, and you have since you were ten years old. So if you need the money of a Nicholas Dantry to make that plan work, what does it matter as long as what he wants you to do is legal? That's all you have to know."

"You're right. Business is business." She fingered one tiny pearl earring. "His money's as good as the next person's. He's lucky just to be around to offer anyone a job, though. Last thing I heard he was in a terrible car crash. He went off the road in France somewhere, and he walked away from this tangled mass of metal with only a few scratches. He didn't even have to stay in the hospital for very long." She wrinkled her nose in disgust, and muttered sarcastically, "He said the car he ruined lasted longer than most of his did. A one-man wrecking crew."

Jon looked at her with a shade of surprise. "I didn't know you kept track of the man's life."

Kate shrugged off his words. "News is news, and it's hard to miss the stories when the press makes such a fuss over him." Kate didn't want to talk about the ways Nicholas Dantry had made the news over the years, so she changed the subject completely. "How does the budget look for next year?"

"Better all the time," Jon said with obvious satisfaction. "We have almost all the money we need for the new construction. Look at this," he said, opening the ledger to show columns of figures put precisely in order.

Kate looked over his shoulder, and while he explained the budget, a picture from a year and a half ago superimposed itself over the columns of figures. A full-color photo of Nicholas Dantry on the "Stars In Our World" page of a national magazine. It had shown a tall, lean man in dusty jeans and a black sweater. A white bandage, stark against bronzed skin, covered his left temple and was partially hidden by errant curls of mussed ebony hair worn a shade too long. His eyes, a startlingly clear blue-gray, looked right into the camera, and a smug smile that seemed to say, "You didn't think I'd make it, did you?" touched his wide mouth with pure pleasure. Dantry stood in front of a white building giving the thumbs-up sign.

The caption accompanying the photo ran along the edge of the glossy page.

Nicholas Dantry, 37, leaves a French clinic two hours after admission for injuries sustained in an accident on a side road overlooking Monte Carlo. Dantry walked away from the wreck of his Lotus with only a slight concussion and facial abrasions. It went out of control on a curve and plunged twenty feet over the side of the road, flipping three times before coming to rest at the bottom of a ravine. "Missing by an inch is as good as missing by a mile. All that matters is that the Lotus isn't the car I'm backing in the Grand Prix tomorrow," Dantry joked as he spoke to reporters outside the hospital.

Kate blinked rapidly, shocked at how completely she had remembered the photo and the caption. She would just bet that no one in this world had ever considered calling Nicholas Dantry stuffy, much less normal or traditional. "Crazy" seemed to fit him very well, however. With more than enough money for any one person, the brains behind Dantry International chose to play games with death. Crazy.

"I'm not good with figures," Kate murmured as she stepped back quickly and brushed a hand over her eyes.

"Suffice it to say that we have more than enough," Jon said as he closed the book and turned to face Kate. He inclined his head to one side. "You know, I'm pleased that you're going to take your doctorate in Los Angeles. Maybe you'll branch out a bit. I've never believed a child of mine could be so focused on one thing." He shrugged. "I thought Mike might have changed that, but . . ." He let the thought trail off, a thought he'd voiced many times before.

Kate had been engaged to Michael Dean for over a year. Yet now, six months later, the man seldom entered her thoughts unless her father brought him up. "All Mike did was make me realize that I didn't really love him," she admitted with no bitterness. "And I really ought to thank him for that. It saved us both from making a mistake."

"Love?" Jon asked softly. "You seemed perfect for each other."

Kate sighed. "Mike *was* perfect." She knew how honest that response was. Michael Dean had been perfect in every way. A professor of science, pleasant looking, kind, even tempered, encouraging her to get her Ph.D. some day. Perfect. Until he informed her that he was going to take a teaching position in Chicago. He'd stood in front of her, calmly saying that they'd move to Chicago after a small wedding ceremony in California. That he'd settle into his position there while she made a home for them. She could teach later, maybe at some small school, and she could go back for her advanced degree after his career was established.

Kate could still remember the moment when she realized she wasn't going anywhere with Mike. Strangely, she hadn't been terribly shocked to realize that she hadn't loved him with the single-mindedness it would have taken for her to put her own goals on a back burner. She doubted that she would ever love anyone enough to change her life completely for him.

Mike. She tried to conjure up an image, but although Nicholas Dantry's picture had come to her very clearly only moments ago, Mike's face blurred and eluded her.

"Mike *was* perfect," she repeated. "Perfect for someone else. He's doing well in Chicago, and I'm doing just fine here."

"You don't regret letting him go?" Jon prodded.

"No, not at all." I'm comfortable here, Kate almost said, then realized that the statement sounded just a bit stuffy, so she settled for, "I'm perfectly happy here with you, and I'll be back after I get my degree. I'm not like Andrew or Mark. I'm not going to desert you."

Jon frowned at that. "Your brothers didn't desert anyone. They both went out into the real world."

"I know, but..."

"You're young. You've got plenty of time to spread your wings, to get out into the world. Who knows, you might meet another man, and the next time it will work out."

Kate shook her head. "I hope not," she muttered and meant it. She knew what she was doing with her life, and she didn't need any distractions, not now. "I'm going to meet with Mr. Dantry. Heaven knows he's no Mike," she stated and began to coil her hair around her finger again. "All I need is to get through this meeting." She shrugged, her thoughts back on a crazy man who thought a brush with death was a joke. "I couldn't cancel it if I wanted to, actually. He said he'll be out of reach of a telephone until he gets here."

Her father watched her carefully. "All you have to do is hear the man out, then decide if you want to take on whatever work he offers you. It's that simple. You're twenty-six and intelligent. You'll do fine."

"Thanks for the vote of confidence." She smiled.

Jon reached for the ledger, then turned back to Kate, his thin face creased with concentration. "I just remembered. I heard something about Dantry recently. Hasn't he been somewhere in South America?"

"He's probably trying to negotiate to run speedboats up the Amazon," she retorted before she could stop her words.

Jon shook his head slowly. "Maybe when you finally meet the man, you'll find out that he's only human, like all of us."

She held up her hands in mock surrender. "You made your point. Anyway, I'm painfully practical, as you've pointed out repeatedly, and I'll be good, I promise. I won't make any judgments until I've heard him out."

"That's my girl," Jon said and turned to go.

Kate watched her father stride out of the room, then quickly crossed the room and stepped into the tiny foyer. She reached for her navy cardigan. A walk in the cool night air sounded inviting. Kate glanced at the wall clock. An hour and forty-five minutes until the meeting.

* * *

As the bell-tower clock sounded eight, Kate approached the house again. The chimes echoed around a campus deserted for summer vacation and blanketed by fog that blurred the shadowed buildings and trees.

She stepped onto the grass of the quadrangle, her low-heeled brown pumps sinking into the soft turf. A cool breeze that came with the fog ruffled her loose hair as she looked up at the house ahead, its lines muffled by fog and darkness. Then she stopped. A dark Mercedes sedan stood under one of the old olive trees that framed the entry gate to the bungalow.

Slowly, Kate approached the car. In the soft light its sleek black finish seemed to shimmer from tiny beads of water that misted over it. Kate hesitated, then walked around the elegant car to the gate and stepped onto an uneven brick path that led to the front steps. As she got closer she saw a dark silhouette waiting near the stairs.

In the weak glow of the porch light, she could make out no more than the large frame of a man who stood at least three inches over six feet, towering over her own five-seven. The man turned to face her as she approached him. Something flared in the darkness, then fell to the ground, and at the same moment, Kate caught the vaguely sweet scent of cigar smoke. Her stomach knotted uncomfortably, but she made herself keep walking.

"Mr. Dantry?" she asked as she approached from the darkness.

He glanced at his wrist. "Yes, and you're right on time," he said in a voice as deep as the shadows.

Kate nodded as she passed him, catching another hint of cigar smoke mingled with expensive after-shave and the crisp freshness of night air. "You said eight o'clock," she tossed over her shoulder as she climbed the porch steps and reached for the door. The cold brass knob sent a chill through her, and she hurried inside. Taking off her sweater, she turned to Nicholas Dantry.

Her first clear look at the man made her think how ineffectively a photo duplicates the reality of a person. Despite his size, he looked elegant in a perfectly cut, midnight-blue suit. His deeply tanned face contrasted sharply with his blue-gray eyes, which were direct, yet totally unreadable.

"I'm sorry to intrude on your weekend, Miss Harding, but I won't take much of your time," he said as he closed the door behind him.

Kate turned quickly, nervousness affecting the steadiness of her hands as she hung the cardigan on the coatrack. "We can talk in here," she murmured, heading into the study.

The room held the faint fragrance of wood smoke, a remnant from the fire her father had started hours ago. Despite the fact that it was the last week of June, the old house held coolness well into the day, sometimes never losing the chill. Across the room from the desk, two leather chairs faced each other in front of the fireplace. Kate crossed to the closest one, sank into it and, without looking up, motioned Nicholas Dantry to the other chair with a flick of her hand.

Moving quietly for such a large man, Nick sat and took his time settling into the wingback chair. He tugged on his starched white cuffs and stretched his long legs out in front of him. If Kate had matched his move, their feet would have tangled somewhere under the tiny table that separated the chairs. Instead, she tucked her feet back protectively, smoothing the pleats of her skirt with restless fingers. Just as she'd expected, she was out of her league with Nicholas Dantry.

Steeling herself, she looked up. "What did you want to talk to me about?" she asked in a voice to which she managed to give a businesslike edge.

His penetrating gaze held her amber eyes just a fraction of a second too long and made Kate slightly giddy. Then he spoke and the world settled. "You don't beat around the bush, do you?"

Kate tensed inside. "No, I guess I don't." Two could play that game. "Maybe it's because I don't have the vaguest idea why you're here. You didn't give me any details on the telephone.''

Nick rested his strong hands on the leather chair arms, his long tanned fingers devoid of any rings. Why had Kate assumed that a man of his sort would wear flashy gold and diamonds? "I didn't expect you to read my mind," he said evenly.

"Good, because I can't."

The tinge of sarcasm was met by the raising of one dark brow, yet he didn't show any annoyance when he spoke. In fact, his voice sounded vaguely placating. "I'm afraid I have an aversion to doing business on the telephone. I like to look people in the eye when I talk to them." He paused. "The strange thing is, now that I'm here, I'm not quite sure how to go about this."

Kate sat back, spreading her hands flat on her skirt to still their nervous movement. "Why don't you begin at the beginning?"

"The beginning? Good idea." A spontaneous smile transformed his face for a fleeting moment; then it died, as if it had never been. Despite his words, he didn't begin immediately. Instead he tugged at his tie. "I hate these things," he muttered, loosening the knot and undoing the top button of his shirt. "I was at a business meeting before I came here. That's why I had to make this appointment so late. As it was, I left some annoyed members of the board behind."

"I could have met you Monday at your office."

"No, this isn't corporate business, and I wouldn't have expected you to fly down to Los Angeles. It was easier for me to fly up."

He had given no hint that he wasn't in the area when he called earlier. "You flew up here?"

He nodded. "An hour flight to San Francisco International, then another hour's drive in a rented car."

The Mercedes out in front was a rented car? She wondered a bit uncharitably why the man had chosen a sedan rather than a sports model. "If this isn't corporate business, then...?"

"Strike all of that." He shook his head. "I'm sorry. That isn't the beginning. You are."

"Pardon me?"

"I came to make you an offer for your services as a linguist to help me with a problem I've come up against."

"A problem?"

He sat straighter. "The beginning is that I want you to know I've had you thoroughly investigated. That needs to be out in the open."

"I . . . you . . . ?" she stammered, shock making it impossible to get anything coherent past her lips.

"Secrecy is imperative for this job, so it follows that I had to make sure I was safe coming to you with my proposition."

Kate tightened with indignation as his words sank in. Did he think the world revolved around him? "I'm not at all sure I want to hear any proposition you might have for me," she said, matching his bluntness.

He held up both hands, and another jolt hit Kate. His palms weren't smooth and soft, but heavily callused and faintly scarred. "That needed to be said because I don't want it to come up later and cause difficulties." He sighed. "Today I seem bent on tackling problems from the side instead of head-on. Will you listen for a minute while I try to explain?"

Despite her indignation, something about the situation had begun to intrigue her. And there was something about the man himself. She didn't understand either reaction, but it couldn't hurt to simply listen. "All right, go ahead."

"Thank you," he murmured, resting his hands on the taut material that covered his thighs. "What I'm about to tell you has to be kept just between the two of us."

He waited until Kate nodded agreement before he continued. "I've approached others with this offer. Some wouldn't agree to confidentiality, and others just wouldn't consider the job. That's why I didn't want to wait to approach you. If you won't do it, I've got to keep looking."

Kate narrowed her eyes slightly, trying to blur the sharp edges of the man. She wished that she didn't feel overwhelmed simply by his physical presence. She'd never felt that way with another man before, and she didn't know how to deal with it. So she focused on one thing—the spot where his shirt parted and his pulse raced at the hollow of his throat. In some way it was comforting to her to know that, despite his cool exterior, the man wasn't totally calm. "Go ahead. What's so important to you, Mr. Dantry?"

Nick released an audible breath. "I need a very good translator to help me with some writings that are completely incomprehensible to me."

"I don't see why you would have a problem—"

"You'll see." He took a breath. "First, I want you to know that you're my last choice, not because of your qualifications, but because of your suitability to the situation. I don't want to offend any feminist leanings you have, but I would have preferred a man for this work. The situation isn't simple, and a man would be better equipped to deal with it."

Kate had never been involved in any feminist causes, but she firmly believed in equal pay for equal work and the value of everyone as an individual. Curiosity pricked at her to find out why a man would have been better for this job. "Why *did* the men you approached refuse your offer?"

"A few refused because of conflicts in scheduling. Others just didn't want to do it. One didn't like the idea of confidentiality. He wanted to write some paper about it, and another considered it until he heard my conditions."

"What conditions?"

"The work has to be done in Brazil, completed in less than three months, and, as I said, kept completely confidential."

Kate's curiosity increased with each word Nick spoke. "Is there more?"

"Not really. As far as money goes, I'm willing to pay a thousand dollars a week until the work is done."

The amount staggered Kate. "A thousand a week?"

"A minimum of ten thousand no matter how quickly you finish. Double pay would be in order if the project comes in ahead of schedule."

Kate swallowed hard as a thought came to her. "Is this legal?"

He looked taken aback, as if he'd never heard the word. "What do you mean?"

"Secrecy, lots of money. That sounds a bit..." She let the thought trail off.

He shook his head. "It's not illegal, not in any way. It's important to me. That's all. And I have the money to pay to get what I want."

Nick watched her intently and found himself actually holding his breath. Legal? Not one of the others had asked him that. He'd even been close before, with that man in Phoenix, until the deal had turned sour. But this woman had been smart enough to ask.

He shifted. A woman. Too bad he didn't have an alternative to the titian-haired beauty in front of him. Even though she was taller than average, she radiated a sense of fragility emphasized by the faint dusting of freckles across her straight nose. Her amber eyes held his, and Nick swallowed hard, inordinately aware of every detail of her. Why couldn't she have been a middle-aged spinster? That was what he'd expected from a teacher of linguistics, at least until he saw the age on the report. Then his wish had been for a plain, intense scholar.

Oh, he knew that she was brilliant in the field of languages. It just didn't seem right that she also had a subtle beauty that became more obvious as each second passed.

He'd thought about the issue all the way up on the plane. How could he take a woman back with him and insure her safety? He exhaled. What would she say about the arrangements once they got to the valley? He'd have to deal with that.

For a moment that thought made him seriously consider leaving and continuing the search for a male linguist. There were enough complications without taking back a woman who could fog his mind with responses he'd deliberately put on hold for months. He didn't need—no, he couldn't *afford*—distractions of any sort right now. He had to maintain control of the situation, and her presence in the valley wouldn't change that. He brought his thoughts to an abrupt end. Katherine Harding was a means to an end. Cold, but true.

"And you obviously have ten thousand dollars to spend any way you want to, don't you?" she asked in a soft voice with a trace of huskiness. And maybe touched with a bit of a reprimand.

"It's my money," he said, nodding. "Ten thousand . . . minimum."

He took a slim silver case out of his inner pocket and flipped up the lid. "Do you mind?" he asked as he selected a slender cigar.

She shook her head, and her hair drifted around her shoulders, coming to rest against the soft silk of her blouse. "No, not at all."

Nick took a few minutes to collect himself while he lit the cigar. After he drew deeply on it, he finally looked at her. His eyes narrowed through the drifting smoke.

The truth of the situation was right before him. Katherine Harding was his last hope, the last on his list of ten. His sources had confirmed how talented she was at translations, better than most of the others. She had few emotional ties, no husband. The fiancé was long gone, someplace in Chicago, and there had been no contact with him since he left. She'd never had children. There was just her father and two brothers. She was basically free to go with him, and she had the skill he needed.

He drew on the cigar again, then sat back, his eyes never leaving her. The bottom line was that he would be willing to pay just about anything to get her to come back to the valley with him. But that didn't affect the businessman in him, who knew better than to oversell. He sat very still and controlled the foolish impulse to offer twenty or thirty thousand dollars. "You'll probably make more than that . . . if you're as good as I've been told."

Ridiculously long dark lashes swept low to hide the expression in her eyes. For a moment Nick was certain her answer would be no, but when she looked directly at him again, it was to ask, "You'd pay that much for a hobby?"

"No, not a hobby, a very important part of my . . ." He stopped himself. He didn't know how far to go in the explanation. "Let's leave it for now that it's important to me." Sitting forward, he drew his legs back and rested his elbows on his knees. Katherine—he couldn't begin to think of her as the "Kate" mentioned in the reports—waited, watching him, and he knew she was taking in every detail about him. He'd had a sense of being under scrutiny since the moment she'd stepped out of the fog, and it wasn't a particularly flattering scrutiny, either.

Actually, he felt relieved that she had allowed him to get this far. But something in him, that part that always chose the bluntly honest path, nudged at him. It did no good to paint pretty pictures, to lure her with money. If she found out he'd lied, or even that he'd made things seem better than they were, she could turn around and leave him in the lurch. He hated taking the chance of putting her off, but he knew better than to withhold anything.

"What you do need to know is that it won't be pleasant down there. It's not paradise, and it's not easy to live with any degree of comfort. It's hot and humid, very nasty at times. There are no cool June days or foggy nights, even though it's their winter. It's the tail end of the wet season, and it still rains a lot." Something stopped him from going into details of what the routine would be at the valley. Later, if she chose to go with him, he could explain. He added simply, "The people and their ways are totally different from those you're used to."

She listened, her eyes never leaving his face, the unusual golden color a rich contrast to her translucent skin. He prided himself on being able to read people by the look in their eyes, and Katherine's hid nothing. Curiosity and confusion showed in equal amounts, with just a dash of what might be fear. "What kind of people?"

"They're Indians, people who don't know, much less care, about what you think of as civilization. You wouldn't be sheltered there the way you have been here. It's the real world in Brazil, a hostile world, not a comfortable, cushiony place. I don't think you could take it, actually." There, it was out.

Her eyes widened, and high color brushed her delicately boned face. "You don't think I could survive there?"

He'd read the reports over and over again. He knew she'd never traveled much, that she'd spent virtually all her life in a closed academic setting. She seemed so delicate, and his stomach tightened to the point that he had a fleeting sense of sickness. He'd never met a woman he'd want to subject to the valley, yet he had no choice. "The report mentioned your life-style here. I've wondered if you could fit into the world down there."

He didn't know what reaction he had expected, but it wasn't this direct gaze that made his skin tingle. "Then why did you bother coming here at all?" she countered.

The situation had gone from bad to worse. He had the immediate idea that he'd better regroup and approach the situation differently. He only wished he could leave the room and walk back in to start all over again. "I need to be completely honest with you about this. I'm not trying to talk you out of it." But I'm doing a pretty good job, he thought ruefully. "I'm just concerned, now that I've met you."

The line of her mouth tightened, and Katherine sat straighter. The color in her face deepened, and her eyes grew brighter. Yet when she spoke, she sounded composed, in control, and that confused him. "I'm not made of china, Mr. Dantry," she said softly. "And I live in the 'real world,' though maybe my definition of reality isn't yours." She paused, and he heard her take a deep breath before she went on. "I've got a feeling that if you can survive there, so can I. If you don't think so, go ahead and look for someone else to help you. Look for a man."

Was it a bluff? The eyes that had been so readable were suddenly baffling. Could she really be passing up the work when such a large amount of money was involved? His reason told him no, yet he didn't have the nerve to call her bluff. So he flicked his all-but-forgotten cigar into the hearth and smiled, a smile that had always been effective with the ladies before. It suddenly seemed important that it work its wiles on Katherine now. "I would hate to keep looking."

She didn't even blink. "Do what you think's best."

And he'd thought she was easy to read. What was going on inside Katherine Harding's mind? He shifted in his chair. She wasn't a woman who could be filed into any clear-cut niche. "You're the last name on my list," he finally admitted, hating the weakness it exposed, so he added quickly, "although I can find others, I'm sure."

He was the one bluffing now. Woman or not, if Katherine was willing to take the chance, he needed her to come with him. "But it would take time, and I really don't have the time to waste." He looked right at her, tried the smile again and put everything on the line. "Will you come with me?"

Chapter 2

Kate held herself in check, ignoring the current of electricity that shot through her when Nicholas Dantry smiled. How could she know so surely that this man didn't smile much, and that when he did, it was probably calculated, meant for his own purposes? She wouldn't be manipulated that blatantly by anyone. But ten thousand dollars—more than enough to finance her doctorate. She could even go back to school a semester earlier than she had thought.

Carefully, she watched the man opposite her. He wanted her to go with him. She didn't need a third party to tell her that, yet he had intentionally almost made it impossible for her to agree. And she could almost feel his uneasiness and urgency to get on with his project.

She studied Nick. She'd meant it when she'd said that if he could survive there, so could she. A man who wore impeccable suits and drove fast cars wasn't into wilderness survival. The Mercedes outside attested to that. The life he lived in Brazil couldn't be that difficult. She knew that it wouldn't be like here, but she didn't doubt that she could endure a few discomforts and get the job he wanted done.

It would certainly make her life easier once it was over. Ten thousand dollars easier.

Until that very moment she had thought it was only a matter of listening to what was offered and then refusing him. Now it was a matter of trying to figure out if it was the right thing for her to do. So what if she *was* stuffy, rational and traditional? She wanted to do it. After all, it would only mean changing her life for a period of a few months.

"Well?" Nick asked, breaking a silence that had been complete for several moments. "Will you do it?"

Despite the increasing tension she felt, Kate had her answer in that instant. She could do it. She *would* do it. She waited a full heartbeat before she nodded.

She didn't know what she expected from Nick—profuse thanks? Excitement? Relief? To her surprise his gray eyes never left her face, not even to blink. Then he asked calmly, "Are you absolutely certain?"

She didn't understand his lack of reaction. "Yes, if you want me. I'll do the best I can for you."

He pressed the tips of his fingers together. "I want you, but I can't allow any slipups. I can't afford to take you down there, then have things fall through."

"I won't expect it to be like home, Mr. Dantry."

"Good, because it won't be," he said quickly. "There's great beauty there, but it isn't like camping in the woods, either."

Was all this going to end with her begging him to take her? she wondered. "Is there another problem?"

He hesitated. "There might be."

Why this hedging? Where had all his bluntness gone? "Are you going to tell me or make me guess?"

The smile flashed again, and a part of Kate wanted it to stay instead of disappearing before it could be fully appreciated. "There's a problem with the way the natives regard women."

She understood. "Women are possessions, another form of property?"

"I'm afraid so. And there's no way around it. Your status there will have to be as my property... at least in their eyes."

No wonder he'd been looking for a man. "Meaning?"

Nick nodded. "If the Indians see you as mine, under my protection, they'll leave you alone. They'll come after me first. That should be enough to keep you safe, but there are never guarantees in this world, are there?"

Kate shook her head, wondering just what she had agreed to. "No, of course not," she murmured. "Just what would it entail?"

"What?"

"Being your property, or at least pretending that's the case."

He considered her with narrowed eyes. "Giving an illusion of obedience to me, of being with me and for me." He held up his hand at the same time that Kate opened her mouth to object. "Just an illusion. That's all. We'll know what the real status of our relationship is." Dropping his hand to the arm of the chair, he shrugged. "It won't affect our work, but the appearance has to be maintained. That's important."

Kate digested what he'd said and had to fight the strangest bubble of laughter that tingled in her middle. His property? She had a sudden mental image of being a racing machine, long, sleek, high-powered. Nicholas Dantry's property. The laughter dissolved into a hard knot in her middle. No, she didn't fit that category.

"I was never good at playacting," she admitted in a voice that had turned strangely flat.

"Don't worry about it. People generally believe what they're told. There's no reason to say more to the Indians than that I bought you, in the literal sense, or I kidnapped you."

The overhead lights glinted off his hair, and Kate knew without having to ask that the man had never had to resort to anything like that to get a woman. "What difference would it make what they think?"

"It would matter. Trust me. It could be a matter of life and death in an extreme case. I told you that the people there are different. And the goodwill of the local inhabitants is a must for what I have to do."

Kate took a vaguely unsteady breath and seized the opportunity to change the direction of the conversation. "Which is?"

"The translations."

"What of?" Kate asked.

"Translations are translations. I know you can do what I need, and I can't go into details yet. Besides, it's easier if you see them yourself. I don't have the background to do them justice verbally."

With that Nick stood abruptly, and Kate scrambled to her feet to face him across the tiny table. He studied her from under lowered lashes, the lines of his face suddenly deeper and more pronounced. "Enough of this. Time isn't a commodity that I have a great deal of right now. I can't guarantee your personal liberty down there, and that's the bottom line." He paused for a long moment, then asked, "Do we still have an agreement?"

Despite everything, an altogether new sensation of excitement tingled somewhere deep in Kate. She knew her own worth, her own value. Did it matter if the Indians didn't see it the same way? This was unlike anything she'd ever considered doing in her life. This was temporary, no emotional ties. Business. And she needed to know something. Did she have a spark of the explorer in her somewhere, a need to go beyond the mere satisfaction of intellectual curiosity? Suddenly she hoped that she did.

Nick, despite his well-cut suit, gave the impression of being a hunter. Kate had no idea how she recognized that part of him, or how she knew that he would doggedly pursue what he wanted.

If he can do it, I can do it, she insisted silently. Aloud, she heard herself saying, "Yes, we have an agreement."

He held out his hand to her. She reached out and was startled by his touch, rough, yet warm and strong. Sure and solid. So unlike the impressions she had had of the man before. It was as if the two images were forging a bond—strange and unfathomable.

"Good." He nodded. The simple word was filled with a world of undisguised relief.

She drew back, pressing her hands together, totally aware of sensations that lingered long after the physical contact had been broken. "I had no idea I would be going off to Brazil with you when you showed up here tonight."

"Your life here must be very... settled," he said. "Very controlled."

"No, it's orderly and sane," she countered.

"What would life be like without a touch of insanity now and then?"

"A lot simpler and safer," Kate breathed.

"And very boring," Nick replied with a smile that lingered just long enough to make its full impact felt.

Two weeks later, at the airport on the outskirts of Manaus, Brazil, Kate waited to begin the last leg of her journey into the upper Amazon Basin. The corrugated tin roof of the dirt-floored hangar gave little protection against the unrelenting midday sun. An ancient soft-drink machine with faded red decals provided the only coolness available.

Kate savored the damp chill of her half-empty soda bottle against her wrist and scanned the dim interior of the building. Empty oil drums had been arranged to make temporary dividers between the four aircraft that shared the space, and an incredible array of spiderwebs connected one overhead metal truss to another. The smell of rancid grease and the pungency of gasoline hung in the humid air. A heavy mustiness overlay everything.

When Kate and Nick had landed on the commercial flight from San Francisco at noon, they had taken their luggage and walked out here. Nick had found their pilot, Valdez, a massive man, well over six feet tall and dressed in white shorts and a crisply pressed shirt. His huge feet were thrust into hemp sandals, and a luxurious mustache more than compensated for the total baldness of his cleanly shaven head.

At first, though Valdez had spoken labored English, he had never once looked directly at Kate, not acknowledging her in any way beyond frowning at her luggage. Finally he had switched to a rough dialect with Portuguese origins, a dialect Kate only had to concentrate on for a few minutes to understand.

But she had one personal rule. Ever since she'd realized that she could understand languages with an ease that most people would never possess, she deliberately avoided listening in on discussions in another language unless spoken to directly. Valdez never made eye contact with, much less talked to, her, so she ignored his conversation with Nick. Two hours later she was still ignoring it as the two men talked while they worked inside the hangar. It was none of her business—yet.

Kate dug at a spot of oil on the packed earth with the toe of her leather sandal, then looked at Nick and Valdez loading supplies into a bright red twin-engine plane. The men worked quickly, the two of them shirtless in the heat, their skin already filmed with moisture. Kate watched Nick lift a box of her reference books. The muscles of his back rippled from the weight, and his powerful shoulders seemed more appropriate for a laborer than a corporate chairman. He was indeed a man of contradictions.

Nick moved again, and sunlight from the open door slashed across the glistening skin of his back. Kate felt her breath catch. Pale, barely visible marks were caught in the light, crisscrossing over his back. More scars like those on his hands? Were they from his accident near Monte Carlo? Or from another time when he'd risked his life for a thrill? She quickly looked away. That was no more her concern than what he said to the bald man working at his side.

After downing the last of her drink, she put the bottle back in the side rack of the cooler and headed out of the hangar. Without a backward glance, she stepped into a blast of suffocating heat. The sun penetrated the thin cotton of her sleeveless blue blouse and shorts, and the accumulated heat in the blacktopped runway radiated through the leather soles of her sandals.

Kate lifted a hand to shield her eyes from the glare as she looked into the distance, past the low airport terminal to the shimmering city on the horizon. "The last outpost of civilization," the travel book had said. This wasn't what Kate had expected from that description. Manaus looked cosmopolitan, clean and white, as if it had a continental flavor. The Rio Negra swept past the city to the upper basin, and a sky of true blue hung over the mixed Portuguese and Indian population.

Kate dropped her hand. As she stepped back into the shade of the hangar to lean against the warm metal of the doorjamb, she closed her eyes against the glare. In the past two weeks she had been drawn along in a whirlwind of activity initiated by Nick—getting her passport and immunizations, sorting through books and clothes, trying to decide what she needed and what she could survive without. And during all of the time she had spent with Nick, both at the college and in San Francisco, she had done most of the talking.

He had a remarkable way of turning around any question she asked him and getting her to talk about herself. If they were walking, he'd give her some vague answer, then touch her arm and ask her where she was going to get her Ph.D. Or he'd announce that all the talking had made him thirsty. "A drink sounds good," he would say with that smile, and before long Kate would find herself sitting in the bar near the college while Nick gave specific instructions for the bartender to shake, not stir, his martini.

The upshot was that she knew little about Nick beyond the fact that his parents had died when he was young, and he'd lived with his grandfather until the old man was gone and Nick had begun to build his business empire. He brushed aside any questions Kate ventured about his lifestyle with, "A life is a life. I live mine the way I want to."

His single-mindedness of purpose about his "project" seemed as intense as Kate had always believed his search for excitement had been. The project. He never spoke specifically about what the project actually entailed. His stock answer seemed to be, "Translations of a puzzle." But what the puzzle was or wasn't never came into his conversation. He simply told Kate there would be no office hours, no regular timetable, and the work would go on until the translations were done.

Her father had been surprised yet pleased at Kate's decision to work for Nick. When the two men met, they had talked for hours.

"He's certainly different than I thought he'd be from what you had said about him," Jon had told Kate when they were alone. "He's smart and intense. And from everything I've been able to find out, he can read French menus."

Kate smiled at the memory. But that smile slipped when she thought back to her last meeting with Nick before the flight out of San Francisco International. He'd been waiting for her in the library, crouching in front of the fireplace, poking at the small wood fire. The night outside had been filled with fog and silence.

Kate had watched him silently from the door for a moment before speaking. He was a man of darkness, dressed in black, from his tailored shirt with sleeves rolled back to his snug-fitting slacks.

Something about him had made her throat suddenly go dry, and she'd had to try to speak twice before she could say his name. As soon as she did, he was on his feet in one smooth motion, turning to her.

It seemed the thing to do to stay by the door, keeping a safe distance between them while they talked. Then Nick came toward her, stopping only inches away.

"There's something else I need to ask you," he'd said, then surprised her by reaching out to her. He touched a single strand of her loose hair, then asked, "Would you cut your hair, Katherine?"

She remembered her own confusion at the request, which had been underscored by his proximity. "P-pardon me?"

"Your hair." He had very carefully lifted the lock of hair, then let it drift off the tips of his fingers. "Will you cut it?"

She'd had to force herself to concentrate on what he was asking and not on what he was doing. "Why?"

"It's hot and humid in the jungle, and you'll be a lot more comfortable with it short."

He'd crossed his arms on his chest, yet Kate had had the idea that at any moment he might touch her again. Her family had never been demonstrative, but Nick seemed to think nothing of making contact with others as he spoke. Fingers on the small of her back, a hand resting on her shoulder while he explained the intricacies of martinis. Kate had found that she braced herself whenever his hands moved. It would take some time for her to accept his touch without being inordinately aware of it.

Right then he had seemed safe enough with his arms crossed, and Kate had tried not to let herself take a step back. She had focused on what he'd asked. No, she wouldn't cut her hair. Changes were coming at such a fast rate, she didn't want one more. Maybe in those last days she had begun to feel as if she didn't quite know herself. Part of her had been filled with excitement about the trip, about going to a new country. Nick had walked into her life and found that part of her. Yet another part had been holding back, uncertain about the changes.

Her hair had been long since childhood, and in some odd way it had become symbolic of the real Kate Harding, the woman who would still be there when Nicholas Dantry was gone. She couldn't let go of that part of herself. It was bad enough that the man insisted on calling her Katherine; she couldn't let herself change the way she looked for him, too. "No, I like it long," she'd murmured, then plunged ahead. "And, by the way, my name is Kate. No one calls me Katherine."

"But it fits you," he'd said matter-of-factly. "To me, you're Katherine."

There had been no room for argument then, and there had been none later. She supposed she could handle being Katherine for the next ten weeks, probably easier than she could handle her long hair, she realized now.

Kate opened her eyes to a runway of shimmering heat. Her hair felt damp and stringy where it had escaped from the fastener that held it in a high ponytail, and the heat felt unbearable against her scalp. For a flashing moment she knew she should have cut it, that she should have listened to Nick's logic. She broke that thought off. No, her time here was limited. She would *not* change who she was.

She turned to go back inside and stepped from the brilliance outside into the gloom of the hangar. Momentarily blinded, she had a flashing sense of movement in front of her and put out her hands in order to avoid a collision. Her palms made contact with sweat-sheened skin and rippling strength. In a flash strong hands caught her by the shoulders to keep her from reeling backward from the impact. As her pupils dilated, Kate looked into amused gray eyes. Nick had slipped his white shirt back on, but he hadn't buttoned it, and her hands were spread on his naked chest. She became aware of taut skin over hard muscle and the rapid beating of his heart underneath her palms. As the contact registered completely, Kate jerked back.

Nick chuckled softly as he patted his middle. "You pack quite a wallop. I hate to think of the damage you could do if you put your mind to it."

Kate fell back another step. "I'm sorry," she mumbled and kept her eyes on his face. It was much more rational to watch his lips until the deeply tanned expanse of his bare chest was hidden by white cotton as Nick finished buttoning his shirt. "I couldn't see for a minute." Rubbing her hands together with more roughness than necessary to dispel the lingering dampness from his skin, Kate muttered, "It's the glare of the sun."

"Down here you'll learn to blame almost everything on the sun or the heat," Nick teased, tucking his shirt into the waist of his jeans with sharp, quick strokes. "We're ready to take off as soon as Valdez taxis to the end of the runway and gets clearance. We'll meet him there.''

The plane's engines sputtered to life at that moment, and Nick walked around Kate to take her by the arm and draw her out into the sun again. They stood to one side as the plane went past; then Nick started after it, pulling Kate with him.

Kate could make out Valdez in the cockpit window, talking into a headpiece, shaking his head vigorously. Even as she watched him, she never quite forgot that Nick still held her arm.

With feigned casualness, Kate moved out of his hold under the pretext of brushing her hair back from her face. She kept walking while she cast a sidelong look at Nick. He was smiling, and his expression annoyed her. ''What's so funny?'' she asked, raising her voice to be heard over the roar of the airplane.

''You,'' Nick shouted back.

Did he know how uncomfortable she felt every time he touched her? She hoped not. ''What are you talking about?'' she yelled, swiping at a trickle of perspiration that trailed down her cheek.

''Your hair. Why didn't you cut it? You're hot and miserable.''

Her relief at the source of his amusement melted her annoyance and allowed her to manage her own smile. ''I've never had short hair, and I like it long.'' Teasing came without her planning it. ''Are the native women as bald as Valdez?''

Nick laughed, a pleasant sound that was lost all too quickly in the roar of the plane. ''Absolutely not. I doubt they ever cut their hair. It's part of the feminine mystique down here. I think Valdez would beat his wife if she showed up bald.''

Her good humor faltered. ''You're kidding! He beats his wife?''

''Well, maybe I am exaggerating a little bit. But don't forget that women's rights don't exist where we're going.''

Nick watched her with a frown. "Katherine, it's important to respect the customs and traditions of these people—no matter how horrifying they seem to you." He stopped walking. "I just thought of something."

"What is it?" Kate asked, turning to face him.

"You wouldn't try to do anything...militant, would you?"

The question threw Kate off balance. "Militant?"

"Trying to get the women to stand up for their rights?"

She almost laughed. "You think I'm going to lead protest marches through the jungle?"

"I didn't mean..."

"Didn't you?" Her smile grew as she looked into the depths of Nick's eyes. "No, Mr. Dantry, I'm here to do a job, not change the world."

Nick looked relieved, but he didn't say anything before he turned to walk slowly toward the plane. It had turned and was facing the runway, ready for takeoff. Nick glanced sideways at Kate, and his mouth moved, but the words were lost in the roar of the engines.

Kate hurried up to him. "Pardon me?"

"I said no one person can change the world. Although Valdez tries." He motioned to the other man and kept walking. "He suggested that I get a female, and then I brought you back. He thinks it's all his doing." A smile touched the corners of Nick's eyes and curved his lips. "And, I might add, he looks on it as a good deal. It has something to do with your chances of having boy-children."

Kate jerked Nick to a stop by grabbing his forearm. Facing him squarely on the runway, she dropped her hand, breaking the impulsive contact quickly. "Hey, that's not funny at all."

"I'm doing my best to let him know you aren't the usual woman. Actually, he thinks you're a bit too thin." Nick seemed to be enjoying Kate's growing embarrassment. "He likes more meat on his women. He says it makes them better for breeding."

"That's disgusting," she snapped.

"Don't look so shocked," he said, leaning toward her so his voice came clearly over the engine roar. "I assured him that neither your ability to have children nor your lack of fat had anything to do with why I brought you down here."

Kate instinctively moved back a fraction of an inch. "Does he think you bought me or kidnapped me?"

Nick shrugged, leaning forward and effectively erasing the bit of space she'd left as a buffer between them. "He can't understand the concept of a man and a woman working together as equals."

Kate felt uncomfortable, so she turned and started for the idling plane. Nick fell in step by her side as she asked, "Why can't he understand? He flies an airplane. That takes brains. He should be able to understand something as simple as me working for you. *He* works for you. I'll have a talk with him and—"

It was Nick's turn to stop Kate in her tracks by taking a firm grip on her upper arm. He spun her around to face him, his features harsh in the unrelenting sun. No humor lingered in the depths of his eyes now. "Oh, no, you won't, Katherine! Valdez is no fool. He's a smart man, and he's a friend of mine, but that doesn't change the fact that he's still an Indian. He's not about to do anything to break their laws." He shouted at her to be heard over the plane's roar. "His relationship with the valley people is excellent. He's like a brother to them. They trust him, and he trusts me. I won't have you upsetting him with your western logic—or your version of it."

"He's not some savage," she yelled.

"That's not the point. He's bound by tradition. If you can't overcome the need to educate him while you're here, maybe you'd better go back." His hold on her tightened, stopping just this side of pain, betraying an intensity for his work that he had hidden all the time they had been readying themselves for this trip. "I won't have anything jeopardize this project," he bit out.

"The project! You haven't even told me exactly what this 'project' is," she countered. "You've told me about the compound, about the housekeeper, Sorrella and her son, Alfredo, who helps you. But you never told me about the work itself—and you didn't tell me about Valdez."

He released her abruptly, and she could see him fighting for control. "If you come with me, I'll tell you all you need to know."

She looked him in the eye. "Tell me again what my status is going to be when we get to your place and the work begins."

He didn't hesitate. "To me, you are my equal. You'll be treated with dignity and respect. And the Indians will value you because you're with me. You won't be hurt or demeaned. Is that enough for you?"

Kate blinked as a trickle of perspiration stung her eyes. "That's it?"

He reached for her again. This time the contact was gentle when his fingers touched her chin, but the rasp of the callused tips brought a shiver that was at total odds with the oppressive heat. "Katherine, isn't it enough to know you're totally indispensable to me, that I'll protect you? I can't control the world. I've tried it before, and I know it's not possible. All I can do is give you my word that I'll always do my best for anyone close to me, and I don't want anyone to get hurt, not Valdez... and not you."

She exhaled, feeling ridiculous standing in the heat debating something that Nick had never tried to hide from her. "That's good enough," she said, shocking herself by the simple truth of the statement. "I'm coming with you."

A deep intensity flared in his eyes just before he leaned toward her, and then his lips touched hers, cool and soft. Her reaction didn't have time to materialize before he trailed his lips along her cheek to her ear. "Thank you," he said for her ears only before drawing back and letting her go. "Now, let's get on with this."

Without giving herself time to analyze what had happened, Kate turned away from Nick and hurried toward the plane. When she paused at the metal step to the side door, Nick cupped her elbow to help her inside. In that moment

Kate would have given the world if he hadn't been a man who touched people, a man who made contact as a way of letting others know he was there. That kiss had definitely made Kate more than aware that Nick was close. Too close.

She was logical enough to realize that the display had been for Valdez's benefit, yet that didn't change the fact that it had left her on edge. She would have to say something to him later.

For now, she knew enough to keep silent as she climbed into the small cabin. She took one of the two back seats in the four-seater space and waited while Nick and Valdez settled in the front. As she sank back she looked at the pilot. Valdez talked to the tower in a form of Portuguese that seemed as fragmented as his English, but Kate understood that they would fly north by northwest, that their estimated time of arrival at a village called São Ana was 4:00 p.m., and that their fuel tanks were full. After a brief static-filled pause, the tower gave them clearance, and the plane started down the runway.

Moments later, as they climbed into the heavens, the land where the awesome river snaked through the jungle shrank away. Kate looked up from the diminishing earth to glance at Nick, who was adjusting something on the control panel. He and Valdez kept up a running conversation, and Kate sat back, content to watch and take in what she could.

She studied Nick. He was a multifaceted man. Without any solid proof, she knew she had been partially wrong about him. She couldn't begin to find the person she had seen in the magazine picture, the driver who had almost died in Monte Carlo. The man with her seemed deadly serious about life. He could be blunt, honest and genuinely funny, and he cared deeply about things. It shocked her to realize that although she didn't really know him or understand very much about him, she trusted him. She never would have come with him to Brazil if she hadn't. Strange that she hadn't realized that until they were almost at their destination.

Instinctively, she touched her fingertips to her lips. It was a show for Valdez, a way of letting the bald man know that she was Nick's. A woman is marked by a man. Was that what the Indians thought? She had no doubt that Nick did mark his women, on one level or another. At that thought, bitterness touched her tongue and she swallowed hard. Right then Nick turned, and Kate quickly dropped her hand to her lap. His clear eyes met hers, and a smile curved his lips.

A wave of pure pleasure at his smile blotted out every other emotion, but it took a moment for Kate to realize that. And by the time her answering smile came, Nick had turned away to talk to Valdez.

A woman marked by Nicholas Dantry. Thank goodness this was all an illusion. Playacting. With that thought to comfort her, Kate turned to the window.

It was five minutes to four when Valdez tapped Nick's arm and pointed west. Kate followed the direction of the gesture and saw a village far below, no more than a postage-stamp-sized splash of white near the tops of soaring green bluffs that plunged down into a deep canyon choked with jungle. A narrow clearing to the south of the village had been leveled for landing, and Valdez banked the plane toward it.

After what seemed to her like an inordinate amount of time the plane touched down and taxied over packed earth to the door of a small Quonset hut that was apparently used as a hangar. The plane slowed, then drove into the deep shade of the building, and as it came to a full stop, Nick stood to reach for the door.

As the door swung back, Kate looked out and found herself facing a very dark-skinned man who held a rifle. And the barrel was leveled right at her middle.

Chapter 3

Rondo! No!" Nick called out from behind Kate as he pushed past her to jump down to the ground in one easy motion. He faced the scowling man who held the rifle and spoke quickly in what was apparently the local dialect. This time it *did* concern Kate, and she didn't even pretend not to listen.

"It is all right," Nick was saying. "I meant for you to watch any strange airplanes that came. Not mine. Do not use the gun. Just watch, Rondo, watch!"

The thin man, who was dressed in green pants and a loose white shirt along with hemp sandals, lowered the rifle. His dark eyes never left Kate. "The female?" he asked in a deep, gravelly voice.

"Mine," Nick said. "Mine. She is with me." He patted the man on the shoulder, then turned to hold out his hand to Kate, who was still standing in the doorway. "It's all right. Rondo is a bit overzealous," he said in English. "Come here."

Kate took the offered hand and felt the roughness of calluses again as Nick's fingers closed around hers; then, in one quick movement, she was on the ground.

Nick leaned toward her, still holding her hand tightly, and kissed her. It was all over so quickly that she hardly had time to take a breath; then Nick whispered to her, "He's got a gun. I really want him to believe that you're my female."

She understood immediately, but that didn't stop her face from flooding with color. "I understand," she said in a low voice and looked at the man. He lowered the gun, but still held it by his side, and he never stopped staring at Kate.

She found herself staying very close to Nick and realized that he was still holding her hand. "Why does he have a gun?"

Nick spoke to the man quickly in the dialect. "It is all right."

With a slanted look at Kate, the man turned and headed toward the door. Nick didn't answer Kate until Rondo was out of the hangar and disappearing into the glare of the sun. "He's a guard of sorts. He watches things here while Valdez and I are gone."

Kate wasn't in any hurry to let go of Nick, not just yet. "Other planes fly into here?" she asked and tugged at her blouse with her free hand to loosen the fabric from her damp skin. She could taste the saltiness of Nick's kiss on her lips.

"No, we're it," Nick said. "São Ana isn't exactly on the main route to anywhere."

Kate glanced around the building, empty except for the plane and an old jeep parked to one side of the doors. The scent of musty earth and heavy heat mingled to tickle at her nose. She returned her attention to Nick. "No, I guess it wouldn't be," Kate murmured. She finally made herself draw her hand away from Nick's casual hold when she had to move to let Valdez get out of the plane. "It's awfully hot," she said a bit stupidly.

Nick nodded. "And it doesn't get much cooler." He looked toward Valdez and motioned to the cargo door. "Let's get everything unloaded."

The bald man twisted the latch and let the cargo door drop open to expose the tightly packed boxes and suitcases. Without a word he and Nick began to methodically transfer the cargo to the jeep.

Kate watched for a moment, then followed Nick to the jeep, where he deposited one of the boxes. "We're driving this?"

"We sure are," he called over his shoulder as he headed back to the plane for another load. "It's four-wheel drive and takes the terrain without too much trouble."

Kate touched the dusty metal fender with its oxidized green paint and looked at the large, heavily lugged tires that held the jeep well above the ground. A black canvas top stretched over heavy roll bars, and a welded luggage rack protruded from the rear. Using a discarded rag that had been draped over the side mirror, Kate began to dust the rock-hard seats.

In a short time everything was packed, and Valdez all but pushed Kate out of the way and swung up into the passenger seat of the jeep. Nick got in the other side, then glanced at Kate, who had taken a step backward to avoid a collision with the big man. He spoke quickly to Valdez in dialect.

Kate quickly translated what was being said. "There is a space in the back," Nick pointed out while Valdez settled into the seat. "Could you sit back there so Katherine...?"

The man's immediate response was a sharp shake of his gleaming head. "Are you touched by the sun, brother? A female riding in the front?" His tone emphasized his shock. "Brother, you cannot do a thing like that, not in front of all the village."

Nick nodded, his whole demeanor placating. "You are right, of course." He turned to motion Kate into the back seat. "Sorry," he said in English, "but..."

She didn't miss the glint of amusement in his eyes. "I understand. A female's place." She pulled herself into the back by gripping the roll bar and swinging up. "Drive on," she muttered as she settled between the boxes.

"Take heart, Katherine, he didn't suggest that you walk ten paces behind the jeep," Nick commented with a quick smile before turning to start the engine.

They drove out of the hangar, across the packed earth of the runway, then turned northward and entered the village. They passed Rondo walking by the side of the road, the rifle swinging from his hand. With a wave at Nick, the man turned off into the brush.

They went forward slowly, passing a cluster of thatched-roof huts built of thick mud, washed a blinding white. Their route took them along a deeply rutted path that meandered under palm and banana trees and through a tiny plaza, where brilliant blossoms cascaded over stone walls and up into the trees. The oppressive heat was incredibly uncomfortable, since little speed was possible on the rough road.

Kate saw only a scattering of villagers, beautiful dark-skinned people with flat features, black eyes and voluminous clothes fashioned from materials in every bright color imaginable. They stood silently in the shadowy doorways of their homes, intently watching the noisy jeep pass by.

At the far side of the village Nick pulled up in front of a house that was a bit larger and nicer than the others. Its narrow windows were draped with lace, vines climbed the thick walls to splash brilliant color on the pristine whiteness, and some emerald-colored ground cover gave the semblance of a lawn between the house and the dusty road.

As soon as the jeep stopped, Valdez vaulted out, landing squarely on the ground, and shouted, "Rosa! Rosa!"

In a flash, a short, plump girl with straight black hair flowing around her childish face and partway down her back came to the door. Valdez's daughter, Kate decided. At the sight of the large man the girl squealed with delight and darted out into the sun. Her vibrant purple shift billowed out behind her as she literally threw herself into his arms. She hugged Valdez tightly before moving back to talk rapidly to him, repeatedly patting his chest with her tiny hand to emphasize her words.

Valdez listened for a moment, his whole attention on the girl. He nodded over and over again and spoke quietly. Finally he turned to point to the jeep. Rosa peeked around Valdez to get a better look at the idling vehicle, cocking her head to one side, and her dark eyes widened as she took in Kate's presence. Her quick glance at Nick was accompanied by a smile before she walked slowly toward the jeep. She stopped, clasped her hands at her full waist and stared at Kate.

"Who is this female?" she asked in the local dialect, her liquid black eyes never blinking in their appraisal.

Valdez came up behind Rosa, resting one large hand on the curve of her shoulder. "Our brother has brought back a female."

"It is about time," the girl said bluntly.

Kate sat very still, afraid to move in case she did or said the wrong thing. She felt lost in a sea of unfamiliarity. The world had changed more in one day than it ever had before in all her life.

A smile flashed under the bald man's thick mustache. "Valdez told our brother to get a female, and he did not make a bad choice, eh?"

"This is good," Rosa pronounced matter-of-factly. "Very good," she said, then proceeded to shock Kate by leaning forward to poke Kate sharply in the shoulder with one finger. "A good female."

Kate couldn't stop her hands from clenching in her lap, and she darted a look at Nick. He seemed to be watching the girl calmly. Kate knew there would be no help coming from him, so she looked back to Rosa, deciding right then that she wasn't going to sit there like a prize animal being judged. "Hello, I am Kate," she ventured slowly in dialect.

Rosa blinked with shock and gripped the jeep with both hands. Up close, Kate could tell that Rosa was little more than a teenager, and she looked as if she might be pregnant. Could she be Valdez's wife and not his daughter?

"Kate?" Rosa asked, giving the short name a strangely abrupt sound. But she wasn't speaking to Kate. "You bought her?" she asked Nick.

Nick reached back to rest his hand lightly over Kate's. "Her given name is Katherine," he evaded neatly, and his thumb moved slowly on Kate's skin, a strangely comforting gesture in the midst of all the turmoil.

Rosa cast Nick an openly affectionate look. "Now there will be babies?" she asked, gently touching her own stomach.

The child was having a child of her own. Kate felt Nick squeeze her hands to stop any response, and he completely ignored the girl's question. "There is a lot of work to do, and a long way to go. We must leave."

A gaggle of small children in various states of dress from simple shifts to nothing at all had come up behind the jeep, silently watching the lady in the car. Kate looked at them, at their huge eyes and questioning expressions, and she tried to smile. They simply stared.

"The female will have babies," Rosa said, smiling. "Much babies."

Kate didn't have a chance to respond before Nick let her go in order to reach in his shirt pocket and hand Valdez some money. "Take care, brother, and be good to your female."

"You have your own to take care of," Valdez said with a gesture to Kate. He smiled at Nick. "You did not tell Valdez. How did you get her? Did you have to fight?"

"Later," Nick said quickly. "I have to go."

Valdez moved back, reaching to encircle Rosa with one arm. "Go. It is getting late."

Nick nodded without saying any more and drove off, heading toward the nearby jungle on a road that was little more than a path that disappeared into the heavy growth. When the jeep penetrated the green wall of the jungle, Nick slowed and patted the other front seat. "Climb over. They can't see us now."

Kate didn't have to be asked twice. She scrambled over to plop unceremoniously onto the hard seat, then sank back with a sigh. "Thank you."

"You're welcome," Nick responded. "Ready to go?"

Kate nodded as she settled on the hard seat. "Yes, more than ready."

Nick shifted gears and drove deeper into the jungle as the day faded into evening without any perceptible lessening of the heat. Kate held on to her seat, trying to relax with each jarring bounce as the tires hit the gaping holes in the crude road.

"They liked you," Nick finally said, breaking a silence that had lasted more than five minutes.

Kate looked at Nick. "Pardon me?"

"Rosa and Valdez, they liked you."

"They weren't exactly what I expected," she admitted. "I had no idea that Valdez and Rosa..."

Nick shook his head, "Yes, she is his..."

"...female?" Kate finished with a touch of humor.

Nick never looked away from the road. "Sorry about that. They can be pretty blunt here."

"I've never been stared at like that before. Even the children stared. Maybe they were waiting for me to faint."

"I thought Rosa would faint when you spoke up."

Kate frowned at Nick. "*I* spoke up? I expected any wife of Valdez's to be mousy and walk behind him. Rosa is a little chatterbox. She *is* his wife, isn't she?"

"Yes, and Valdez indulges her sometimes. In fact, he's so fond of her that he's easily wound around her little finger."

Kate liked the girl and was amused by Nick's answer. "She certainly says what she thinks."

Nick cast her an amused look. "She certainly does."

"It's hard to believe she and Valdez are married."

"They're very married." He fought the wheel to get the jeep out of a deep rut. "Rosa is his third wife, I think. The others died before I met him."

Kate clutched the seat as the jeep surged out of the rut. "That's awful."

Nick shrugged. "I suppose so, but these people accept death as part of life. They aren't like us, hoping to sneak past death somewhere down the road."

Kate watched him closely, not missing the nerve that jumped erratically in his jaw. "That's a strange thing to say."

"But true," he said, passing it off with a smile that was gone so quickly that she wondered if it had ever existed. "How old do you think Rosa is?"

"I don't know, but she looks awfully young. I thought she might be Valdez's daughter at first."

"Young enough to be. As far as I can figure, she's somewhere around fifteen."

"How old is Valdez?"

"Thirty-five."

"That old?"

That brought a genuine laugh. "That must make me ancient at thirty-eight."

"No, of course not," she said quickly. "But Rosa is just a girl . . . a child."

"She's old enough to have children herself. That's very important around here."

"So I heard," Kate murmured. "All she thinks about is babies."

"She's thrilled to be having a baby for Valdez."

"She obviously cares for the man."

Nick slowed the jeep to a crawl when the road began to climb sharply. "I'm very impressed."

"About the fact that she could love a man with a bald head?" she teased.

"No, that you picked up the language so easily."

"It's crude, but it has a Portuguese root. If you listen for the repetition of vowels and their patterns—"

"I don't understand any of that," Nick cut in. "All I know is that it's very difficult for me to use and understand."

"Where did Valdez learn his English, such as it is?"

"There used to be a mission school around here. Rosa went there, and Valdez was some sort of handyman."

"What happened to the school?"

"You were in it. It used to be in the airplane hangar. The two women who ran it left a few years ago, and the school closed. It sat empty until someone else came out here and bought it. I bought it from him."

Kate sat back, a bit disheartened. "That's too bad. About the school, I mean."

"As far as I know, the women got too old to keep doing it, and there wasn't any money to bring in new people. Maybe nobody wanted to come. I'm not really sure."

Kate felt the depth of the loss the village had experienced. "That's a shame."

"That's life," Nick murmured flatly.

Kate turned away, vaguely depressed by his offhand sentiment. A school could have meant so much out here, and she felt a sadness she couldn't fully define.

She turned to the jungle that surrounded the jeep, to the towering trees that lined the road, their trunks gnarled and mossy, their branches laced with clinging vines and creepers. Glossy-leafed plants hugged the ground, and huge ferns clumped together, growing higher than the jeep, their fronds partially covered by a brown, furry matting.

There were no signs of animal life, yet she could sense an eerie presence, a suffocating feeling that was enhanced as they drove deeper into the untamed jungle.

Kate had never seen land like this before. She had never seen greens so green, nor blossoms large enough to dwarf the hand of a grown man. There was nothing familiar, nothing to hold on to. She truly felt like a stranger in a strange land.

She turned to Nick, his dark hair ruffled by the hot breeze, his bronzed skin sleek with moisture. He was rapidly becoming her anchor. "Tell me more about your home," she said. "About the compound and the valley." She suddenly needed to hear the sound of his voice.

Nick held on to the steering wheel, the plastic hot and sticky under his fingers. Home? He had never actually thought of the valley as home, yet it was, a place to come to, a place to find what he needed. "It's simple and safe. The power's generated by the local waterfalls. There's hot and cold running water. Well, not really cold, sort of tepid, but it's fresh."

"Sorrella and Alfredo—where did they come from?"

"From the valley—the bottomland."

"Bottomland?"

He'd never tried to describe the valley before, and the words came with difficulty. "Their tribe comes from the valley floor, a secluded area, extremely isolated."

"Isn't that where *you* live?"

He glanced at Katherine, at her gentle features and appealing softness. Could she really understand about the valley? "This valley isn't like any you've known," he began. "There are no hills, no fertile farmland. It's literally a hole in the ground. It might be thirty miles long, no one's really sure. And I've never found the eastern wall. Each time I think I've found the other side, I go along it and find that it's a finger of land splaying into the valley. All I have to do is go around it and there's more valley. That's happened twice. My place is on the southern rim, above the deepest end. The north end seems to get shallower the farther you go. I've managed to explore about twenty miles north."

"It does sound . . . different," she said softly.

Nick killed a strange urge to reach out to her, to tell her that no matter what happened in the valley, he would see to it that she got back to her home safely. He glanced at her profile, at the slightly sharp line of her chin, the sweep of her neck, her skin glowing with moisture. At that moment something clicked inside him, an awareness of Katherine that staggered him, an echo of what he'd begun to feel the first night he met her. Yet now it was stronger, as if he had known her forever, instead of two weeks.

Stop it, he told himself and turned back to the road. This was only one more reason he should have hired a man, instead of this woman, who seemed able to stir him without even trying. Damn it, wait until she heard the one last thing he hadn't told her.

"Is this the right time for you to tell me some specifics about your project?" she asked.

He didn't look at her—he didn't dare. He filled his mind with what he had to do, and why he had to do it. A project? No. It had become a vital piece of him, a piece that would validate his worth—the payment of his debt. "I'm sorry for not being more forthcoming before we left." He brushed a hand over his face as he thought about his worth. What would it end up being? "This 'project' is at the bottom of the valley, in some caves that I've found in the western wall."

"It's archaeological?"

"No." He had to fight to control the jeep on a slippery spot of trail. When he had it back on course he said, "I'm only interested in what's been written in the caves—caves that are holes cut into the granite walls and used for tombs."

He remembered Alfredo's initial reaction to the caves. *"Brother, this is not a hole. It is a grave, a burial site. We cannot violate it."* Precious time had been lost convincing the frightened boy that it was not only right, but imperative, to enter the caves. After that first find, there had been six more. "I think you need to know some background," Nick said aloud.

"Please. I'm getting terribly curious."

He could remember his own curiosity when Alfredo had balked at looking inside. "I can't leave without looking inside. This could be what we have been searching for," he'd told the boy, and he had been right. The first clue had been cut into the wall—the start of it all. He focused on facts, on filling Katherine in.

"Until forty years ago this valley was virtually unknown to the outside world. Even local tribes didn't get too close. You've heard of lost tribes?" When he sensed her nod, he went on, "Well, this valley is the home of a tribe that has never seen the outside world—'the edge of life,' as they call it.''

"What's the name of this tribe?" Katherine asked.

"The best translation I can think of is 'the Rain People,' or maybe 'the Mist People.'" He repeated the word the tribe used for themselves and felt vaguely pleased when she told him that his translation was as close as she could come. "The Rain People are unknowns, and the farther you get from the valley, the more fearsome the tales of the Rain People become. Rumors grow and grow around here, fed by legend and imagination."

He stopped, taking a moment to get back on track with his explanation. "Just after the Second World War, some renegade Indians stumbled into the valley and plundered a cave they found. They took everything out to sell on the black market. Their first stop was Manaus. There was some interest, but it took second place to world events, and the stuff was pretty much forgotten about. Recently a few of the old pieces resurfaced, and rumors began to grow about where they came from."

"What sort of pieces."

"Gold and silver coins, and some statues cast in gold. Things that make men greedy. That greed brought in mercenaries, who are out to find the valley and strip the caves of anything valuable." It all sounded so simple and clear. It didn't show the heartache and heartbreak, or the danger that was always there.

"I thought you said this wasn't archaeological?"

"My interest isn't." He didn't want to get into everything now. Keep it simple, he cautioned himself. "What I'm most concerned about right now is the safety of the valley and its people."

"Is that why that man had a gun when the plane landed?"

He didn't try to hedge. "Yes. The Indians of the valley could be destroyed by greed from the outside world."

"And greed isn't part of what you want to do here?" she asked with a touch of disbelief.

He turned to her and couldn't help smiling. She looked hot and sticky, impatient with his explanations. And he couldn't blame her. He wasn't being very clear. That was something new for him, too. Since that day, clinging to life on the valley wall, he'd changed more than he had ever thought possible.

"Please, let me help you. The rope, hold to it," his rescuer had called to him in the native language. A hallucination, he'd been certain, until the rope touched him. Rope, burning his wrist, his whole body stretching, his weight horribly heavy on the tendons of one arm. No, don't remember that right now, he told himself. Don't dwell on the past, only on what you need to do. He glanced at his wrist, at the faint scar that circled it like a bracelet. Rope burns took forever to fade.

"What I want to do is get you to translate the writings in the caves. As near as I can tell, they're a combination of riddles, pointless scratchings and broken gibberish. They boggle my thought process."

"What do they have to do with the items in the caves?"

Everything. "The gold and silver are by-products, things left with the dead. They aren't important to me. The riddles are what I'm interested in, the riddles and what they say."

"I can't wait to see them. How do we get down to this bottomland?"

No, she couldn't be exposed to that. Nick had made the decision long ago that he wasn't going to endanger anyone's life but his own. "*We* don't. *I* do. I reproduce whatever I find, then bring it up. You stay at the top. That land below isn't fit for man or beast."

"Why?"

It smells and it's miserable, he wanted to say, but didn't. He went for more acceptable words. "The origin of the tribe's name comes from the perpetual rain forest down there, produced by the waterfalls. Some fall from the very top of the valley walls, some from partway down. They form pools at the bottom and send up a thick mist. The Indians call the place the 'Valley of Veils.' Its beauty is breathtaking, but the humidity mixed with the rotting vegetation can be a bit much.'' What an understatement. And it didn't matter, anyway. Katherine would never see the bottomland. ''Living down there isn't very pleasant. I don't quite understand how the natives have adapted to it, but I suppose anything is possible when you don't have any choice.''

Katherine hung on every word intently. Nick could feel her eyes on him. ''Why do this? You don't need the money you could get, even if you meant to plunder the caves.''

''I don't want—''

''I know. You told me this is entirely legal. I believe you. I'm just saying that whatever is down there, your money could buy it ten times over. Why do this?''

People always thought of money as the reason behind everything in the world. ''It's not money, just something I have to do.'' He paused, then admitted to one of his most basic traits. ''It's a challenge. And I can't turn away from it.''

''Why did you ever come and build here?''

He didn't even try to explain about the bet with his friend. ''Of course I can exist without people for two months,'' he'd boasted, his drunken state only emphasizing his sense of power. A challenge was a challenge. He had known he could do it. Now he simply ignored Katherine's question. ''I took over the house of a doctor who probably fantasized about being another Albert Schweitzer. He didn't last a year. He had dreams of having a clinic somewhere in the area, but he didn't have the strength to see them through. A friend of mine found the place, I don't know how, and I bought the hangar and the compound from the doctor.''

''If the doctor couldn't make it out here, what makes you think you can?'' she asked bluntly.

It seems he didn't have a corner on the market for bluntness. ''I won't let this land beat me.'' He flashed her a smile to take the edge off his words. ''I can do it. I thrive on a challenge.''

"And you don't think that your pride in being able to do it could be a false pride?" she asked.

"Is pride all bad?" he countered.

"It comes before a fall," she responded without hesitating.

What a choice of words. Nicholas, his mother had said, never let pride bring you down. A fall? He'd certainly fallen, but he'd survived. "I'll remember that," he said and slowed the jeep even more.

When he looked at Katherine, she smiled, a stunning expression that lit up her amber eyes. He felt its impact deep in his being. "You're a fast learner," she murmured.

He looked away out of self-protection and snapped on the headlights, their brilliance arcing through the gathering dusk. He certainly didn't feel like a fast learner. It had taken him a lifetime to learn some things, and he knew that there were others he would never understand.

He'd almost had to die, completely alone in this land, before he realized he wasn't immortal. He had accepted a stupid bet and come to this place, only to find out that he could never win the wager, and that he hated losing more than anything in the world. He'd taken on a debt that he had to pay back; then he'd realized that he needed help to rid himself of the obligation. For thirty-eight years he hadn't known he would ever need anything from someone like Katherine. He learned, but not quickly enough, it seemed.

"Hold on tight," he said, never looking at Katherine. "The ride gets rough from here on out."

Chapter 4

Ouch!'' Kate yelped when the jeep hit a gaping hole in the road and her elbow struck the door frame.

"Are you all right?'' Nick asked quickly as he braked to a stop and reached for her. He touched her elbow and gently probed it with the tips of his fingers.

Kate sat very still, the tingling in her arm nothing compared to the jolt to her being every time his strong fingers pressed her skin. "It's just a bruise,'' she managed. "No real damage.''

Nick lifted his eyes to hers, the contact so direct and riveting that for a moment it made Kate incapable of drawing a full breath. Then he sat back and gripped the steering wheel again. "I know it's bad traveling, but does it help to know that we've only got about five minutes of driving ahead of us?''

Kate nodded, her relief allowing her smile. "I feel better already.''

"Good,'' Nick said. "Brace yourself, and we'll get this over with.''

"By all means, let's get it over with," Kate said and grabbed the sides of the seat again.

Nick pushed the gearshift into first and pressed the gas pedal enough to make the jeep resume its slow progress along the rough trail.

Kate looked away into the deep twilight that shadowed the land. "How can you tell where we are?"

Nick pointed to the side of the trail, to a tree caught in the glare of the headlights. A two-by-two-foot chunk had been hacked out of its rough trunk. "Alfredo makes markers and renews them periodically. Each mark means something, and that particular cut means we're close. It's the last one."

Kate looked ahead, and at first she thought the faint glow above the trees was an optical illusion. But it grew and became more defined as the jeep kept going. Two stone pillars showed in the headlights, stacks of rocks that framed either side of the road. They drove between them, past a thick stand of trees and into a clearing covered with crushed stones.

After the oppressive closeness of the jungle this open space made it seem easy to breathe again. The fifty-foot-long expanse, defined by towering trees on either side, allowed them a sight of the sky and intensified the glow that Kate could now see came from the other side of a ten-foot-high, vine-covered wall twenty feet ahead.

Nick brought the jeep to a stop in front of a solid metal gate, shut off the motor and turned to Kate. "We made it."

She relaxed on the seat and asked, "Did you doubt we would?"

"You never know," he murmured and swung around to get out, leaving the headlights on.

Kate stepped out of the jeep, onto the gravel that pressed against the thin soles of her sandals. She followed Nick and, in the glare of the headlights, watched him manipulate a heavy latch and push back the broad gate. Curious about her surroundings, she reached out toward one of the shiny leaves on the vines that covered the fence. With no warning Nick spun and knocked her hand away. "No, don't!"

Kate jerked back, holding her stinging hand to her middle. "Wh-what...?"

Nick reached out and took her hand in both of his, then turned it palm down and gently ran his fingers over the back of it. "Damn, I'm sorry."

Kate stared at him, unable to absorb what had happened. "Why did you do that?"

He held her with one hand and reached with the other to lift a leaf gingerly and expose tiny thorns hidden on the pulpy stem. "Sharp, like needles. They puncture the skin too easily." He let the leaf fall back into place, covering Kate's hand with his again. "I didn't mean to hit you, but they hurt something awful if they break your skin. And the swelling is terrible. Some people have a horrible reaction to the poison in the thorns. I have medicine for it, but it takes time to work."

"I didn't know...."

"Of course you didn't. There are so many things here that look beautiful until you see their underside." He shook his head, his hold on her tightening perceptibly. "The Indians used to torture their enemies by wrapping them in the vines, then leaving them alone. The vines broke easily, and the poor fools thought they had gotten away with a few puncture wounds and scrapes...until the pain started."

Kate didn't miss the faint shudder that ran through him before he released his hold on her. "The victim usually ended up killing himself to stop the agony."

Kate pulled her hands back, pressing them together as tightly as she could, and she grimaced at the vine. "Why have it here at all?"

"For protection." Nick moved back and pushed the gate open farther. "For the same reason there's gravel outside and the trees are cleared for twenty feet from the fence."

Kate took one quick glance around the clearing and turned to duck her head and hurry past Nick, giving the vines a wide berth. She stepped into what Nick had called his "compound," a place with no trees inside the fence and loose gravel paving the open areas. She turned back to Nick, who took his time driving the jeep inside, then fastening the gate. She couldn't stop herself from asking the obvious question. "Protection from what?"

"From cats and strangers."

As Nick turned to look at her, Kate strained to see him in the shadows. Was he making a joke? "Cats?"

"Not house cats, Katherine, wild cats—dangerous cats. VanderFeer, the doctor, made sure nothing could get in unless he wanted it to—man or animal."

Kate shivered despite the heat and turned to face the place where she would be staying with Nick. In the center of the open area stood a sprawling building, the source of the glow, with golden light blazing from every window facing onto a full-length porch. The walls looked like rough logs stacked one on top of the other, and several chimneys stuck out of the steeply pitched roof. Fine-leaved vines twined around the corner posts of the porch, two shallow steps led up to a screened entry door, and massive insects beat frantically against every window where light spilled out into the night.

As Kate fell into step with Nick and headed for the house, the door snapped back and a young man stepped out onto the porch. He squinted into the night, his tall, extremely thin frame silhouetted by the lights at his back.

"Senhor Nicholas?" he called out.

Nick moved ahead of Kate to stop at the foot of the porch steps. "*Sim*, Alfredo. It is me."

As Kate drew close to Nick's back, she could see Alfredo more clearly. Dark-skinned, and no more than eighteen, the boy was dressed in white pants and a loose shirt knotted at his diaphragm. Iron-straight hair fell from a central part well past his shoulders, and a bright red headband held the black strands back from his flat-featured face. His wide-set eyes narrowed on Kate, and he spoke quickly in the local dialect. "Who is this female?"

"Alfredo, Katherine came with me to—"

Nick didn't get a chance to finish his explanation before Alfredo cut in. "Why did you not tell Alfredo that you went off to buy a female?" He grimaced at Kate and muttered petulantly, "Alfredo would have found you a good one."

Nick shook his head. "I had to do this in my own way, Alfredo. I found her myself." He spoke very deliberately and casually put his arm around her shoulder.

Kate tensed, wondering if he was going to kiss her to prove his claim again. But it didn't happen. He simply held her close, so close that she could feel the keys in his jeans pocket pressing into her hip.

The boy came quickly down the steps, his black eyes never leaving Kate, who stood rigidly. She would endure this. She would get it over with; then it wouldn't have to happen again.

"Are you certain you want this one?" Alfredo poked Kate sharply on one shoulder, and Nick's hold on her tightened even more. "Too thin, too pale," he mumbled.

Kate clenched her teeth, enduring his prodding the way she had Rosa's, waiting for Nick to say something, but he didn't. He held her and watched. Alfredo walked around her, appraising her from head to foot before coming back to stand in front of her and Nick. "Next time, you ask Alfredo. Alfredo will get Nicholas a good female." He snorted derisively. "Alfredo will show what is best."

"Thank you," Nick said, and Kate didn't miss the barely contained humor in those two words. The man had obviously begun to enjoy this.

She cast him a look that should have brought him up short, but he let her go without looking at her. Then he began to speak to the boy about the luggage and supplies that needed to be brought inside. Kate watched silently as Nick laughed. "*Sim*, it is very good to be back here."

Alfredo turned to Kate again, poking her one last time. "*Sim*, good enough for now." Then he walked past Kate to head for the jeep.

Kate waited until he was out of earshot and spoke to Nick in a low voice. "I don't want him or Rosa or anyone else doing that to me again!"

"Doing what?"

"Poking me as if I'm some animal he's judging."

"Alfredo doesn't mean a thing by it. Females out here are—"

"At least *you* can use the word 'women,' and I know...women aren't people," she finished with real exasperation. "The boy thinks you own me." She rolled her eyes. "Everyone probably thinks you kidnapped me."

"There are other ways of getting women out here. I didn't want to go into them before, but..."

"No," Kate muttered. "Don't bother. Create your illusion any way you want. You know what you're doing." She rubbed at her hip. "Your keys hurt me."

"Sorry." Nick touched her shoulder, a fleeting, gentle contact. "I didn't mean to hold you so tightly. Let's get inside and get over the last hurdle. Sorrella."

A strange sort of sharp energy had infused Kate during the trip, but she could tell by the weariness in Nick's expression that he hadn't been so lucky. "I can put up with anything after having a gun pointed at me," she said.

"I think you can," he agreed. "Let's go inside."

Kate followed his lead and went up the steps after him. She swiped at the furry wings that brushed her face as soon as she stepped into the circle of light. When Nick opened the screen door, Kate ducked into a large, low-ceilinged room that seemed to take up the whole center of the house. From its wide-planked flooring and log walls to the heavy beams that supported the roof, this place seemed a part of the land.

Kate looked to her left. A fireplace. Odd. A leather sling couch and two chairs flanked the stone hearth, and hemp drapes covered the windows on either side of the room. Natural tones were everywhere, except for a tapestry on the far wall, a weave of brilliant greens, reds, yellows and oranges. Kate nudged at the rope rug under her feet, then looked up to see tiny gnats circling the single electric bulb overhead.

She inhaled the heavy scent of lemons, wax and dampness. "A fireplace?" she asked, turning to Nick, who was still standing in the doorway.

"It counteracts the dampness during the rainy season." He smiled ruefully. "The lesser of two evils, either the dampness or the heat."

She brushed a hand over her damp face and hair. "How do you work here?"

Nick had never wondered about working when he first walked into this room. He'd wondered only how he would survive and win the bet. Even now, work seemed so minor compared to what he had to accomplish here. "I converted the doctor's outbuilding into a study of sorts. It's small, and not usable during the high sun. I also do a lot of work in a room across from the bedroom."

A door to the right of the hearth swung back, and Sorrella walked into the room. Nick smiled, genuinely happy to see the tall, lanky housekeeper. Her face lit up with greeting, and Nick had the feeling of being welcomed by family. "I'm back, Sorrella," he said.

Her hands smoothed her coal-black hair in its severe bun, then dropped to brush at the skirt of her flowing red shift. "*Sim*, Senhor Nicholas, you are back." Proud of the English she'd learned, she didn't revert to dialect. "Sorrella is happy, eh?"

Nick opened his arms to her as she hurried across the room to him. "Sorrella, it is good to be back." He hugged her; the scent of soap and wood smoke that clung to her was sweet and fragrant, welcome after the odors of the world. A bit reluctantly, he held her back. "The world is not a kind place."

Her dark eyes widened. "*Sim*, not kind." Nick knew she had never been farther than the village, but her idea of the outside world never changed. Beyond the two old ladies that had run the school, she knew the outside world was filled with people she didn't know, who didn't talk the way she did, or look the way she did, and people who would never welcome her. "Not kind at all."

Nick nodded, then attacked his introduction of Katherine to Sorrella without waiting any longer. He reached for Katherine and held her to his side again. This time she seemed to expect it and didn't tense. Strangely, he couldn't quite think of what to say. Soft and delicate under his hand, Katherine stood very still. Her lack of movement gave him time to gather his thoughts. Very deliberately, he spoke to Sorrella.

"I have brought this female to my home," he said to her, weighing his words carefully. "She is my number-one female." If Sorrella bought Katherine's appearance here, if she bought the fact that Katherine was his female, the bottomland Indians would probably follow suit. "My number-one female," he repeated.

He felt Kate tense as he spoke, and he held her a bit tighter.

"She is your female?" Sorrella asked abruptly.

Careful. "Yes, she is my number-one female."

With the petulance of a child, Sorrella compressed her full-lipped mouth into a pout. "Number one, eh?"

Nick nodded, hoping Katherine would continue to keep silent. "Number one."

The woman frowned as she came closer. Nick knew what she was going to do, but before he could stop her, she poked Katherine sharply in the shoulder. He felt Katherine tense even more, and he tightened his hold on her. For Sorrella to accept Katherine, she had to see that the new woman wasn't a threat to her own position. Sorrella's one real fear was going back to the bottomland, back into a life where a woman her age without a man would be at the mercy of the others. She would be little more than a slave.

Sorrella reverted to dialect and spoke rapidly. "She might be your female, but she is no good. She is too thin. She will not be able to cook and clean like Sorrella." She jabbed Katherine again. "Send her back to your land."

Nick felt Katherine flinch again, but she didn't knock the woman's hand away. "Sorrella, she is staying," Nick said, falling into dialect to make sure the woman understood completely. "She is very good, a good help for me. But she is not here to take your place. She cannot cook or clean. She is here for me, to read with me and help me in ways that you can't." That wasn't lost on Katherine, and she seemed to stiffen a bit in his hold.

But Sorrella's expression eased. "Sorrella can stay?"

"Yes." Nick smiled. "Sorrella must stay. I need you."

"Are there more females coming?" Sorrella asked warily.

"No more females. She is the only one."

"Sim, sim." Sorrella nodded, her relief obvious now that she felt secure in her place in the house.

Nick switched back to English. "Take Katherine into the bedroom and show her where the bathroom is." Katherine hadn't moved, hadn't spoken, and he knew what such control had cost her. He found himself offering her a prize of sorts. "Take a bubble bath, if you like. You deserve a treat after riding with the luggage."

She looked at him a bit blankly, the tightness lingering at her mouth and eyes. "A bath?"

"Yes, an honest-to-goodness bath."

Without warning the tension was gone, and she grinned, a teasing expression that lit up the amber depths of her eyes. "I'd almost forgotten about being consigned to the luggage area."

She's going to fit in here, he thought with real relief. Even the man in Phoenix wouldn't have fit in as well. "That'll teach me to keep quiet," he said, and as her smile deepened, it hit Nick hard.

"You're enjoying all this, aren't you?" she asked in her husky voice.

"Who, me?" he asked with mock affront.

"Yes, you, and don't deny it."

He touched her cheek, the feel of her silky skin sending a shiver through him that he barely contained. What would have happened if they had met some other time, some other place? He cut off that thought before it could grow and blossom. He had one priority in life right now, and this woman didn't have a part in it beyond what she could do to help him obtain his goal. "I find it great fun to see this place through the eyes of a newcomer—to see your reactions."

"Senhor Nicholas?"

He had completely forgotten about Sorrella, losing himself in the exchange with Katherine. "I'm sorry, Sorrella. What was it?"

She shook her dark head. "Your female wants to wash?"

Katherine had been accepted. He nodded with a smile. "In the bathtub, please."

Nick nodded to Katherine. "Go take your bath, bubbles and all. Sorrella will show you where everything is kept."

When her smile died, she suddenly looked very tired, as if the day had caught up with her all at once. Silently she turned and followed Sorrella down the short hallway toward the bedroom. Nick watched her go; Sorrella might not have existed for all that he noticed her.

Katherine claimed every atom of his attention. He appreciated everything she'd done today, and now that he took the time to simply look at her, he felt the awareness of her that had surfaced in the jeep spiral into full bloom. His eyes took in every inch of her slenderness, and he was struck by the milky tone of her skin. He narrowed his eyes and let them linger on her bare legs just before she disappeared into the bedroom with Sorrella.

At the village, in the airplane hangar, her lips had been soft, parted with surprise. He shook his head sharply. Enough of that. Thoughts were one thing, but that was as far as it would go. Nick yawned, covering his mouth with one hand, and turned toward the kitchen.

Kate could literally feel herself sag. Her energy was gone and weariness surrounded her like a second skin. It took an inordinate amount of concentration to simply step into the large bedroom. An ornate poster bed by the door was hung with gauze curtains and a canopy. A natural-linen spread covered the high mattress. Rope mats were underfoot, a monstrous dresser stood on the wall to the left, four high windows lined the back wall, and the scent of lemon and wax hung even more heavily in the air in here.

Sorrella circled the bed, crossing to a closed door on the right. She pushed it open. "Hot water," she said as Kate followed her. "Towels." The woman's eyes never made direct contact with Kate's and her voice held a distinct coolness. Kate looked into the square room with its claw-foot tub, antique commode and vanity on the back wall. A large bottle of bubble bath stood by the sink. Nick hadn't been kidding.

Kate turned, making a real effort to smile at Sorrella. "Thank you for everything."

Sorrella moved abruptly, stepping into the room quickly and using her sandaled foot to crush a huge spider that scurried out from under the tub. "Senhor Nicholas will call when he wants the female," she said, grinding her sandal on the wooden floor.

As Sorrella stepped back, Kate tried desperately to keep her smile intact. "Thanks for killing it, Sorrella. I hate bugs."

Sorrella slanted Kate a considering look. "Bugs?"

Kate pointed to the stain on the floor. "That. Bugs."

One dark brow lifted, and Sorrella finally looked right at Kate. A faint smile touched her lips. "There are lots of...bugs here." She held her hands up and separated them by two feet. "Big bugs." She waved her arms in a wide sweep that took in the bath and connecting bedroom. "All around. Big, big bugs." She paused for effect. "Bugs."

Kate couldn't stop a spontaneous shiver or the way she backed out of the bathroom into the relative safety of the bedroom. "Don't you have some spray?"

The woman stayed where she was and looked confused. "Spray? What is spray?"

"Poison to kill the bugs. You put it on the bugs and they shrivel up and die."

"Step on them," Sorrella muttered with a touch of disgust. "They die, sure thing." She bent and turned on the faucets in the tub. She stood and looked right at Kate, who stayed by the open door. "Big bugs," she pronounced, then moved quickly past Kate and left.

Kate stood very still for a long time after the other woman had left, then, cautiously, went into the bathroom and closed the door. What on earth had she gotten herself into?

Chapter 5

Even during her soothing bubble bath, Kate kept her sandals within reach. Before she finally got out of the water she looked around the room, checking the corners for signs of life. When she felt reasonably satisfied that she was alone, she got out, reached for a large towel and rubbed her skin briskly, then tucked the towel around her.

When she turned to face her reflection in the small mirror on the back of the closed door, she felt vaguely taken aback by the image. The pale girl with limp, clinging hair and deeply smudged eyes bore little resemblance to the way she'd looked just that morning. No wonder Sorrella and Alfredo had second-guessed Nick's wisdom in choosing a female like her.

A sharp knock sounded at the closed door. "Yes?"

She opened the door to find the housekeeper holding out her overnight case.

"Senhor Nicholas said to bring this," Sorrella said, glancing over Kate and not missing the sandals Kate had donned the minute she stepped out of the water.

Kate took the suitcase quickly and smiled at the woman. "Thank you so much. I needed fresh clothes."

"Sim," Sorrella muttered, and would have left if Kate hadn't stopped her.

"Sorrella?"

"Sim?" the woman said, using what appeared to be a multipurpose word meaning yes, no, or of course.

"My name is Kate, and I don't want you to serve me. I can take care of myself."

Black eyes flicked over Kate. "Senhor Nicholas says for Sorrella to do for the female."

"But you don't have to."

"Sim. Sorrella do what Senhor Nicholas say."

Kate felt as if she had hit a brick wall. "Sorrella, I am Kate, just as you are Sorrella, and—"

The lanky woman shook her head sharply. "He say Kat . . . Katreen."

Kate swallowed hard. "You can call me Kate."

"Katreen," Sorrella said slowly, deliberately, the word touched with what might have been pity for a poor female who didn't even know her own name. With a bob of her head, she turned and left. The sound of Sorrella's feet hitting the wooden floor sounded in Kate's ears; then the bedroom door shut with a sharp click, and silence fell.

Kate rolled her eyes with exasperation. "Katreen," she mumbled to herself. "Katreen." She shook her head.

When Nick knocked softly on the closed bedroom door, he felt clean and refreshed after a cold shower at the makeshift faucet outside the back door. After a soft, "Come in," from inside, he stepped into the bedroom.

Katherine stood at the bathroom door watching him. A sleeveless blouse and blue shorts worn with leather sandals made her look amazingly fresh and cool. Her loose hair and face free of makeup only added to the impression. He spread his hands apologetically. "Sorry to disturb you, but it wouldn't do for Sorrella to find me knocking loudly to get into my own room." He smiled at her. "She's not very understanding right now."

Katherine came closer, then stopped to look up, her fingers tucked in the pockets of her shorts. The scent of soap and freshness clung to her, washing over him at the same moment she spoke. "Do you know what that woman's calling me?"

Nick knew very well what Sorrella called Katherine. He'd just listened to a long tirade about it in the kitchen. "Yes, I know."

Her slender shoulders lifted in a slight shrug. "I thought you might."

"Sorrella is beside herself that you were correcting me. She's annoyed with you for saying it and with me for bringing a female here who is so..." He tried to translate the word as closely as he could. "Forward."

"I knew I shouldn't have tried to talk to her." She shifted nervously from foot to foot in front of him. "I wanted her to understand, that's all."

"She didn't." Nick had absorbed the brunt of Sorrella's outrage, choosing to endure it rather than have the Indian woman take it out on Katherine. "You can't expect her to begin to understand your values or ideas," he murmured as he leaned back against the closed door and absorbed one more disturbing thought about the woman before him. On top of everything else, he felt an uneasy sense of protectiveness. Why couldn't that man in Phoenix have taken the money and forgotten about wanting to write some damned paper on the project?

"Stupid, wasn't it?" she asked sheepishly.

"No. You don't have any background to help you understand these people. I didn't when I came." He flinched inside at what his ignorance had almost cost him. "We all make mistakes."

"Thanks for understanding," she murmured without a trace of sarcasm.

"Actually, Sorrella might be the one person here you could relate to. Despite the fact that she poked and prodded at you—" he didn't pause to let Katherine comment about that "—she's more flexible than most of the bottom-land people. She helped at the school for a while, and she even began to learn how to read." He didn't miss the sudden rush of interest that glowed in Katherine's eyes. He held up one hand. "Don't get the wrong idea. She's not looking for a teacher. She still recognizes Santeen as her headman. And no matter what, she'll still call you a female."

He didn't want to disappoint Katherine, and he was relieved when she simply shrugged it off. "Who's Santeen?"

"The chief, the headman of all headmen. He's regarded as a type of deity."

A faint frown line formed between her eyes. "He's pretty powerful?"

"He could order our deaths with a wave of his hand. He's the main reason we have to make very sure that everyone around here sees you are under my protection. He's dangerous, and filled with a sense of his own power." He knew how direct and frightening that sounded, yet he couldn't afford to hide it from her. It could mean the difference between life and death for both of them.

Her frown deepened, her lashes sweeping lower over her eyes. "He respects you enough to stay away from your female?"

So she understood completely, he thought. "Yes. I hope so."

"Aren't you afraid he'll kill you?"

"That doesn't bother me, not now."

"What is it with some people that they're willing to put their life in danger on a whim?"

She was talking about him. He knew it. And a year ago he would have had a simple answer. The thrill was worth the danger, and the sense of complete victory when you survived topped everything. But things were different now. "This isn't a whim."

She considered him intently for a long moment. "I've read about your life, about the way you constantly put

yourself in danger, as if you have a death wish. In Monte
Carlo, when you went off the road—"

"That was over a year ago," he cut in. A lifetime ago.
"This is different. *I'm* different. Santeen is what's important now. As far as he's concerned, nothing will happen if
we understand that these people are loyal, unique and committed to their own. We're aliens here, not them, and it's up
to us to conform." He stood straight, uneasy with the
memories of his past foolishness. I'm different, he'd told
her. He'd heard about people changing, but he'd never
thought he would be that sort of person...until it happened. He kept talking to distract his own thoughts. "It's an
ego thing with Americans, always expecting others to adapt
to our ways, use our language, even when we're the invaders."

Katherine simply nodded. "A friend of mine who did
translations in India told me the same thing once. She called
it 'American cultural ignorance.'"

Nick blinked, taken aback that Katherine had understood his ramblings. "Yes...exactly. That's it."

"You made it clear before that we have to fit in here.
That's why I didn't haul off and hit Sorrella when she
started poking me. But..." She cocked her head to one side,
her eyes so direct that her gaze made his insides knot—
though not unpleasantly. "...I refuse to walk ten paces
behind you."

Is she for real? he wondered. He stopped himself from
moving toward her and heard himself saying something that
sounded almost childish. "You're a good sport."

"Thanks."

A sharp knock on the door saved Nick from having to say
anything more than, "Come in!"

Sorrella pushed back the door enough to peer around it.
"Senhor Nicholas, the food is for eating now."

"Thank you. We'll be right there."

The woman's eyes flicked to Kate, but her words were for
Nick. "The female is eating with you?"

Nick spoke quickly, not wanting anything to spoil this understanding between himself and Katherine. "Yes, Sorrella, with me."

Her mouth drew into a tight line of disapproval, but she nodded and silently slipped back out, closing the door behind her.

Nick looked back to Katherine. "The female eats with me," he said, smiling. He realized that he hadn't done this for a long time, teasing and being teased. The last year had been so intense, so focused—a whole year since he'd felt the least bit free.

He studied Katherine as her own smile answered his. "We'll have to think of another word for Sorrella to use," she said softly.

Nick couldn't stop staring at her. What was it that made her different from the other women he'd known? She wasn't stunning. Pretty? Yes, but not ravishingly beautiful. Smart? Probably close to genius level, but he'd known intelligent women before. He took in the richly colored hair, loose and flowing around her shoulders, and the single strand she twisted around and around her finger—no rings, no nail polish. Slender legs. What was it about her that was so unique? He actually found himself hoping that the two of them could be friends, real friends. That was certainly a first! Friendship had never been high on his list of priorities with any woman he'd known before.

"Nick?"

He blinked, tugged away from his questions by the fact that Katherine had been talking to him. "I'm sorry. What did you say?"

"Where do you say you work in the house?"

He shook his head sharply to clear his thoughts. "Work?"

Kate looked up at Nick, trying to figure out where he had been a moment ago. He'd almost smiled at his own joke; then the expression had fled, leaving a strange seriousness in his eyes. "Yes, work."

"Oh. Follow me." He turned to open the door and spoke without looking back at her.

Kate hurried out of the room after Nick and stopped beside him when he opened a door across the hall. She leaned forward to look past him into a small room lined with floor-to-ceiling bookshelves. A single curtainless window on the opposite wall looked out over the front of the compound, and under it stood a couch with loose cushions. A desk filled the center, sitting on a hemp mat.

"It's more comfortable than the shed during the day," Nick said.

"I'll get my books unpacked tomorrow." She glanced at the full shelves. "Although I don't know where I'll put them."

He turned, brushing her shoulder with his. "Anywhere you want to. Stack my books on the floor, if you like."

"I don't want to upset Sorrella by making a mess. I could leave mine in their boxes."

Nick cupped her chin, the gentleness of the contact tempered by the roughness of the calluses on his palm. For a moment it made her feel giddy, and she had to concentrate when Nick spoke. "Sorrella never comes in here. Don't worry about it."

Kate was close enough to see the burst of gold in the gray around the pupils of his eyes and the faint scar that cut across his right temple and disappeared into his thick hair. She wished that she didn't feel so light-headed. Jet lag, she told herself. A good, simple explanation. "Okay. Shelves, not boxes."

"Good. Now, the food is for eating," he said, finally letting go of her chin. "Come on."

The table under the back windows in the living room held pottery filled with fruited chicken covered with a simmering sauce. Kate sat opposite Nick, and though a lack of appetite had plagued her all day, she found that she was almost ravenously hungry now.

After one taste of the delicate chicken and fresh fruit, she ate with relish. When she finally paused she looked up at Nick and found him smiling at her.

"Excuse me?" she asked.

"I was just watching you pack away the food." His smile deepened. "Most of the women I know eat like birds."

She sat back, fascinated by the way the low overhead light cast blue reflections in Nick's hair. "My father used to joke about taking out a mortgage to feed me. I've got a healthy appetite."

"So I noticed."

She lifted her fork. "I was thinking about the valley. I really need to see it myself."

Nick spoke abruptly. "No."

She dropped her fork on her plate and looked right at Nick. "If it's this Santeen person, I—"

He shrugged that off. "You aren't going down, and Santeen never comes up. I don't want you ever to have a face-to-face confrontation with him."

Kate looked down at her plate before meeting Nick's gaze again. "You never did tell me why he hasn't killed you."

Nick speared a chunk of pineapple. "I've got an arrangement with him," he said cryptically, and that was that. He silently ate the pineapple, then methodically began to cut up his chicken.

"Can't we talk about this?" Kate finally asked.

Nick tossed his napkin down beside his plate and stood. "No, we can't," he said as he walked away from the table and disappeared through a swinging door by the hearth. Kate watched until the wooden barrier swung shut before pushing back her own plate. Her appetite was completely gone now. Without waiting for Nick to come back, she stood and headed for the bedroom.

Her luggage had been emptied and neatly stacked by the dresser. Opening the drawers one at a time, Kate found her clothes lying neatly side by side with Nick's. Later she would rearrange them, once he took his things away, but for now she left them. After taking out a short, yellow cotton nightgown and her white terry-cloth wrap, she went into the bathroom and locked the door.

After a careful inspection of the room Kate took off her already damp clothes, tossed them on the vanity and put on her nightgown. She smoothed the light material over her hips, enjoying the crisp coolness on her skin. Then she put the robe on over it, tied the belt at her waist and leaned back against the vanity.

What had she done? She had left everyone and everything she knew. From now on, just getting ready for bed included "bug patrol." Heaven knew what was lurking under the tub, ready to scoot out at the first chance. And now she'd been told that someone called Santeen could kill her if he took the notion.

A wave of homesickness for all the safety and comfort she had left behind washed over her so strongly that it all but took her breath away. She'd never thought she'd do something like this, that she'd be off in the wilderness with a man like Nick. And on top of it all, Sorrella thought she was stupid and probably hated her. She bit her lip hard.

Enough is enough. She stood straight, pushed back her shoulders and took several deep breaths. *I'm here, and that's that. And I'm going to make it work for me.* She turned, opened the door and would have gone back into the bedroom, but she stopped when she saw Nick at the dresser. His back was to her. He took something out of a drawer, closed it, then turned.

"I didn't know you were here," he said.

"Where else would I be?" she asked, surprised by the sharp edge to her words.

"Good question." The look of weariness in his expression brought Kate up short. "I don't know what I was thinking. Sorrella and Alfredo have gone to their house at the back of the compound, and I'm tired. Are you about ready for bed?"

Kate stepped farther into the room. "Sure. I'm exhausted." She looked at the huge bed by the windows. "Where are you going to sleep?"

"In the bed."

Nervously, she pushed her hands into the large pockets of her robe. "What bed?"

Nicked tossed his pajamas on the dresser top before crossing to where Kate stood by the door. Here goes, he thought. The last condition to their arrangement. "The only bed in the house." He motioned to the bed with a nod. "And that's it."

She frowned up at him, and he knew she was angry. "And where do I sleep? Out in the jungle?"

He pointed to a rough mat that had been carefully laid over the hemp rug on the floor at the foot of the bed. He knew he'd been right to keep silent about it. She would never have agreed to it beforehand. "Sorrella made what she thinks is your bed."

"Oh, no," Kate said and held up both hands, palms out. "You're kidding."

"I'm afraid not."

"Why didn't you say something before this?"

Nick looked down at Katherine, at the slightly sharp chin lifted a bit defiantly. Should he at least tell her the truth now? No, he had to let her believe that it was unimportant to him, that he could handle the situation without any problems. He hoped he could, because there wasn't any alternative. "I'm sorry. I meant to. It just slipped my mind."

She stared at him—hard. "You're serious, aren't you?"

"Yes. I'm afraid it's either the mat or the bed with me. I have no intention of sleeping on the floor." He crossed his arms on his chest and found himself softening his voice. "What will it be?"

Kate crossed her arms on her chest, echoing his stance. She wasn't going to give in without an argument. "What about the den? It's got a couch. It could be used for a bed. I'd be very comfortable—"

"Now do you understand why I really wanted a man for the job? As part of the illusion that you're my number-one female, you have to sleep in my room. I can't take the chance of anyone finding out otherwise."

She eyed the bed, then looked at Nick. "I have to share it with you?"

"Yes. It's either the mat or the bed. I give you my word that I won't touch you. You can have your half completely to yourself." His words sounded so sane and rational. "I'll stay on my own side. Besides, I'm only up here for a night or two at a time. I spend most of my nights on the valley floor. The bed will be yours alone most of the time." He looked at her directly. "It's your choice. I recommend the bed, but it's up to you."

She weighed her choices carefully for a long moment, then said, "The floor."

He nodded, then changed the subject completely. "I wanted to say something to you."

Kate rubbed at the rough rug with her toes, noticing how hard the floor was. "What?"

"I didn't mean to cut you off when we were talking at the table. But your going down into the valley isn't negotiable. Santeen is off limits, and the valley bottom is his domain, so that makes *it* off limits, too."

"How safe are you?"

"Safe enough. The man has a certain sense of honor," he said. "Besides, I know the rules, and I'm a man." He shrugged sharply. "And I watch my back all the time I'm down there."

Her hands closed tightly in her pockets. "But what if something happened to you down there?"

Nick studied her intently for a long moment. "I don't plan on anything happening," he said. "But if I don't come up, Sorrella knows what to do."

Kate had to swallow once before she could talk. "I stay up here and worry? Is that the idea?"

"No, you stay up here and work."

"Sure...work," she echoed, her stomach knotting more tightly as they spoke. With a deep breath Kate forced herself to ask, "When will you go down again?"

"Tomorrow. You'll have the bed to yourself for three, maybe four days."

Kate tensed. "That soon?"

"I have to get on with things. This winter has been mild, little rain, no real storms, and I need to take advantage of it."

She didn't know why she felt as if she were being abandoned; she should be relieved that he was leaving. But she found herself protesting. "You can't go alone."

"I won't. Alfredo goes with me. He's a nephew of Santeen's, so he's got a place down there—a relatively safe place."

Kate nibbled on her bottom lip. "I feel so helpless staying up here."

"You'll have plenty of work to do."

"All right. I'll stay up here and work...as soon as you tell me what that work is going to be."

"Sleep for now. Get some rest, and I'll brief you in the morning before I leave." He turned from her, crossed to pick up his pajamas from the dresser and headed for the bathroom. With one hand on the doorknob, he looked back at Kate. "Make up your mat, Katherine," he said, and then he was gone.

Kate stared at the closed door for a long moment, then looked around to see a pile of bedding on the floor by the dresser. Quickly she laid out a double thickness of sheets on the bottom and covered them with a light blanket. At least the pillow was full and soft. She slipped off her robe, stepped out of her sandals and quickly got under the blanket. On second thought, she reached out until she found one sandal, then laid it right by the pillow within easy reach and settled back.

When the bathroom door snapped open Kate closed her eyes tightly, but that didn't keep her from hearing Nick moving around. Then the light was turned off and the bed sighed under Nick's weight.

She lay rigidly on the ungiving mat, the blanket clenched in her hands, and finally, when no sound came from the bed, she opened her eyes. In the darkness she stared up into the shadows. Somewhere in the distance, beyond the sounds of insects and night birds, she could hear a low roaring that never stopped. She'd noticed it before and meant to ask Nick about it. But she certainly wouldn't ask now.

She pulled the blanket higher and rubbed her chin on the soft linen. The scream of an animal off in the distance rang through the night. Or maybe it was human. She didn't know. She scooted farther down. She had never dreamed that keeping up the illusion of being someone's property could be so taxing.

She was so tired that she could have cried from it, yet her eyes stayed wide open and her whole body felt rigid. Her father thought she should get out into the world. And where did she end up? On a mat on the floor. She forced her eyes closed.

She heard Nick shift in the bed, then settle down with a sigh. Stillness filled the room. Then, from somewhere close by, a horrendous scream shattered the night.

Kate sat bolt upright, and when another scream came, worse than the first, she scrambled to her feet. "Nick?"

"Mmm?" came the murmur from a dark shadow on the right side of the bed.

"I've changed my mind. I'm going to sleep in the bed."

She didn't know what she had expected, but it certainly wasn't the simple, "All right," that she heard.

Quickly she tugged back the sheet and climbed into a softness that seemed almost indecently luxurious after the floor.

She stretched out flat on her back, close enough to the side that her hip touched the edge of the mattress. She folded her hands on her stomach and closed her eyes. Nick moved, she jumped, and then he settled back again.

Kate released a breath and tried to relax, but it took a long time after Nick's breathing turned slow and even for her to feel that first tug of approaching sleep.

Chapter 6

Kate knew it was a dream as soon as it began. She'd had this dream since childhood in one form or another. In it she floated somewhere over the action, watching herself. This time she was alone in the tree house she and her brothers had built years ago behind the white bungalow in the hills above Santa Barbara. She was an adult, though, sitting on the floor, in a corner, watching the doorless entry.

Outside rain fell—hard, driving rain that shook the tiny shelter and made the old oak tree sway back and forth.

The dream always started the same way—with her waiting. From above she watched herself, with her hair plaited in a braid down her back, her clothes a blur of blue. Her arms were wrapped around her bent legs, and her huge amber eyes stared at the door.

Kate never really knew what would happen in the dream until it began to unfold, but she was never surprised as the dream went on. She knew something or someone was climbing up the crooked steps to the tree house. Not a monster, she reasoned in the dream. Because I'm not afraid.

She wanted to see the intruder, and she leaned forward. A hand came in the door to grip the floorboards; then a wrist was exposed, a wrist with a faint scar around it. Backed by a flash of lightning, Nick looked in the door at her. Nick. No surprise. Yet he'd never been in her dreams before. "Are you hiding from the storm?" he asked.

Had she been hiding from the storm? Or had she been waiting for him all along? She thought she might have been waiting, but she wasn't certain. "I don't know," she admitted.

"I'll stay here with you," he said quietly and sat down in front of her.

She could see scars on his chest, a crisscross of pale lines, almost like decorations on his tanned skin. "How did you get those scars?" she asked.

"Sorrella knows. Ask her."

"But she won't talk to me."

"She wants you to go home."

Kate stared at Nick while the tree house shook in the storm. Home? "I'm not going," she said. "Even if there are bugs here."

Alfredo came from nowhere to squat beside Nick and poke Kate in the shoulder. "She goes. She goes now."

"No, I'm not going," Kate said, swiping at the boy's hand.

He poked her again. "She goes."

"Make him stop poking me, Nick," she demanded, "or I'll start poking him."

"It's his way," Nick said simply. "We can't change his ways."

She looked away from Alfredo and found her eyes on Nick's chest again. The scars. She found herself reaching out to touch them. The beat of his heart vibrated under her fingertips. Smooth skin. Body heat.

No one was in the tree house anymore but Nick and her. She moistened her lips, enthralled by the energy that seemed to ripple from Nick through her fingertips and into the deepest parts of her being. His gray eyes gleamed in the dim light from the storm outside. It's a dream, she told herself. She tingled all over from the caress of his eyes on her skin. A dream.

Slowly, ever so slowly, she became aware of a pulsing sensation, a need that flickered, then grew into a searing flame through her. Her hands moved on his chest, whispering over the scars, then drifting lower to the narrow line of soft, dark hair that led down to his navel.

Lifting her lips to Nick's seemed the most natural thing in the world. So right. Mouth against mouth, flesh to flesh. There were no barriers. Her body molded to Nick's hard strength. It was wonderful the way dreams made so many things possible, and the way the fire that blazed through Kate seemed to devour her, yet made her more real at the same time. She tasted Nick, her tongue swirling around his, and there was no taste but him, no touch but his. She knew she could lose herself in the essence of this man.

Lightning flashed around the tree house. When Nick began to caress Kate, the energy in the skies seemed to shoot into her with his touch. And she embraced it, holding to it as tightly as she held to Nick, falling back with him onto a rough hemp mat. She felt no fear. Why had she expected to be afraid?

Then the floor was gone, and they were outside on a down mattress, under a tormented sky, surrounded by storm, yet untouched by the rain. She was safe, surrounded by the hard strength of Nick's arms. Nick was over her, all around her, in her.

She spun crazily out of control in his arms and arched toward him. Then the fear did come, and she didn't know why. With that fear came the sure knowledge that she had lost control. Nick wasn't safe. She knew that. Why had she thought he was? No, she didn't want logic to intrude, and she tried to hold more tightly to Nick and to the dream.

Yet the harder she tried, the more elusive the dream became. Nick began to slip out of her hold, and she found herself unable to touch him. She reached out, but he drifted back just beyond her grasp, and she called out to him.

With a smile that sent more lightning through her, he whispered, "Katherine, Katherine," then dissolved into nothingness.

Her loneliness was insurmountable, and she felt weak and painfully dissatisfied. Her whole body ached with the knowledge of what might have been, and she began to cry.

A dream. It was only a dream. And she wanted it back. She called out to Nick, but he didn't come back. Her tears were silent.

"Katherine?" Nick asked, but she couldn't see him, couldn't reach him.

"Nick?"

She heard her own voice, and in that moment she knew she was awake. She could feel her heart racing, and something was holding her still.

She tried to move her arms, but something warm pinned her left arm to her side and her right arm across her stomach. Struggling against the restraint, she forced her eyes open and froze. Nick was so close he was almost a blur, and his arm lay across her, while his body trapped her other arm against her side.

"Shh," he breathed. "Katherine, it's all right."

What was happening? Why did he have her pinned down like this?

In the dim morning light that filtered into the room, she stared up at him. "Wh-what's going on?" She gasped and tried to pull back, to free herself of his hold.

Nick let her go immediately and moved back to support himself on one elbow. His hair was tousled, his eyes narrowed with concern. It was a dream, wasn't it? she asked herself desperately. Her heart thundered against her ribs, and she felt caught between fantasy and reality, not at all certain which was which until Nick spoke to her.

"Sorry, I didn't mean to startle you. But you were thrashing about, and I didn't know what was wrong." He lifted one brow. "A nightmare?"

"Yes, I . . . I guess so," she mumbled, unable to meet his gaze, her dream too fresh in her mind. She tugged the sheet back into some semblance of order, then started to push her tousled hair off her face. She stopped when she felt wetness on her cheeks. Tears. That part of the dream had been real. Nervously, she swiped at her face with both hands. She had always had vivid dreams, but none had been so real as the one she just left. Or more disturbing and unsatisfying.

"I...I'm fine now," she heard herself saying and eyed the bathroom door. She wanted to stand under a hot shower until she totally dissipated the lingering effects of the dream.

"Good. It's time to get up anyway," Nick said and moved abruptly, rolling away from Kate to get out of bed and head for the dresser.

Relieved to have distance between them, Kate wiped at her face again, then looked up. Across the room Nick was rummaging through the drawers, and she couldn't keep from wondering if his skin was as smooth as it had been in the dream. He turned to her, shattering her thoughts with a direct gaze.

"I promised you answers. We need to talk before I head down to the valley," he said.

"Yes. We do," she murmured. She looked away, but her gaze fell on his chest, a chest free of scars. But the memory of the narrow line of hair at his navel had been real, a path that fanned out just before it disappeared into his pajama bottoms. She swallowed hard and abruptly clutched the sheet to her, sat up and leaned back against the headboard.

"What time is it, anyway?" She kept her eyes on the floor. It had been a stupid dream to have. An unsettling dream. She almost touched her tongue to her lips to check for Nick's taste, but stopped herself.

"Somewhere around six, I suppose." She heard the dresser drawer open again, and then Nick added, "I need to get going, and I promised to brief you before I headed down."

She looked up at his back. "Thanks," she murmured, and found herself facing another reality from the dream. The scars were not on his chest, but on his back.

His deep tan emphasized the network of fine lines that ran from his shoulders to his waist. It was on the tip of her tongue to ask him about them, but she stopped herself. She didn't really want to know if the car crash in Monte Carlo had left more of a mark than anyone knew. Kate pulled her knees up and circled them with her arms. "When are you leaving?"

"Soon."

It was sleeping in the bed that had done it, she told herself. Nick was nothing to her. It was the semblance of intimacy without the reality. Her mind was playing tricks on her.

A sharp rap sounded on the door, and Nick called, "Come in."

Sorrella pushed back the door and stood in the opening holding a wooden tray with covered dishes on it. Despite the brilliance of her shocking-pink shift, the woman looked darkly somber, with her face stamped by a deep frown and her hair pulled back in a tight knot. She looked from Kate to Nick, then back to pin Kate with an annoyed gaze. "The female is with sickness?" she asked Nick.

"No, she's not sick," Nick said, leaning back against the dresser. "She's tired after the long journey."

Sorrella shook her head, as if despairing of the female Nick had chosen. With a sharp nod she muttered, "Eat," and stepped in. She handed Nick the tray and, without another word, crossed the bedroom, opened the bathroom door and disappeared inside.

Nick set the tray on the dresser and spoke over his shoulder. "Sorrella is a terrific cook."

Kate felt herself settling back to normal until a loud thump from the bathroom made her jump. After a second Sorrella appeared, her arm extended straight out in front of her.

Caught between her thumb and forefinger was a wildly wiggling reptile, several inches in length. It was a lizard, with iridescent green and orange skin, and it was thrashing back and forth, fighting against captivity.

"Lots of big bugs," Sorrella announced as she stepped into the room. That Sorrella didn't know the difference between a bug and a lizard mattered little to Kate. They both scared her to death.

"Good morning, good morning," Sorrella chanted, slyly watching Kate cringe against the headboard. With a sharp nod, the Indian woman went to the door and left with her captive still held between her fingers.

Kate closed her eyes for one brief moment, then looked at Nick. He was standing at the dresser, pouring coffee into a heavy ceramic mug. He put the pot down, then turned with a gooey nut roll in his hand.

"Do you want one?" he asked, holding it out to Kate in much the same way Sorrella had held the lizard.

Kate shook her head sharply. "What was that thing Sorrella caught?"

"A lizard."

"I know, but where . . . ?"

"They come up through the drains sometimes."

"The drains?" Kate shook her head. A sandal wasn't a fit weapon for protection against that thing. "They come in through the drains?"

Nick nodded, then held the roll out to her again. "Want some?"

The dream was completely forgotten now. "No, I don't." She darted an apprehensive look at the open bathroom door, then back to Nick. "Can't you fix the drains and stop them from coming in?" It sounded perfectly logical to her.

But he didn't seem convinced. "They don't hurt you. They're more afraid of you than you are of them, and besides, it would take forever to figure out where the outside end of the drainpipe is. The best thing to do is close the bathroom door at night. That keeps them out of here." He popped half the roll into his mouth. "These are delicious," he mumbled as he chewed the other half. "Sure you don't want one?"

The thought of food made Kate distinctly sick at that moment. "I'm not hungry, and I . . . I want to get up."

"Get up while I'm in the tub."

"The tub?"

"The bathtub."

"In the *bathroom*?"

"Yes, the bathroom." His smile grew. "Do you always do that in the morning?"

"Do what?"

"Question everything anyone says to you?"

She shrugged sharply, uneasily looking around the room for any flash of movement in the corners or under the furniture. "I don't know, and I don't care," she muttered.

"Irritable, aren't you?"

"I'm not irritable...." She drew a deep breath. "I just want to get up."

"And I need a bath," he said. "And I don't want to use the shower I used last night."

"Why?"

"It's outside the back door, and I want hot water this morning. Would you refuse me a warm bath?" he asked. "I'll check for lizards, if you like."

"Go ahead, take your bath, and...yes, please, check to make sure you're alone in there."

"Sorrella makes a clean sweep of the place every morning," Nick assured her as he rummaged in the dresser drawers for clean clothes. "She seldom misses anything." He gathered his things up in his arms and crossed the room, pausing for a moment at the foot of the bed. "Are you getting up?"

He's a morning person, Kate thought with an inward sigh. He's a toucher, and a morning person. He's wide awake and full of good humor when most people are struggling to get their minds cleared of sleep. And he invades dreams. She would just bet that he'd slept like a log last night. She took a deep breath and found that she could actually manage a slight smile. "Go on, take your bath, and I'll get up."

He considered her for a long moment. "You really were terrified of that lizard, weren't you?"

"They make me uneasy," she said with a masterful sense of understatement. "Lizards and bugs. Things that move too quickly and look ugly."

"That about covers everything around here." He smiled.

"I guess it does," she agreed. "Are you going to take your bath?"

"Yes, I am," he said and strode into the bathroom.

When the door clicked shut and the water began to run, Kate sank back against the headboard. She let herself gradually take in everything around her, the dresser with the tray of food, the smell of the coffee, the scent of cinnamon that touched the air. She sat there until Nick began to sing some unidentifiable song. Whatever else he did well, singing wasn't one of his talents, she thought with a smile when he hit a particularly flat note.

She got out of bed and shrugged into her robe, then pushed her feet into her sandals and walked to the windows. When she pulled back the curtains she found herself facing a lawn of sorts that disappeared from sight thirty feet beyond the back of the house. Beyond, a great emptiness was haloed in mists, and the green lushness of the jungle in the distance shimmered in the clean morning light.

Off to her right, Kate finally saw the source of the roaring sound she'd heard last night, the crest of a massive waterfall, its blue-white foam cascading downward into the valley.

Kate leaned closer to the window to stare out at this land of iridescent mists. A perfect rainbow flashed at the top of the falls, hanging in the air for several long moments before dissolving and dying.

Kate knew without being told that she could only see a fraction of the valley rim, yet its breathtaking beauty almost canceled out the heat, the discomfort and... she was about to add lizards until she thought about the one Sorrella had caught, and shivered. Almost, but not quite.

Nick watched Katherine for a moment from the bathroom door before he said anything. Last night had been

strange. He'd been certain he could handle the situation. In
fact, the hard part had been talking Katherine into sharing
the bed. The actual act hadn't bothered him. Nothing to it.
Except for the fact he hadn't been able to sleep with her
there. At every movement, every sound from Katherine, his
whole body had tensed. If he hadn't known how uncomfortable the mat was, he would have lain down on it himself just so he could relax. And when she'd cried out, he'd
reacted instinctively, trying to comfort her, but he'd only
succeeded in confusing himself. Getting out of bed had been
the only solution.

He watched her stand on her tiptoes to get a better view
out of the window, and he knew he had to get on with
things. The hemp hammock waiting for him down in the
valley would at least let him get some sleep. "Special, isn't
it?" he asked.

Katherine jumped, startled by the sound of his voice, and
turned. While he buttoned the work shirt he had put on with
his jeans, he walked over to her. He did the last button up
just as he reached her.

"I love to see it first thing in the morning," Nick said. "It
looks so unspoiled, with beauty hiding the dangerous side
of nature." He looked past Katherine. "It never ceases to
fascinate me."

Kate stepped to one side, all too aware of the scent of soap
and after-shave mingling with his clean body heat. Despite
having been engaged to Mike for almost six months, she'd
never felt at all easy with this sort of intimacy. "It doesn't
quite make up for lizards," she mumbled as she ducked past
him to walk into the still steamy bathroom.

His pajama bottoms were lying on a wicker hamper by the
door. His toothbrush and double-edged razor sat by the
sink. Kate looked around the room with great care, and
when she was quite sure she was alone, she threw the bolt.
Then, in one motion, she pushed the razor and toothbrush
to one side and dropped a damp towel over them.

In less than fifteen minutes she felt fresh in lemon-yellow
shorts and a loose white blouse, with her hair combed up

and off her neck into a tight twist. Then she took a deep breath and went looking for Nick. As she entered the living room, she heard a muffled sound outside on the porch, and she crossed the room and opened the screen door. Heat, which had been tempered by the thick walls of the house, hit her full force. She squinted into the painful glare of the strong morning sun and spotted Sorrella farther down the porch, trimming potted plants with long shears. The woman saw Kate immediately and straightened, waiting silently.

"Good morning, Sorrella," Kate said, smiling. "I was looking for Nick."

"Behind the house," Sorrella said, stooping over the plants again.

Kate hesitated, then stepped closer. "Sorrella?"

She stood immediately, her coal-black eyes narrowed. *"Sim?"*

Kate couldn't stand this silent hostility, and she said the first thing that came to her mind. "Nick told me you used to be at the old school."

"Sim." She wiped her free hand on the bright pink cotton of her shift.

"Were you there long?"

Sorrella frowned. "Long?"

"Were you there a year? Two years? More? How much time?"

The older woman shrugged. "I do not know."

Kate tried again. "What did you do there?"

"Do?"

"Did you work there?" Kate persisted.

"Sim."

Kate looked into the steady black eyes and blinked. What should I say now? she wondered. She took a breath and tried again. "Do you remember much about the school?"

"Remember?"

Kate repeated the word in dialect, and Sorrella frowned. She answered in English. "I remember things in here." She tapped her forehead.

"What is in there?" Kate asked carefully.

"Words. Pictures. Stories." Her voice seemed to be losing some of its tightness. "Did you go to school?"

Kate smiled, feeling a sense of accomplishment that Sorrella had asked a question. "Not to your school, but I go to a school far away. I teach there. I teach words and stories."

"The female teaches?" the woman asked.

"Yes, I teach." She touched her head. "In here, I have many things to teach. I lived a long way from this valley, but I have stories."

Sorrella dropped the shears on the porch and came closer to Kate. "You know Miss Anna?"

"Who?"

"Schoolteacher. She had hair like that." She pointed to Kate's hair. "But she had many years, many years."

"No, I'm sorry, I didn't know her, but I would have liked to."

Sorrella stood very still. "Miss Anna is gone."

"Yes, I know. Nick told me about her and the other lady."

"Miss Edna." Sorrella shook her head. "Miss Edna is gone."

Kate nodded. "Yes, but maybe we can talk about the school sometime, and you can tell me all about Miss Anna and Miss Edna."

The dark-haired woman hesitated. "Talk?"

"*Sim.*" Kate nodded, claiming the word for her own. "I would like that very much."

"Do you read books?" Sorrella asked abruptly.

"*Sim*, I do. Do you?"

"Sorrella tried. Miss Anna or Miss Edna used a book. Sorrella has it." She narrowed her eyes on Kate. "You can read the book?"

One look at Sorrella's face and Kate knew what she was asking. "Would you like to read it with me sometime?"

The woman bobbed her head sharply. "It is hard for Sorrella."

Kate felt absolutely joyful. She had found her link to this woman. "Soon we will read together. Very soon."

"Good," Sorrella said, and her expression eased. She didn't smile, but there was a softening of her frown and the lines at her mouth and nose. Progress, indeed.

Kate hated to break things off so soon, but she had to hurry. "I need to see Nick before he leaves."

"Alfredo and Senhor Nicholas go quickly."

"We can read when they're gone." Kate hesitated, then allowed herself to briefly touch Sorrella's arm. "It will be good to read with you, Sorrella, very good."

Sorrella looked down at Kate's hand. *"Sim."*

Kate smiled, then reluctantly turned and walked away.

"Katreen?"

A name. She'd used a name instead of *female*. Kate turned back to Sorrella. "Yes?"

"The bugs?"

Kate frowned. "Yes?"

The lanky woman shrugged, spreading her hands, palms upward. "Sorrella will take care of the bugs for you."

Kate recognized the peace offering for what it was and took it without a second thought. "The big ones, like this morning in the bathroom?"

Sorrella tipped her head to one side. *"Sim*, the big ones."

"Thank you, Sorrella, that would please me a great deal."

"Sim," the woman said with a bob of her head, then turned back to her plants before Kate could say anything else.

"Thank you, Sorrella," Kate said softly and walked quickly to the end of the house.

The huge white blossoms on the vines that covered the fence were waxy and bright, a startling contrast to the deep green of the distant trees. The sky shimmered overhead with the unrelenting sun, and the heat bounced visibly off the gravel. The discomfort hadn't eased a bit, yet Kate's heart felt lighter and touched with happiness. She might have a friend here after all. She smiled to herself. A friend who was willing to kill the bugs for her.

Stopping at the end of the porch, Kate looked to the rear of the compound, where a squat, thatched-roof building sat near the drop-off. Its walls were blinding white, its windows were high slits, and the door was open. Kate stepped down onto the gravel and walked toward the building, humming softly under her breath. By the time she reached the open door her good humor had been tempered by the heat, which had sent rivulets of perspiration trickling down her face and made her blouse cling damply to her back. Flushed and uncomfortable, she hurried inside.

The interior was a dim blur until her eyes adjusted; then she could make out walls lined with empty shelves, an overhead fan that moved in lazy circles, and a desk facing the door. Nick sat behind the desk, bent over an open notebook. Kate cleared her throat.

He looked up immediately. "Sorry, I didn't hear you coming." He sat back. "What's the smile for?"

"I've been talking to Sorrella, and guess what!"

"What?"

"I think we're going to be friends. We talked about the school." She moved forward and leaned toward Nick, her hands resting on the desktop. "She wants to read with me. She even offered to kill the bugs for me."

"Read all you want with her. You're going to need someone friendly up here while I'm gone."

She took a breath. "Yes, I will need someone up here."

"If anything happens, Sorrella knows how to contact Valdez. He'll get you out safely. He's totally trustworthy."

Kate stood back, her happiness seeping away. "How about you? Who goes down after you?"

Nick shrugged off the question. "I can take care of myself. And don't worry, you'll be paid no matter what happens."

"I didn't ask because of the money," she countered, his words making her insides tighten.

"Surely it was a passing thought," he said sardonically.

Kate could feel her expression stiffen, and she couldn't stop her own sarcasm from surfacing. "Aren't you worth helping unless someone's being paid to do it?"

Slowly, deliberately, Nick sat back and released a long breath. "Most people reduce this life to money, one way or another."

Obviously Nick did. And she *had* come because of the money, though she could honestly say that she hadn't thought about it since arriving at Manaus. "I guess I'm not like most people," she said quietly.

"I guess you're not," Nick said just as softly; then he swept the whole discussion to one side with a wave of his hand. "We need to talk about other things right now."

She nodded, a little relieved to stop whatever was happening before it really began. "All right, where are these writings you've found?"

Nick pointed to the open notebook. "I sketched these when I went down. You can start here. Maybe you can make some sense out of this mess."

Kate circled the desk to look over his shoulder, getting her first glimpse of the work ahead of her. The sketches were perfect, clearly defined, but she saw nothing that looked like words or hinted at a definable sense of language. When Nick stood, Kate slipped into his chair to stare down at the pages. "I expected words."

"I didn't know what to call them," Nick said from behind her.

Kate slowly traced the drawings with the tip of one finger. It looked as if two or three letters had been strung together, then cut off abruptly. Two or three letters of gibberish. "These were in the caves?"

Nick leaned over her shoulder and pointed to the longest series of letters, six figures strung together with no rhyme or reason. "This was at the head of a burial bed in a small cave on the southern wall." He indicated several additional pieces. "These were there, too. And these—" he turned the page "—were on the two pieces of land jutting from the east. The caves were stripped of everything. Another cave in the eastern section was untouched, but had only two figures on the wall."

"I don't know what to say. These aren't any sort of dialect. They aren't even symbols."

"But someone was trying to say something with them
and I have to know what the message is."

Kate stared at the paper, asking a question that had been
plaguing her from the first. "Are you going to tell me what's
going on now?"

"What?"

She turned to look up at him. "I need to know exactly
what's going on, and I want to know now, before you head
down to the valley."

"There's a riddle I want to solve. I told you, I like to finish what I start."

"Then why start it at all? Why be here, in this place,
worrying about a valley you said is barely habitable? Why
have a man with a gun watching for strange airplanes?" She
shook her head. "Why?"

"Can't you accept that I simply want to do it?"

"No."

He stood back and raked his fingers through his hair.
Gray eyes met amber, and neither gaze flickered. "Why do
you have to have answers? Just solve the mystery for me."

"I need to know everything to solve your mystery. Whatever your reasons for doing this, I promise you, they'll go
no farther than this room."

He turned away abruptly, then ran a hand over his face.
Finally he turned to face her again and leaned against the
empty shelves on the side wall. "All right. I'll tell you."

Kate shifted in her chair until she faced him. "Go on."

Nick looked at Katherine, at the impatience and determination on her face, and wondered where he should begin. "I'll try to make this as simple as possible. There's a
treasure beyond what was taken from the caves, a treasure
hidden in the valley, and its location is somehow linked to
the writings on the walls."

Her golden eyes widened, but then a frown settled on her
face, drawing her finely arched brows together. "This is all
some . . . some stupid treasure hunt?"

She almost spat out the last four words, and he didn't know what to say, so he hedged. "Sort of."

She stood to face him, and he could see that she was trembling. He couldn't tell whether she was angry or upset, but from the look in her eyes, he voted for anger.

"I asked you about the gold and silver in the caves, if you were after them, and you said you weren't. And I believed you! Now you're telling me that you dragged me down here to this place to play some stupid, self-satisfying *game*? Some rich man's idea of fun! And as for it being legal, you can't just take things out of a country for your own gain. That's looting!"

"Will you let me explain?"

Katherine hugged her slender arms around her body and cocked her head to one side challengingly. "Will it be the truth?"

That shook Nick. If she doubted his honesty, how could they work together? "I've never lied to you," he said, hearing more defensiveness in his voice than he liked.

"Isn't lying by omission still lying?"

"I've told you things on a need-to-know basis." His own anger showed in his tone. "And it's *my* business to decide *when* you need to know something. You work for *me*."

He hated the words as soon as they were spoken, and he wanted to pull them back—until he saw her lift her chin. Any worry about hurting her had been foolish.

"I've never forgotten that, Mr. Dantry. All I'm asking for is the truth. The full truth."

He didn't know why, but he wanted her to trust him, to believe him. But he'd gone about things in the worst possible way, he realized. If he made the same mistakes in his business, he'd be bankrupt in no time. I'll tell her the truth and let the chips fall where they may, he decided.

"All right. You want the truth. I'll give you the truth."

Her eyes widened slightly. "Thank you."

"Don't thank me. Just remember that this is just between the two of us."

She nodded, and he could have sworn she was holding her breath, waiting for his explanation.

He took a deep breath and laid the truth out in front of her. "The truth is that I killed a man, and I have to pay for it."

Chapter 7

Nick watched Katherine sag heavily into the chair. The color had drained from her face and deepened the richness of her shocked eyes. "You...you what?"

"You heard me. I killed a man. And finding the treasure is the price I have to pay." There, he'd said it. He'd shocked her, horrified her, but she'd wanted the truth.

Kate stared at Nick, unable to take in what he said to her. "H-how?"

"It started with a stupid bet," Nick said. "A bet with a friend. I used to do that all the time, and I always won...until last year." His gray eyes never flickered. "You heard about Monte Carlo? I lost that bet. I had to get down the road without using my brakes. I could have died then, but I didn't. The car flipped, and I was out walking around a minute later.

"A few weeks after that, the same friend made me another bet. I was a bit drunk, and I couldn't refuse the challenge when he bet me I couldn't stay completely alone for two months. That's how it all began ... with that bet."

Kate couldn't breathe. A bet? He'd killed a man on a bet?
"How did you kill—"

"I'm trying to explain," he interrupted. "Let me do it."

She sat back, unable to quell a trembling that had begun
deep in her being. What had she gotten herself into? "All
right. You can explain...." She tried to take a breath. "Then
I'm leaving."

That hit home. His lips thinned, and he walked closer to
lean across the desk. "What?"

"You said Valdez can get me out, and I..." Her words
died under his unblinking gaze. "If you think I'm going to
stay with you, you're crazy," she managed finally. "Just
plain crazy."

Nick didn't move for a long moment; then he stood back
and lifted his shoulders in a sharp shrug. "Maybe I am
crazy. Who knows?" he muttered. "Just hear me out. Then
you can do whatever you feel you have to do."

She nodded without saying anything.

"The bet intrigued me—to stay completely alone for two
months. My friend had it all planned out. He'd heard about
this place the week before from someone who had known
the doctor's family. They wanted to get rid of it, so he made
that a condition of the bet. Buy it. Come down here and stay
for two months—by myself, without knowing the language. He'd drop me off and come back and get me when
the time was up. If I wanted to give up, Valdez could be
reached by shortwave, but if I called for any other reason,
or if I even went to the village, all bets were off."

A rich man's idea of a game. "How much were sixty days
of your life worth?" she found herself asking, her voice
tight and hard.

He stood very straight, his arms crossed over his chest.
"That doesn't matter. Let it be said that I came cheap,
Katherine, very cheap. What matters is that I came, I stayed,
and after two weeks I felt like I was going crazy." His voice
tightened with each word. "I understood snatches of the
language, but I couldn't talk to anyone. Drinking alone
doesn't hold great appeal for me. A solitary cell couldn't

ave been more isolated. I never knew how much a person ould miss the world—as defective as it is.''

He ran a hand over his face and took a deep breath before continuing. ''One day I just walked out the gate. I don't now where I thought I was going, but I left, found a side ail and followed it.'' He held up a hand to stop her from aying anything. ''I don't need to be told what a fool I was. admit it. I live with that fact every day. To make this short, didn't see that I was near the edge of the valley until I fell ver.'' He spoke quickly, as if wanting to get it over with. ''I nded up tangled in some growth near a high ledge. I found ut later I had dislocated my hip. I was there for hours.''

The scars. Now she knew about the scars. Her eyes never eft Nick as he walked to the open door. He pressed one and flat on either side of the jamb and stared outside. His oice became lower and more intense. ''I finally did something I'd never done before. I faced the fact that I could die. t wasn't a game. I wasn't going to emerge seconds later covered with glory. I was sure I was going to die in this god-orsaken place.'' His chuckle held no humor. ''Death. The great leveler. But I didn't die. An old Indian passed by and heard my shouts . . . my curses . . . my prayers.''

Kate watched in silence, her anger and outrage slowly changing to disbelief and shock.

''Torga,'' Nick said softly. ''An old man, brother of Santeen, he heard me. He came up from the bottom from time to time to see Sorrella and Alfredo. Unlike his ancestors, he knew about white men. He'd seen the doctor and the women at the school, and he had no illusions about white people being like gods. Somehow he managed to crawl down, tie a rope on one of my wrists and pull me up himself.''

Kate stared at Nick. ''He saved you?''

He turned back to her, his eyes narrowed as if he couldn't quite bear to look directly at her. ''Yes, and he's dead. I killed him.''

She sat stunned. ''I . . . I . . .''

"Getting me out and carrying me back here was too muc[h] for him. He had a stroke, or a heart attack, or somethin[g] There was no way to get help in time." He turned to face he[r] again. "I killed that man, Katherine," he said with vibra[t]ing intensity. "I as much as put a gun to his head because o[f] my stupidity, my selfishness."

Kate felt confused by the look of pain in his eyes and th[e] tension on his face. "No, he helped you. You're alive to[day—"

"Because he's dead. And what's my life worth?"

"It's worth everything," she whispered. "You'[re] worth..." She bit her lip. "If someone dies for you, yo[u] have to have value, or that person's sacrifice is worth noth[h]ing."

"I don't want to hear platitudes," he bit out, striking th[e] desk with a sharp slap. "All I know is that Torga is dead[,] I'm alive, and I have to pay the debt."

Kate blinked rapidly, unnerved to find her lashes moist[.] She didn't understand. "You risk your life all the time. I'v[e] read about it. Why...?"

"I can risk my own life, but when someone else is kille[d] because of what I do, that's different. I've never put any[-]one else in danger. And I hated what I did to that old man."

"How can you possibly make up for a life?" she asked.

"By finding that treasure."

"But...?"

"Torga knew he was dying. He talked to Sorrella, going on and on about his younger days, about his forays into the deeper sections of the valley. Then he began to ramble, going in and out of consciousness. He kept talking about the caves, about tombs he'd found with secrets in them. He didn't understand the secrets, but he knew that something was being said about a treasure that was brought into the valley a hundred years ago."

"Nick, the man might have been delirious or..." She hated to say it, but she made herself go on. "He might have been mad."

"I thought about that myself, but his story fits too neatly into an old legend that's been told in the valley for years."

"A legend?"

"The story goes that bandits robbed the missions along the river just before the turn of the century, then fled to the upper basin. They stumbled on the valley. They were probably Dutch or Portuguese, pale and tall. Anyway, their looks saved their lives, because the Indians thought they were gods, fallen from the sky.

"They stayed—maybe they couldn't find the way out. Who knows? One finally left, but he never came back, and the others lived out their lives in the valley and were buried in special tombs made by their leader. That's where the gold and silver were found. That's where the writings are.

"The story goes that when they died, they went to a secret place, then came back as trees, overlooking the valley, the people, and their treasure."

Kate tried to concentrate on what Nick was saying instead of on her own churning emotions. "How can finding the treasure make up for Torga's death?"

"It could give his people everything they need to survive. I could give them a new life and make up for taking Torga's."

She sought for logic. "But you've got money. You could..."

"No, I couldn't. They wouldn't take it or want it. But if it's their treasure, theirs alone, it'll work."

Kate looked away from Nick's eyes to his hands, and she saw the scar, the bracelet of pale skin on one wrist. *He pulled me up by one wrist.* She moistened her lips and looked back at Nick. "You...you're all right now?"

"I healed," he said flatly as he straightened.

"Why is there a time limit?"

"The mercenaries I told you about. The reason for Rondo's gun. I made some stupid inquiries in Manaus when I first heard about the treasure, and it tipped off the wrong people. They're looking for the valley, and for the treasure.

I don't have any idea when they'll come, but they will. Sooner or later, someone will stumble on the valley.''

"It could take someone else years...."

"Or days," Nick countered. "That's why I have to move fast."

Kate felt the urgency radiating from him. "If you fell before...?"

"I didn't know what I was doing then. I do now. And I know that the caves—all hand hewn—hold the answers. Torga said that *'in death the men could tell the secret,'* and each tomb contains writings. They're the places of the dead, and the clues were written above the corpses' heads."

Kate looked down at the black lines on the white paper until they began to blur in front of her eyes. "If this is all true, and the writings *are* the clues to the main store for the robbers' treasure trove...?"

"I accept that it's true," he said firmly.

"That's all that matters." If he believed it, she would do anything she could to help him. She frowned at the paper in front of her. "But this won't be easy."

"I've learned one thing over the past year: nothing worthwhile is easy. I have to get into the protection of the valley before the heavy heat comes," he continued. "Sorrella knows how to use a gun."

That brought Kate's head up. "A gun?"

"She won't use it on you," Nick said with a wry smile.

"I didn't think she would," Kate countered, but her own smile felt forced.

"Stay inside the fence at all times, and let Sorrella search the bathroom before you get out of bed." He hesitated. "Are you going to stay?"

She didn't have to think twice. "Yes."

He lightly brushed her cheek with the tips of his fingers. "You know, Katherine, it won't be half bad knowing you'll be here when I come back up."

Killing the impulse to take his hand, she said softly, "I'll be here."

"Take care, and with any luck, I'll be back with more writings in a few days. Until then, the bed is all yours."

With that he turned and was gone before Kate could even say, "Be careful."

"I never knew it could get so dark," Kate said softly into the night.

Sorrella shifted on the porch step by Kate. "*Sim*, it is dark."

"Very." Kate rested her chin on her forearms, which were crossed on her bent knees. "Do you go to the village very much, Sorrella?"

"*Sim*. I see Rosa." Sorrella chuckled softly, a gentle sound in the shadows. "Her child is near."

Kate remembered the way the girl had looked. "Yes, she's getting big."

"Valdez is pleased."

"Very pleased," Kate agreed. A sound off to the north caught her attention, a shrill scream that brought her to her feet. She strained to see into the night. "What was that?"

Sorrella stayed seated. "Animal. It is pained."

"Hurt?"

"*Sim*, hurt."

Kate sat down beside the other woman, but her hands stayed clenched on her thighs. "When will Nick and Alfredo be back?"

"Soon," Sorrella said softly.

Kate hoped that was true. In the four days since the two men had left the compound, time had dragged, falling into a set pattern. Sorrella came into the bedroom every day at dawn and, while Kate watched from the safety of the bed, searched for invaders. The woman was still somewhat reserved, but she had lost her earlier coldness.

After a light breakfast with Sorrella, Kate went into Nick's study and pored over the notebook with its enigmatic symbols—elusive scratches that filled her waking hours.

Now Kate jumped when a moth brushed its furry wing against her cheek. She swiped at it, more annoyed than afraid, then sat back and concentrated on imagining what Nick might be doing in the valley she had never seen.

"Sorrella?"

"Sim?"

"The valley... what do Nick and Alfredo do there?"

"Look for holes."

That didn't help at all. She wanted to be able to visualize a cave. "Have you ever seen a cave... a hole?"

"No. Sorrella stays at Senhor Nicholas's home."

"You don't go to the bottomland?"

The woman was silent for so long that Kate turned to look at her. The shadows had all but swallowed her up, but they didn't hide the stiffness of her posture. "Sorrella goes down just for a remembering day."

"What's that?"

The woman reverted to dialect and said something that could only be translated as, "When life comes."

Kate understood. A birthday. "You only go then?"

"Sim," she said. "Sorrella stays with Senhor Nicholas... and with Katreen, now."

Kate wondered why Sorrella didn't go below more often. She had come from there. She recognized Santeen as her headman. But Kate kept her questions to herself, sensing that Sorrella didn't want to talk about the bottomland anymore. She changed the subject by saying, "We will read soon."

"That is good."

Kate looked forward to the time before bed when she read with Sorrella. By chance the book from the school had been *Robinson Crusoe*, the story of a stranger in a strange land. Sorrella didn't understand a great deal of English, so Kate found herself randomly translating into the local dialect, strengthening the bond between herself and the other woman. The reading also boosted Kate's morale. Once a teacher, always a teacher, and it was a diversion for her, too.

It gave her a break from the hours she spent on Nick's sketches, hours when she found nothing. Absolutely nothing made sense. The letters didn't fit any pattern, produced no cadence. A half hour ago she'd given up, changed into fresh clothes, found Sorrella and come outside.

What she really wanted was to run, to stretch her legs, to feel genuine physical exhaustion instead of frustration and intellectual weariness.

She turned to Sorrella. "I'm going to get a book I left in the small house."

Sorrella nodded and stood. "The food is to eat."

"In a bit. I'll be right back."

She went back to the hut, found the book she had left out there earlier and came back to sit on the porch. Sorrella had gone inside and turned on a light in the living room. The glow drew the insects to the screen, actually pulling them away from Kate, and the light gave just enough of a glow for her to read by.

Distractedly, she began to flip through the pages, until something stopped her. On one glossy page a symbol struck a chord. Slowly Kate outlined the figure with her finger. It wasn't like Nick's writings, but something seemed familiar. She read the caption. *Portuguese Death Inscription.* The combination of vowels seemed familiar.

"Sorrella?" Kate called.

The woman came immediately, wiping her soapy hands on an apron she wore over her loose yellow shift. *"Sim, Katreen?"*

Kate had actually come to like the sound of her name on the woman's tongue. "Do you see this?" Kate asked, holding up the book.

The woman stared intently at the page. *"Sim."*

"Have you ever seen anything like this before?"

"Sim."

"Where?" Kate prodded.

Sorrella pointed back to the house. "On papers that Senhor Nicholas keeps."

So, the other woman saw it, too. "Does it mean anything to you?"

"Mean...?"

"Does it say anything to you?" Kate rephrased.

"No."

Kate closed the book, holding it to her chest. "Have you ever seen it in any other place?"

The black eyes never blinked. "No."

That would have been too much to ask for, Kate thought with a sigh.

"Katreen?"

"Yes?"

"Rosa says she wants to read out of a book, like you do with Sorrella."

"Rosa? How did you get to talk to her?" Neither of them had gone outside the fence since Nick and Alfredo had left.

"On the radio Senhor Nicholas uses to speak to Valdez." She smiled conspiratorially. "You will not say Rosa speaks on it, will you?"

"No, of course not. It isn't hurting anything."

"Can you read with her?"

"I don't see how, Sorrella, not that I wouldn't like to. If we could be together, like we are here, but not with her in the village."

"On the radio, you could do it."

The idea was tempting.

"I will not tell."

"No." Kate smiled at the woman. "I will tell Nick and get him to agree. It couldn't hurt for a few minutes now and then. I don't think he'll mind."

Sorrella beamed. "*Sim, sim.* I will call Rosa and tell her." She reached out uncertainly to pat Kate on the shoulder, then said, "Thank you."

Kate watched her go into the house. The woman had never thanked Kate for anything, had always wanted to serve. "It's my pleasure," she whispered when the door snapped shut.

Kate stayed where she was, thinking about Robinson Crusoe stranded on his island. This was like an island, just as isolated, but Kate had people here, people who touched her in the most unexpected ways.

She looked down at the book. She wanted to figure out this puzzle, wanted to help Sorrella and her people. But she needed Nick here. She needed him to help her sort out her impressions and give her some input on this find. Almost instantly, the door snapped open, and Sorrella rushed back out.

"Katreen, they have come back!" Sorrella said in a rush. "I see the lights!"

Kate scrambled to her feet, filled with tingling excitement. "Are you sure?"

Sorrella bobbed her head emphatically, "*Sim*, they are home." With that she hurried off to disappear around the corner of the house into the night.

Kate stayed where she was, clutching the book. After a long moment she heard Nick's voice, "Sorrella, it's me!" He sounded weary, and Kate waited.

She kept her eyes on the shadows until Nick stepped onto the porch and into the light.

He walked slowly, a drained version of the man who had left four days earlier. Grime streaked with sweat filmed his skin. Crusted mud hid his ebony hair, and his clothes had become dead gray. He came toward Kate.

Despite the aching weariness that filled his body, when Nick looked at Katherine, he felt like smiling. She looked so appealing in her pale shorts, holding an oversized textbook.

"Are you all right?" she asked in a breathless voice.

He knew how he looked; he'd faced it often enough in the mirror after one of his treks to the bottomland. He knew how he smelled, too. He told himself that was why he didn't give in to an inexplicable impulse and grab Katherine in a hard embrace. Four days of hard, backbreaking work and not a thing to show for it. He had felt like screaming in

frustration when no cave turned up in the eastern site he and
Alfredo had found.

"I just need a bath and twenty-four hours of sleep, and
I'll be good as new," he said, coming close enough to sense
her freshness. Then he said something he'd had no intention of saying to her. "Do you know how good it feels to
just look at you?"

A blush rose in her cheeks, a delicate flush that only enhanced her beauty. "Should . . . should I run you a bath?"

How long is it since I've seen a woman blush? he wondered. "Please," he whispered, beginning to sink from fatigue.

"Alfredo?" Sorrella asked.

"At your place. You go and see to him. Katreen will take
care of me."

The woman didn't argue, only turned to hurry to the
house in the rear of the compound that she shared with her
son. Nick watched her until she melted into the shadows;
then he turned to Katherine.

It was the relief, Kate reasoned, that was making her heart
bounce against her ribs. Or it could have been the heady
sense of joy flooding through her, or the way she could
breathe easily again, after four days of almost holding her
breath.

"I . . . I'll see to the bath," she said aloud and turned to
go into the house.

By the time the bath was full, Kate heard Nick moving
around in the bedroom. She turned off the water and went
into the other room. Nick was standing in the middle of the
floor, his pajamas in one hand, his shirt untucked and un-
buttoned. A line of grime ringed his throat, and red welts
showed on his chest. He came toward Kate, his steps heavy
and filled with weariness.

Kate had to clench her hands behind her to keep from
reaching out to touch the welts. It was too much like her
dream, a dream she hadn't had again while she slept alone
in the huge bed. "Are you hurt?"

He followed her gaze to glance down at his chest. "No. I'm in one piece."

"But . . . ?"

"Vines. They can hit you like whips sometimes."

Kate forced her eyes up to meet his gaze. "The bath is ready, and there are plenty of towels."

"I really appreciate it. Thank you." He exhaled a shuddering sigh. "That climb up from the bottomland gets steeper every time I come back."

Kate took in his condition, the hair that clung in muddy coils at his neck and temples, the prickly growth of beard filled with crusting dirt, perspiration that left tracks on his skin, and the smell—as if something had died.

"What's that awful smell?" she asked, crinkling her nose.

"I fell in one of the stagnant pools on my way back." He grimaced. "I only hope a bath will be enough to take care of it."

"Did you find anything?"

"No."

The stark flatness of the single word stopped Kate from asking any more. Since she didn't have a thing to show for her four days of work, she didn't have the heart to probe Nick about his time down below, so she stepped aside to let Nick walk past her into the bathroom. When the door clicked shut behind him, Kate hesitated, then knocked. The door swung back open.

"What is it?" Nick asked, his shirt discarded now and the welts fully exposed, red and raised.

Kate had to swallow hard before she could talk. "Food? Are you hungry?"

He seemed taken aback by her offer, an offer she hadn't considered making until it came out. "Thank you. Maybe some coffee?" He smiled, a heartrendingly boyish expression. "And a few of those rolls that Sorrella makes. Are there any?"

"Sure. She made some this morning."

"Good. Good." His gaze held hers for a long moment before he stooped to barely brush her lips with his cool mouth. Then he stepped back to close the door.

The couch in the study was as hard as a rock in the humid night, and Kate sat in there, unable to make herself go to the bedroom and get into the bed. She shifted to look out at the night, at the huge moon hanging in a sky of velvet blackness. She glanced at the clock on the desk—two o'clock. It had only been three hours since she'd come in here, yet it seemed like forever.

With a sigh, she stood and stretched, the movement tugging her short, white cotton nightie halfway up her thighs. She hadn't picked up her robe before she left the bedroom, and she didn't want to go back there just yet. Instead she snapped on the small desk lamp.

Kate flipped open the textbook and looked down at the writing, but her mind went in circles, circles that always came back to Nick. She turned the page, pushed back her loose hair and stared at the symbol she'd found just before Nick came home. Something nudged at her, but the thought remained elusive. She felt edgy and nervous. And that spontaneous kiss from Nick hadn't made her any calmer.

"Just a clue. All I need is a clue," she whispered.

Waiting for a breakthrough wore her down. She tossed the book onto the desk with a loud thud. "Just a clue, just one clue," she said into the stillness and stared at the book.

A moment later the door opened, and Nick, wearing only pajama bottoms, squinted into the room. "Is something wrong?" he asked in a voice thick with the remnants of sleep.

"No, nothing. I was just trying to think, that's all."

"What were you thinking about?"

"Things. My mind goes in circles sometimes."

Nick leaned against the jamb with one shoulder, crossing his arms on his bare chest. "Should I offer you a penny for your thoughts?" he asked around a yawn.

"You'd be getting cheated," she conceded softly. "And you need your sleep. I'm sorry I woke you. I didn't mean to."

"It wasn't you, just the crashing of books being thrown across the room that broke into my sleep."

She smiled faintly. "I tossed it onto the desk. I'm sorry."

"And I was teasing." He glanced past her at the clock. "I've been sleeping for seven hours. I'm feeling a little bit better." His gaze came back to meet Kate's. "Why aren't you in bed?"

"I couldn't sleep, so I thought I should try to do something useful." She shrugged. "No such luck."

"Thanks for bringing the coffee and rolls. I'm sorry I was asleep when you brought them in."

Kate had wanted to talk, to try and sort out her thoughts, and she'd been the one to be sorry to find him sound asleep on top of the bedclothes. His skin had been scrubbed, the welts had faded considerably, and his jaw had been clean shaven. She had stood by the bed for a moment simply looking down at him, watching the rise and fall of his bare chest.

She had felt like an intruder watching him sleep, but he had fascinated her. An unsuspected vulnerability had been exposed by the simple act of giving in to sleep. She had been stirred by a sense of protectiveness, but she had also been aroused. He was a strong man who probably never needed anyone to take care of him. He confused Kate more and more. Maybe that was another reason she hadn't gotten into bed, but had chosen to put a hallway and two doors between them. It had seemed the simplest thing to do at the time.

The memory made her feel awkward to be wearing only her nightgown, although the material was far from transparent. Yet her first reaction to seeing Nick in the doorway had been to cross her arms over her breasts. "I suppose your coffee is freezing by now?"

"Nothing freezes here. It's just unappealingly tepid."

Surely, she told herself, Nick was used to seeing women with less on than she wore now. The thought had been meant to comfort her, but it only made her feel more uneasy. To take her mind off the subject, she asked, "Since you're up, would you look at something for me?"

Instantly alert, Nick asked, "You found something?"

She shook her head quickly. "Nothing much. But it might help."

Disappointment stamped his face, but he asked hopefully, "What is it?"

Kate turned and flipped the book open on the desk, and when Nick came up behind her, she pointed to the Portuguese symbol. "This. It's Portuguese, a version of a death blessing, usually used for royalty."

Nick was so close that Kate could feel the heat of his breath on her bare shoulder as he asked, "And?"

Kate shrugged nervously, tucking her loose hair behind her ears. "It's the arrangement of the vowels, I think. Something about it looks familiar."

"Maybe," Nick said softly, then stood back. "Did it help you with the translation?"

She hated to say the word. "No. But it seems to underscore the fact that the writing might be some form of Portuguese." She closed the book and turned, almost hitting her chin on Nick's shoulder. She pressed back against the desk, the heat of the man all around her, and looked up. "I haven't found anything important."

"I knew you hadn't." He ran a hand across the back of his neck. "You would have told me when I first came up, wouldn't you?"

"Of course."

Nick sighed heavily. "I had hoped..."

"...for a miracle?"

"I'm afraid so. You'd think I'm old enough and cynical enough to know that miracles just don't happen."

"It never hurts to want one," Kate murmured.

Nick shrugged his bare shoulders sharply. "I'll let you hope for the miracles, and I'll stick to cold, hard reality."

Kate watched his face and asked something she'd wondered about since she'd found out about the existence of the treasure. "What are you going to do with the treasure when you find it?"

"Turn it over to the government to be put in trust for the Indians."

Her perception of Nick changed again. Why had she thought that Nick would want to be the one to dole the money out, to play benefactor? "That's very..." She wanted to say nice, but she didn't. "Practical."

He nodded. "I can be practical when I put my mind to it."

Kate saw the twinkle of laughter in his eyes and answered it with a half smile. "Even rich people can be practical. I know that. I'm not a snob."

"You could have fooled me," he countered softly. He lifted his hand as if to brush at a lock of hair that had fallen across her cheek, but stopped when Kate gasped.

Impulsively, she reached for his hand and turned it palm up. It looked raw and sore; small cuts were everywhere. His chest had been nothing compared to this. "Oh, my..."

"We spent most of our time recutting paths that had gotten overgrown. We made it to the second finger of land to the east, to the end of it and around the other side. We thought there might be a cave on the far side, but there wasn't. We couldn't go any further, not this time."

Kate wanted to do something, but she didn't have any idea where to start. "You...you can't go on like this." Her hand trembled where it held Nick's. She touched her tongue to her lips. "You can't."

He curled his hand shut over the damage, tangling his fingers with hers. "I can, and I will," he said softly, then let her go.

Kate drew back, hiding her hands behind her back. "Don't the Indians help?"

"No. They stay in certain areas of the valley, and when they go into the deep jungle, they don't cut paths like I do. They just slip through the growth."

"For four days you cut paths?"

"I did make one discovery while I was down there. I always thought the valley was relatively contained, but now Santeen says that it goes north forever, probably into the area of the Pico da Neblina rise and on into Venezuela or Colombia."

She frowned at him. "How did Santeen know that? Has he gone north?"

"He has, but never past the great falls. Some of the young men went hunting and traveled for days and never found the end. They had just gotten back when Alfredo and I saw Santeen. They said the waterfalls end, but the valley turns into a deeper, more rugged cut in the land."

Kate nibbled on her bottom lip. "Could the treasure be that far away?"

"I hope not. I sincerely hope not," he said. He barely stifled a yawn. "Sorry. I guess I should get back to bed."

Kate stopped him before he could turn to leave. "Nick, I want to ask you something."

He leaned against the doorway, startled by a wave of weakness that robbed him of strength. "What is it?"

He heard her take a breath, and watched the way her breasts lifted the light material that only hinted at their high fullness. "Sorrella and I have been reading together at night, and I'm translating things for her as I go along." Her tongue shot out to touch her lips. "What I want to know is if I can use the shortwave radio?"

He shook his head to clear his mind of the woman in front of him. It was hard to follow a conversation when all he wanted to do was to curl up in bed with her and hold her. She'd been wise to come in here instead of getting into bed earlier. He'd brought her here to work, not to make love to him. He ran a hand over his face. "What on earth for? It doesn't reach very far."

"Rosa heard about us reading, and she'd like it if I could read to her, too. She understands English, and she went to the school, and I..." Katherine looked confused for a minute, then looked at Nick and asked simply, "Can I use the radio?"

With no hesitation, Nick nodded. "If you want, but it seems like a lot of bother just to read to Rosa."

She began to twist one strand of her loose hair around her finger. "It's no bother. I want to do it."

Nick straightened, then waited to make sure his legs would hold him. He needed to lie down again, but he was reluctant to go back to the room alone. But somehow he knew that Katherine wouldn't come, not just yet. "So, you and Sorrella found some common ground after all. What are you reading with her?"

"Robinson Crusoe."

That tickled Nick unexpectedly, raising the image of Katherine as Friday. He couldn't help reaching out to touch her shoulder, asking, "Do you see yourself as my Man Friday?"

She smiled, a gentle upward curving of her full lips. "As your helper. Maybe as your partner in the search," she said softly. "How do *you* see me?"

How did he see her? Damn it, he couldn't go into that without completely confusing the issue. She felt so soft under his hand. He drew back. Get to bed and get to sleep before she comes in, he told himself sternly. "As a great help...and a partner," he said, then had to cover another yawn. "Valdez should come up tomorrow with the mail. If you want to write home, this is your only chance for a while."

Home. How long had it been since Kate had thought more than fleetingly about the school and her family and friends? She didn't know. "Thanks, I need to write to Dad." She thought of something. "Should I ask Valdez for permission to read to Rosa on the radio?"

"Good thinking," he said with the hint of a pleased smile. "I think you're starting to understand these people."

She was, slowly but surely, and she was starting to understand this man in front of her, too. "Yes, I think I am."

His smile was gone, and his eyes were filled with a disturbing intensity. "Do I have to tell you how good it was to see you here when I came up to the top tonight?"

The world narrowed precariously for Kate, encompassing just herself and Nick. "I was glad to see you come back," she said, amazed at what an understatement that was. Would she ever forget those first moments of staggering relief that Nick had made it back? "I kept thinking about you down there, wondering what you were doing."

Damn it. She held him to the spot as surely as if she had bound him to her with bands of steel. "I was working," he said softly. "Very hard." He wanted to leave. He knew he should, yet he found himself reaching out to touch her loose hair and curl one silky strand around his finger, an echo of the habit he had recognized in her. "I thought about you up here, about everything that this project means," he breathed.

He was too tired to fight any battles tonight, least of all with himself, and he simply drew Katherine to him. For a single moment, he held her tightly. Nothing had felt this good to him in a very long time. Comfort? Support? What did he need from Katherine right now? His brain seemed fogged with weariness, and with a need to hold on to the woman with him. He drank in her presence, her softness pressed to him, and he closed his eyes tightly. He wished he understood himself, understood the needs that seemed to come from nowhere to fill him.

Kate let Nick hold her. She rested her head in the hollow of his shoulder and felt the rhythm of his heart against her breast. But her awareness didn't stop there. Suddenly she felt everything about Nick, down to the heat of his breath ruffling across her hair. And it made her knees suddenly weak.

"I wish..." Nick began, but stopped when Katherine drew back and looked up at him, her eyes wide with an expression he couldn't begin to understand.

What did he wish? he asked himself silently. The answer came from the presence of the woman in front of him. He wasn't wishing for comfort or support. No. He dipped his head to claim lips softly parted in question, lips that he realized had been tantalizing him for a very long time. But the contact was barely made before he broke it. This was reality, not a land of granted wishes. What little control he had left went into making him draw back.

He even felt a certain sense of pride in his control, in his ability to murmur, "Good night," and actually turn and walk away.

Kate watched the door close behind Nick. She didn't move for a very long time. The feeling that had sprung to life when Nick's lips touched hers refused to go away. It had come from nowhere to explode all through her.

That fleeting contact had made her totally, achingly, aware of her womanhood. She forced herself to take a deep, unsteady breath. Why didn't her body understand the difference between acting and reality?

Acting and reality. Those two words brought everything under control for Kate. With relief she mentally arranged her situation with Nick—employer, employee, maybe friends. And that was all. But logic couldn't make it possible for her to go to bed until the first rays of dawn had crept into the study.

Chapter 8

"They are back, Katreen," Sorrella called as she rushed from the house. "They are back!"

That scene was played out four times in the next five weeks, when Alfredo and Nick came up from the valley bottom. And three times there was an air of celebration when Nick produced more writings from the caves.

After each excursion below, Nick stayed at the compound for a day or two, only long enough to recover emotionally and physically before heading back to the bottomland. During his days at the compound, Kate worked side by side with him, and they talked. Long into the night, they lay in bed, the shadows and half the bed separating them, speaking in low, hushed tones.

"I don't have any family," Nick had said once, after lying in silence for a while. "I'm alone, but not lonely. There's a difference."

Businesses he'd spent years building had been dismissed with, "They run themselves, pretty much. I've got a good staff. I don't have to be there except in emergencies, and I pay people to make sure there aren't any."

"Don't you care about them?" she'd asked.

"I cared until the challenge was gone," he'd admitted through the shadows. "Challenge. Excitement. Making the impossible happen. That's all that matters. That's what makes life worth living."

She hadn't known what to say.

"What's important to you?" he'd asked Kate unexpectedly.

"Getting my Ph.D., then teaching," she'd said without hesitation, looking into the darkness. "That's my challenge."

"That's enough?"

"Yes."

"But you know you'll get your degree and that you'll teach. There's no challenge there. Just the question of when."

"It's hard work. And it's satisfying," she'd countered, confronted suddenly by incontrovertible proof of how different their lives were. "Safe and satisfying."

"It would drive me crazy," he'd admitted softly. "But if it's what you want, go for it." He'd reached through the shadows to touch her hand where it rested on the sheet. "Your life is only what you make of it."

"And what will you make of your life after you find the treasure?" she'd asked, not pulling away from the contact.

The answer had been so long in coming that she'd thought he'd fallen asleep. Finally he'd spoken. "Exactly what I want to make of it. They told me a long time ago that I'm like my father. He was restless, always looking for something more to life, something beyond the present. I understand that." There was another long silence; then he let go of her when he spoke. "My mother hardly fit into his life. She was gentle and soft, very structured." More silence, then, "She needed constants in her life, I think."

"Don't you miss having a family?" she'd asked the night before he went back down on his last trip.

He'd considered that for only a moment. "I've never really thought about it. I'm on my own, and I like it that way." His deep sigh had drifted into the warm night air. "I only have to worry about myself. No one worries about me. I don't have that on my conscience. When this is done, I can go anywhere or do anything I want to. Freedom. How do people live without it?"

Commitment, Kate had thought. How do people survive without *that*? Nick was committed now, to this project, but what about later? What about before this happened?

"Why did you break things off with your fiancé?" Nick had asked without warning that last night.

"He wanted a life in Chicago. I didn't," she'd said simply.

The bed had shifted, but Kate had kept her eyes on the canopy. "That's not good enough," Nick had said.

"What do you mean?"

She had been able to sense Nick, who had risen on one elbow and was facing her through the shadows, watching her. "You might not have wanted *him*, but Chicago should have been the least of your worries."

Kate had considered that for a moment. "Chicago seemed like another world to me."

"And you like the familiar...the safe?" Nick had prodded, using her own words against her just before his hand touched her shoulder.

Nick was a toucher. In the nights when they talked, he'd often brushed her hand with his, or touched her while they talked, as if getting his bearing in the dark. Kate lay very still. "Is something wrong with that?"

"No, not for you. I don't suppose it's wrong."

She absorbed Nick's words, thinking about them deep into the night after he fell asleep and his deep, even breathing drifted over to her. Was it wrong to want to be safe, to know what you were doing, where you were going? Was it wrong for the kind of life Nick led to scare her?

She and Nick were poles apart in everything but their desire to find an answer to the puzzle of the valley. That was their bond, their joining. And Kate worked on the pieces of the riddle day and night.

Her only breaks came for meals, for dreamless sleep, and for the occasional letters that came from her father. Valdez rode out to the compound on a huge gray horse with a string of pack animals behind him. He brought supplies, along with the mail. Another break came when Kate spoke to Rosa every other day on the radio, reading short excerpts from *Robinson Crusoe*. A bond had grown between the two women. Valdez simply nodded whenever Kate spoke to him about the readings, and occasionally even smiled. Kate found herself liking him more all the time.

Kate read her father's letters, long, diarylike missives that told about the life she'd left. They only made her feel more removed from the outside world. They talked about a life where news was being made worldwide, where discoveries and tragedies abounded, a life that receded farther from her with each day she spent on the valley rim.

On the fifth day of Nick's last trip down, Kate sat alone at the dining table reading her father's latest letter. She ignored the food on her plate while she read and reread the pages.

Just think. You wouldn't go to Chicago, but you'll go all the way to Brazil. People grow and change all the time, don't they?

She read that two more times before she was able to figure out why she had been able to come here, yet Chicago had been wrong for her. She hadn't wanted to make a commitment to Mike. It was so simple to understand that now, but it hadn't been so simple then. Here she felt a commitment to the work that outweighed the discomforts of life.

She looked back at the letter. *I'm sure Mr. Dantry will succeed at his "project," whatever that may be. He seems to be the type to thrive on a challenge.* How could her father know that? Surely she hadn't said so in her letters. *I miss you, darling, but you sound very excited about your work there, excited about something outside these walls...finally. Just be careful. When a person becomes involved in another person's obsession, it can either be very fulfilling, or very dangerous.*

Kate squinted at the last sentence. An obsession? Was that what this was for Nick? Probably. And her father had realized it before she had. She let the paper fall onto the table and sat back in her chair. Either he'll find the treasure or die trying. That brought the situation into very clear focus for Kate, and tension knotted in her stomach.

How she wished she'd found a key, something to unlock the mystery of the writings. But no answers had come, despite the three new finds. She dreaded the moment when Nick would come back up and ask her what she'd discovered. His disappointment wouldn't be stated out loud, but his true feelings were easy to read in his eyes. She rested her elbows on the table and buried her face in her hands.

"Katreen?"

Kate looked up to find Sorrella standing over her. "Yes, Sorrella?"

The tall woman motioned to Kate's nearly untouched meal. "Is the food not good for eating? Are you sick?"

"No, it's fine, and I'm not sick." Kate sighed, sitting back in her chair. "I'm just worried about Nick coming back. I haven't found a thing to help him." She ran a hand over her hair, which was confined in a tight knot at the back of her head. "It's so hot, and my hair's a mess again."

Sorrella cocked her head to one side to study Kate. "Cut it."

"You have long hair."

"Sorrella is used to it. Katreen is not. Cut it." Kate was ready to refuse, but just then a trickle of moisture ran down her forehead. "Yes, it might be a good idea if I could figure out how to do it so I didn't look ridiculous."

"Sorrella will do it."

Kate thought about Nick's repeated suggestions that she cut it and the way she'd refused. But she hated the way it felt. "Could you really do it?"

"*Sim*. Sorrella will do it fine."

Kate took a deep breath and nodded. "All right."

Sorrella hurried back to the kitchen and returned with a large pair of scissors in her hand. She motioned toward the front porch. "Outside."

Kate walked outside and sank down on the top step. Sorrella crouched behind her and silently began to take the pins out of Kate's hair so the heavy tresses could fall loose. Sorrella smoothed it, then began to systematically snip at the coppery strands.

As the shadows of evening began to gather, great clumps of hair fell around Kate. Her resolve began to weaken, and she tried to bolster it a bit. How bad can it look? she asked herself. Hair grows. It isn't like having plastic surgery. More hair fell to coil on her bare legs and the pale blue of her shorts. It will grow out sooner or later, no matter how it looks when Sorrella finishes. One damp curl floated to the ground by her sandaled feet, and Kate closed her eyes. She didn't open them again until Sorrella spoke up. "It is finished."

Kate raised a hand, and her heart plunged when her fingers touched what was left of her hair. She stood slowly, turning to face Sorrella. "It's all gone."

"*Sim*, it is pretty," the housekeeper said with a smile. "Pretty."

A sheared sheep. Kate nervously fingered the fringe at the nape of her exposed neck. "Are you sure?"

"*Sim.*" Sorrella bobbed her head enthusiastically. "Very pretty. Go see, Katreen."

Kate hesitated, not at all sure she had the nerve to look in a mirror. "I suppose I should," she murmured.

"*Sim, sim,*" Sorrella prodded.

With more than a little apprehension, Kate slowly stepped into the house. As she went down the hall and into the bedroom, her steps slowed even more. "Just look at it," she told herself aloud, and went into the bathroom.

With an action that was second nature to her now, Kate scanned the small room for bugs. When she saw it was clear, she took a deep breath and turned to the mirror over the sink. Wide-eyed, she looked at her reflection. Instead of the heavy mane of auburn, a softly fringed pixie cap framed her face. It lay lightly over her scalp, fringed above her eyes and around her ears, and parted naturally off center. Kate shook her head, twisting from side to side to get a better view.

"Not bad," she breathed with growing relief.

She ran her fingers through the feathery strands and they fell back into place. It wasn't what she'd imagined—no sheared sheep, no need to wait for it to grow out. And it felt so good.

She flashed a grin at her reflection, then hurried back outside to Sorrella. The housekeeper was bent over, picking up Kate's discarded curls. "Sorrella, it's wonderful. Thank you."

The housekeeper kept working, picking up each coil of shorn hair, but she smiled at Kate. "Pretty. Senhor Nicholas's number-one female is pretty."

"Thank you." Kate ran her fingers through her hair again. "I hope Nick likes it."

Sorrella laughed, an expression of amused indulgence that Kate had never heard from the woman before. "Do not worry. Senhor Nicholas likes anything Katreen does."

Kate looked at the woman. "What?"

"Katreen does not clean, or cook, or sew, or have babies, and still Senhor Nicholas smiles all the time he sees you." That must have been unheard of for Sorrella, yet it amused her. "Smiles, smiles, smiles," she chanted. "All the time."

Kate shrugged, not wanting to think about Nick's smiles right then, or her own lack of accomplishments. "I wish he would get back."

Sorrella sobered. "You are alone too much."

"We both are, Sorrella," Kate said.

"We can read?"

"Yes, in a while," Kate agreed, turning to the softness of the early evening sky while Sorrella went inside. She walked along the porch, watching the pinks and yellows flood the distant heavens. The heat that had been tempered by a torrential shower that morning had come back in full force.

The ground had absorbed the water with an ease that seemed remarkable to Kate, but the humidity had only increased.

She stepped down onto the gravel and headed for the hut out back. The ever-present mists wreathed the land in deceptive softness, and the rushing of the falls echoed around her. She fingered the shorn hair at her nape and wondered where Alfredo and Nick were now.

She ducked into the hut, closed the door, snapped on the light and went to sit in the chair. The stickiness of the wood reached her through her shorts and cotton blouse, but she stayed, staring at the writings Nick had retrieved from the caves.

The caves in the eastern section had held a wealth of findings, yet nothing fit. She stared at the figures until they began to blur in front of her eyes. Concentrating, searching for some key to the mystery, she almost jumped out of her skin when a piercing animal cry cut through the night. She never got used to that sound, and she froze when it was repeated. Goose bumps rose on her arms as the cries died out.

Kate got up, shut off the light and stepped out into the deepening night. She stood alone, listening, and from somewhere outside the compound fence she heard a noise. The soft whinny of a horse came clearly, then low voices and shuffling footsteps, and Kate knew what was happening.

She followed the sound with her eyes. First the entry gate squeaked on its hinges. Next, she knew, the horses were secured in a protected area to the north, near the house Sorrella and Alfredo shared. Movement came in the deeper shadows by the fence; then Nick emerged from the darkness.

His face was a dark blur, but as he came closer, Kate could tell that he looked as he always did—exhausted and dirty. His clothes clung to him, darkened beyond recognition by grime and sweat; his shoulders sagged under the burden of weariness; his feet scuffed the gravel.

She ran toward him. "Nick!"

He heard his name being called at the same time that he saw Katherine moving through the night to meet him halfway between the hut and the fence. He stopped. Four days of frustration and useless searching for another cave had left him drained and disappointed. He hurt all over, in his arms, his legs, his back, his shoulders, and his head pounded. He couldn't stand up to questions or bubbling enthusiasm. He braced himself, feeling both happiness at seeing Katherine and a wariness at what she was going to say.

"What are you doing out here?" He knew his voice sounded harsh, but he couldn't draw back the words.

Katherine stopped abruptly. "I was in the hut when I heard you coming." She stopped several feet away and looked past him. "Where's Alfredo?"

"Finishing with the horses." He stood very still, staring at her, uncertain how one person could be such a welcome vision, yet draw up every nerve painfully inside him. Ducking his head, he went past her on his way to the house. She hurried to his side, keeping pace with him. For an instant he caught the scent of her perfume, a light flowery sweetness; then it was gone, and the odor of his own dirt and sweat filled his senses.

She didn't have a thing to tell him. He knew that with a depressing certainty. If there were news, she would have blurted it out as soon as she saw him. Four days of hard work—for both of them—and nothing had changed. He stepped up onto the porch, and Katherine ran past him to the front door. In the light that spilled from the windows she looked slender and graceful, instantly appealing, as she pulled back the screen and called, "Sorrella!"

Then he saw her hair.

The sight stopped Nick at the door for a moment. Then he kicked off his dirty boots and brushed past Katherine to step into the house. Sorrella came rushing out of the kitchen.

"Senhor Nicholas," she said with a big smile; then her expression faltered. "Where is Alfredo?"

"At your place," he muttered, his impatience with everything intensified by his shock at Katherine's new look.

"You are sure?" she asked as she came closer.

Nick looked at Katherine, at her wispy cap of hair, then back to the housekeeper. "I told you, he's at your place," he snapped. "Go and see for yourself if you don't believe me."

He heard Katherine take a sharp breath, but when she spoke, her voice was soft. "I'll start a bath for you."

"Forget it." Why was he doing this? He took a deep breath of air, hoping to ease his tension. In that instant, he would have given anything to believe in miracles.

He didn't understand himself why he was so short with Sorrella, why he wanted to strike out at everyone, and why it irritated him to have to talk and think. It had to be the heat and his total weariness. They clouded his thinking, taking away the ability to reason. He turned, leaving the two women standing in the living room, and headed for the bedroom.

"Go to Alfredo," he heard Katherine saying to Sorrella. "He needs you."

Sure, tell my housekeeper what to do, he thought with irritated pettiness. He stepped into the bedroom, a room that seemed heavy with the scent that Katherine used. An invasion of his world, that's what he decided she was, when all he'd wanted was a linguist.

"But I must help Senhor Nicholas," he heard Sorrella saying.

"No, I can take care of him."

"He is angry with Sorrella."

"No, he's been gone too long, and he's tired, not angry. Go and see to your son. Just be thankful they're both back safely."

"*Sim,*" Sorrella said immediately; then the front door clicked open and shut.

Nick felt his insides drawing up painfully. She's apologizing to Sorrella for me! he thought angrily. With sharp movements he began to unbutton his shirt, tearing one buttonhole by tugging until the button popped off and fell onto the floor. He stripped the stinking cotton off and dropped it at his feet.

"You ruined a perfectly good shirt," Katherine said, and Nick looked up to see her standing in the door. A disapproving frown drew delicate lines between her amber eyes.

Now that he could see her clearly, a surge of real anger coursed through him. The silky auburn veil had disappeared, leaving a wispy memory to frame her delicate features and darkly lashed eyes. It took him off balance to react so violently to a change he'd been the one to suggest in the first place, and his voice came out hard and cutting. "I heard what you said to Sorrella, and I don't need you explaining my actions to my servants!"

Katherine closed the door quietly, then crossed to stand toe-to-toe with him. Her own anger was evident in her low, vibrant voice. "You had no right to treat her like that! Alfredo is all she has. You could have taken a few minutes to reassure her."

Nick took in every detail of her appearance. "It's none of your damned business how I treat her," he muttered tightly.

"It *is* my business—because she's my friend."

Nick frowned at her, narrowing his eyes so he couldn't see the satiny curve of her cheek so clearly. "Just when I think I have you all figured out, you go and do something really stupid!"

Her eyes widened. "What is that supposed to mean? Just because I won't let you hurt someone I care about, that doesn't mean..."

He reached out to touch the shorn hair at her temple. He almost drew back, but finally he allowed himself to make contact with the silky fringe on her brow. "No, your hair." He shook his head. "What happened to it?"

"Sorrella cut it for me."

His reaction was stupid, and he couldn't justify it, so he didn't try. "And you let her do it?" He couldn't stop his fingertips from brushing back her bangs, then trailing down to the hollow of her cheek. He stopped abruptly when he realized that what he really wanted was to hold Katherine. The memory of the night in the study came to him clearly, along with the times when he'd told himself that it was only to support the illusion that she was his number-one female that he touched Katherine, dropped his arm around her, or kissed her.

This wasn't part of any illusion. It was a real need, and maybe that was why he pulled back. The need was too strong, too immediate. He forced himself to return to their earlier conversation. "You let her cut it all off?"

"You let her cut *your* hair," she countered in a voice edged with huskiness.

He forced his hands behind his back. "That's entirely different. I'm a man."

"That makes it okay? That doesn't make sense."

His anger began to dissolve, and he realized it had been directed mostly at himself—at his own failures. "I'm tired and dirty, and I don't have to make sense," he found himself saying with a petulance no child could have bested.

Suddenly Katherine laughed, a gentle, soothing sound that touched him to his soul. Her whole face glowed with delight, and Nick felt as if a heavy weight had been lifted from his back. "And that doesn't make any sense, either," she managed.

His own smile grew slowly, tugging at the corners of his lips until it couldn't be denied. "How did you get so smart?" he asked softly.

Dark lashes swept low over the richness of her eyes. "Practice."

Reason deserted him, and Nick gave in to his own needs. He'd hold her for just a minute, he told himself. Just long enough to balance his emotions. But when he actually touched her and drew her to him, the contact stunned him. Her slenderness fit every angle of his body, and the comfort in her all but overwhelmed him.

He didn't move. He simply held Katherine tightly to his bare chest, and she let him. She rested against him, her arms circling his waist, her hands spread across his back. The beat of her heart against him felt like an echo of the blood coursing through his own body. Drenched in sensations and the scent that clung to her hair, he impulsively touched the top of her head with his lips, then had to close his eyes to get his bearings.

Comfort? No. This was passion. Every inch of his being throbbed with life. What had begun under the guise of comfort sped up his breathing, increased his heart rate, and made images come to his mind that sent urgent messages to other parts of his body.

Let her go, he told himself, but when he would have drawn back, Katherine spoke softly in a muffled whisper.

"Everything will be all right," she said.

Nick had to blink rapidly and literally force himself to hold her away. The air felt cool as it brushed his chest. Strange, how it actually chilled him. "I'm sorry for everything," he whispered.

She gently spread her fingers on his chest, the touch light but compelling. "That's all right. I know you're tired."

Don't patronize me, he thought, but he said only, "Yes, very tired."

She touched her lips with her tongue, her eyes never leaving his face. "I'm just trying to help."

"I know...I know," he breathed, horribly aware of a heaviness in him that had nothing to do with fatigue.

Her lips parted softly, and Nick couldn't handle the understanding he saw in her eyes. He didn't deserve it. "Don't look at me like that," he said, trying to clear his own mind. "I don't have any answers for what I'm doing tonight." He drew back, breaking the physical contact between them, but that didn't kill the memory of her body pressed to his. "I...I'm going to take that bath," he mumbled, making his escape before his own body embarrassed him. He hurried into the bathroom and shut the door firmly behind him.

He stood very still on the other side of the wooden barrier, took a deep, cleansing breath, then crossed to the tub and turned on the water full force. He stripped off the rest of his clothes, tossed them into a heap on the floor and stepped into the soothing water, sliding down to rest his head on the back of the porcelain tub. He closed his eyes to block out the sight of what his errant emotions were doing to his body.

He concentrated on the past days, on the trails he'd cut, the jungle that had been tamed for a brief moment. But Katherine wouldn't leave his mind. She's helping, that's it, he told himself. All I can ask of her is to translate the puzzle. But desire couldn't be killed with reason, and he felt heavy and uncomfortable, even in the buoyancy of the water. She's beautiful, but she's off limits, he cautioned himself, then had to ask why. The answer came on its own, an answer that took him off guard. Because she's a friend, a real friend.

Nick had always been drawn to women on a sexual level, but not once had he been friends with a woman first.

The admission made him feel a bit stupid. If I make my relationship with her into anything more, it's going to ruin everything between us. He knew that without question. My life-style isn't hers. There's nothing between us except this job. He'd learned a long time ago that physical desire didn't compensate for real differences. She was off limits. No matter how erotic the idea of doing more than kissing her was, he couldn't risk everything for that.

An affair would never be enough with Katherine—or for her.

He didn't want to do anything to hurt her. He made himself stare at the wall over the tub. I should have used cold water, he thought with wry humor. Really cold water.

Kate didn't move until she heard the sloshing sounds die out; then, with a sharp shake of her head, she turned and retreated to the kitchen. In the tiny square room, she looked down and saw the dirt smudging her clothes, the dirt that had rubbed off from Nick. Ignoring the stains, she set a tray out on the wooden counter under the series of windows on the back wall. She put out a plate of sweet rolls, a jug of water and a small pot of coffee, which Sorrella had already prepared.

Back in the bedroom, she put the tray on the dresser and stooped to pick up Nick's dirty shirt. The small button was still on the rug, where it had landed earlier, and Kate scooped it up. She rubbed the plastic disk between her fingers, feeling the remnant of knotted thread still clinging to it, much the same way she had to cling to composure around Nick. With an exasperated sigh, she put the shirt and the button on a tiny table by the door.

She wiped her hands on her bare thighs and crossed to the bed to pull back the sheet and blanket. She didn't want to think about what had happened between herself and Nick, and she refused to squarely face the fact that the man had become unnervingly important to her.

Important? What an inadequate word to describe her reaction to him. She bit her lip. She had to keep a distance between them. He had his needs, and she had hers. She had never considered the possibility of developing deep feelings for someone like Nick. The men she had known in her life had all been cut from the same cloth—serious scholars from the academic world. A safe world for her. Like Mike. But even Mike had faded out of her life. And Nick, too, would fade back into the world he knew best. He had his life. She had hers.

She smoothed the sheet and fluffed the pillow. He'd go back to what he'd done before, and so would she. He would go back to a life where he surely had someone. She stopped and frowned. She didn't know if he had any emotional ties to anyone. The information had never been offered. He'd never married, but he wouldn't have been a monk.

She smoothed the pillow again. She wasn't about to leave a part of herself with this man. She hadn't left any part of herself with Mike. She hit the pillow with the flat of her hand, once, twice, three times.

"Don't kill it."

Her hand stopped in midair, and she turned to find Nick in the doorway, tying the cord of his pajama bottoms. His skin looked flushed from the heat of the bathwater, and his eyes were empty of any humor. "May I say something before you destroy the only extra pillow I have here?"

Kate grabbed the victimized pillow and clutched it to her chest. "Yes . . . of course."

Nick ran careless fingers through his damp hair, setting the spiky strands at odd angles around his deeply tanned face. His gray eyes seemed to grow paler yet more penetrating as his tan deepened. "I owe you an apology. Ours is a working relationship and, I hope, a friendship. That's important to me. I had no right to act the way I did." His gaze flicked over her, and the shadow of a smile played around his lips. "And I like your hair. It came as a shock at first, but now I realize that it's very becoming."

Kate felt her face warm. "I guess I owe you an apology, too."

"Why?"

"You told me to cut it earlier, and I should have. It did get hot and heavy."

"I guess we cancel each other out. And Sorrella did a good job."

Kate nodded. His apology and the softness of his voice were hard for her to handle. "Yes, she did, didn't she? She's quite remarkable."

"And she's grown very fond of her 'Katreen,'" he said.

"Don't you love that name?" Kate asked, finding the tension in her easing. "I do. It's really special."

"You're special to her."

She hugged the pillow more tightly to her breast. "We have so many things in common. I would never have dreamed it could work out this way, but Sorrella . . ." Her words faltered when she realized she was simply filling space with them.

"I really should apologize to her, too."

Kate could see the tension at his mouth and eyes. "Is something else wrong?"

"Wrong?" he echoed. "Nothing . . . everything . . . I don't know." He glanced at the dresser, then crossed to pour hot coffee into the heavy ceramic mug. He took a sip before he looked back to Kate. "Want some?"

"No, thanks. None for me."

Nick cradled the mug between both hands and slowly sipped more of the steaming liquid. When Kate couldn't bear the silence any longer, she tossed the pillow on the bed and moved to the windows. When she pulled back the drapes she could see a huge moon cresting over the valley, soft mists rising to ring it in a gentle halo. She kept her back to the room and finally asked, "Do you want to talk about it?"

His breath hissed softly. "You didn't figure anything out, did you?"

Kate hated herself for failing. "No. I'm sorry."

"So am I."

Turning, she saw him cross to sit on the side of the bed. "What happened down below?" she asked.

He stared at the mug, then looked up, to some spot beyond Kate. "Nothing."

"I know something happened. Are you going to tell me what?"

His bare shoulders moved sharply. "There's nothing to talk about. Days in that land for nothing." Abruptly he crossed back to the dresser and put the mug down with a crack on the wooden top. He pressed both hands palm down on the dresser, lowering his head and hunching his shoulders. "And I'm tired." He turned, his hands held palm up to expose the raw skin. "This is nothing, but the tiredness goes to my soul. This need I have to find the clues, to make sense out of the old man's death . . . it eats at me and makes me do things I never thought I could do. I owe the old man and his people." He closed his hands into tight fists. "Damn it, I don't know if I can repay the debt or not."

Wide-eyed at the despair she heard in his words, Kate whispered, "You work so hard." She tried not to look at the welts that hadn't quite faded from his chest and arms. "It takes a toll."

He looked directly at her, his eyes filled with weariness. "Not hard enough."

"You're doing everything anybody could."

He chuckled with a cutting harshness that held no humor at all. "I should have stayed down longer. I found nothing, no cave, no writings, just jungle and more jungle, confined by hard granite walls." He came back to sink onto the edge of the bed, and he exhaled heavily. "I should never have come up without something for all the pain and all the work . . . instead of settling for nothing."

Her whole being responded to him. His need to settle what he perceived as a debt was staggering. He would either find the treasure or die trying, she realized. His was a dangerous obsession. She could barely look at him, but her mind raced. It was the sense of being helpless that was eating at him, the feeling that he couldn't meet this challenge. She had to think of something, anything to give him hope so he could pull back, so he could rest and regroup.

"You're doing all you can," she found herself saying as she crossed to sit beside him on the bed.

"For all the good it's done," he whispered, staring down at his hands. "Damn it, I have to do this. I have to."

Kate grasped at straws, saying anything that came to her mind. "We need to think, to approach this from a different angle. What if we've been wrong about the writings? We keep thinking that they're some strange language, some distorted use of an odd dialect."

She stopped dead, and in a blinding flash she knew the answer. "Nick, what if the pieces of the puzzle are just that—pieces of a puzzle?" Nick looked at her blankly, and she scrambled off the bed to run into the study. She grabbed the sheets with the symbols on them and hurried back to Nick.

She sat down beside him again and began to methodically tear each symbol free of the others until she had a scattering of papers piled on the bed. Then, catching her tongue between her teeth, she concentrated, moving the papers around, putting them in one order, then rearranging them, until she saw what she'd been guessing at. "Nick," she said. "Look at this."

He moved closer. "What?"

She switched another two symbols, then another pair, and suddenly everything fit. "That's it," she whispered, tears burning her eyes, blurring the figures in front of her. "That's it!"

"What?" Nick asked tensely.

Kate pointed to what she'd done. "Alone they mean nothing—partial words, quarters of words, chopped segments. But when they're joined just right, like a puzzle, they make phrases. It's an offshoot of Portuguese. Grammatically, they're incorrect, horrendous, but the words are there."

Nick leaned closer still, his dark hair brushing her auburn cap as she bent over the paper. "What do they say?" he demanded in a strained voice.

Kate stared at the pieces of paper, then closed her eyes and caught at possible words. "I think the verb is misused, but..."

"I don't give a damn about verbs! What do they say?"

She looked up, amber eyes meeting gray. "A rising moon...shadows...the shadow of a tree, or maybe trees."

Nick moved so quickly that the papers shifted, and he demanded, "Trees? What trees? Where?"

"I don't know." She settled the papers in order again. "Trees and shadows. Whatever it means, it's the break we've been looking for, the break that makes some sense out of everything."

Nick stood abruptly. "No, it doesn't make sense."

Kate tilted her head to look up at him. "Yes, it does." She looked at the pieces of paper and saw another word. "A rising moon, the shadow of trees—water." Turning her gaze up to Nick, she impulsively reached out to touch his arm. "Nick, it's here. You're going to do it. You're going to find the answer and the treasure." He glanced at her hand, then down into her eyes, and Kate drew back, desperately wanting that physical link, yet wise enough to know that a simple touch would never be enough. "Words, real words. This is terrific."

Nick watched her carefully, his eyes unblinking. "Words that make no sense?" he asked softly, no ridicule in the question.

She didn't hesitate. "They will."

He shook his head. "No doubts at all?"

"None."

"The rest, figuring it out, how long will it take?"

She stood to face Nick, seeing him so clearly that it sent shock waves through her. "I don't know, but this is a start."

One brow lifted. "A start," he said softly. "A start. And more than I've ever had before. A great deal more."

Kate felt an odd trembling deep in her being, a quaking that didn't show on the outside. "Rain, trees, shadows. The first parts of a puzzle. And you'll find more and bring them up, and they'll fit in, too. Soon you'll know what the old man wanted you to know. You'll find the treasure and be done with your debt."

He ran his fingers through his hair. "It will all be finished."

Finished. The single word caught at Kate somewhere deep inside her and increased the unsteadiness there. Finished. This would all be over. Nick would walk out of her life and she would go back to her own world.

Nick stared at her, then lifted a vaguely unsteady hand and touched her cheek. "You've done it, Katherine. I knew you could. Thank you."

Kate felt riveted to the spot, as if there were more strength in the touch of his finger than if he had held her with both hands. "More pieces might fit, but I'm not sure..." Kate looked into his eyes and felt a dangerous shifting in her, a flicker of heat that she'd ignored so many times before. "I'll know more later."

Nick dropped his hand, but he kept staring, studying her intently for so long that Kate asked, "What are you thinking about now?"

The question brought Nick up short. What *was* he thinking about? Getting the treasure? Making good on his debt? Relief, joy and thankfulness? He had gone through all of those, but right now he was seriously considering the consequences of doing more than just kissing Katherine Harding.

A friendly kiss of thanks? That would never be enough. He wanted her for a friend, and he was thankful *to* her and *for* her. But this need wasn't based on anything quite that pure. This need grew from the way the translucent beauty of her face was touched by pleasure at solving a part of the puzzle, the same pleasure that made her lips part softly—invitingly—her golden eyes widen, and her high breasts rise and fall rapidly under the soft cotton of her blouse.

Blatant desire. That was what it was. So much for the resolve he had formed in the bathtub. "You don't want to know," he muttered roughly, forcing his eyes away from the rhythm of her breathing.

"Is it that terrible?" she asked, looking genuinely concerned.

Laughter welled up in him, the first easing of tension he'd felt in days. "Terrible? God, no, it's not terrible...just terribly tempting."

Friends be damned, Nick thought, and in one fluid motion he pulled Katherine to him. He had the fleeting impression of soft curves and swells against the length of his body. Then, before she could do more than gasp, his mouth found hers. He claimed her with all the chaotic emotion in him, his mouth searching and demanding.

He felt the soaring, the power, the instantaneous ignition of passion, a startlingly pure sensation that he'd never had to deal with before. For a split second he was quite sure it would devour him.

Chapter 9

Kate had never been struck by lightning, but she was quite certain that this kiss was akin to that sensation. The heat, the searing awareness, were so strong that she knew no way to respond to them, so she stood very still and absorbed the sensations. She let them fill her and wash over her, drawing unspeakable delights from every region of her body.

No man had ever done this to her before. Mike had never come close, so how could she have known that any person could draw something so elemental from her, something that seemed as old as the ages, yet as new as this moment?

Her feelings raced just ahead of reason and logic, and she knew that if she let herself go, she would drown in the sensations that almost overwhelmed her. A tug-of-war inside her left her dizzy. She shuddered as Nick's mouth explored hers, as if her dream had come to life. She ached and needed, she wanted, yet she knew she shouldn't. Then she felt his hands on her, urgent and searching, searing through the thin material of her blouse, finding the full sensitivity of her breasts.

Buttons slid silently open until calluses rasped on the softness of her skin. The beat of her heart was under his hand, and she felt Nick catch his breath at the same moment that it became impossible for her to breathe.

Nick buried his face in the heat of her throat, on the delicate exposed skin near the fringe of her hair. Had he ever wanted a woman so completely, so desperately? He couldn't remember. He wouldn't remember. Katherine swelled under his touch, her heart raced, and when she moaned deep in her throat, his body felt as if it would burst.

Desire, potent and encompassing, blotted out everything. The world fell away, and, unsteadily, Nick eased the light material off her shoulders.

When his lips began to trail fire down her throat and onto her shoulder, Kate was finally able to move, to do more than just respond to this onslaught on her senses.

"Nick," she sobbed, and when he would have claimed her mouth again, she lifted both hands to frame his face. It was the only thing she could think of to break whatever spell was being woven in the silent heat all around her. All she knew for certain was that she had to stop this madness. That a line was approaching, and if she crossed it, she could never go back. She had to stop Nick, to control what was happening.

She faltered, then held him back and looked into his eyes, which were dark with passion. That was when the fear came, a primitive aching that spread through her body, blotting out the pleasure. It took every ounce of willpower for her to force herself to put space between herself and this man. Just a half step back, then her hands dropped, balling into unsteady fists. No dream, not this. Just impossible.

"No," she whispered. "No."

She could see the thundering rhythm of his heart in the pulse at the hollow of his throat, an echo of her own. And it frightened her. She tugged at her blouse, holding it closed. This was crazy. Her body might not know what reason was, but her mind did. If she could only stop what was happening and put things back in order, back in perspective.

If only she could recapture sanity and safety. If only...

"Katherine," he whispered, his voice as unsteady as she felt.

"No," she managed. This couldn't be happening. She wouldn't let it happen. She could taste fear. "Don't do that..." she uttered in a voice she barely recognized as her own.

"Why?" Nick asked, his eyes narrowed, so his expression was totally unreadable. "All I did was kiss you. Call it a celebration kiss, if you want."

Just a kiss? That was like calling the atom bomb just another firecracker. Kate moved back another pace, desperately needing more space as a buffer. "A kiss that shouldn't have happened. This is a job, a working relationship. And I can't just..." She bit her lip hard. You scare me, she thought. My own body scares me. She hugged herself tightly as a shaking began in her. I can't handle this. I can't. She had never had to try before. Mike had been so safe, their physical relationship sane and ordinary. This almost made her wish he had never gone to Chicago. "I can't stay if we... if you..."

Nick held up both hands so quickly that he almost struck her. "Don't say that."

She willed her breathing to steady, her heart to slow. "I've never been..." She sought for a word. "Casual. I'm not..."

His hands dropped, and his voice tightened. "I know what my reputation is. But, believe me, I'm not into casual sex. I never was." He hesitated. "It won't happen again. Just don't even consider leaving."

She felt the heat scorch her face. She was completely out of her depth. And she wanted her own life back. Her sanity. She wanted it desperately. She wanted safety and familiarity, a world that she understood. Not this gray-eyed man who set her whole world on its ear.

"It won't happen again," Nick repeated tightly, his eyes narrowing further with a sweep of his dark lashes. "You will stay, won't you?"

Soon she would leave, but not now. She had to finish what she had begun. Unable to put her agreement into words, she simply nodded.

Nick stood very still, able only to say, "Thank you." Then he turned and strode out of the room.

Nick stayed in the den for a long time that night, sitting on the couch and staring into space until he finally got up and began pacing. He walked back and forth, a caged animal in a space that wasn't big enough to reduce the strain that knotted his muscles.

He stopped by the desk and closed his eyes. That was the wrong thing to do. All it accomplished was to bring a remembrance of Katherine, of her softness, the taste of her so fresh on his lips that he knew he had only to touch his tongue there to renew the flavor. She could affect him even when walls divided them. And a bath wasn't going to do any good.

He chuckled softly. A bath wasn't what he needed, he admitted, opening his eyes before he drove himself any crazier. He pushed aside a stack of books on the desk, then sat on one corner and ran both hands over his face.

Damn it, why couldn't I have left her alone? he berated himself. Why couldn't I settle for friendship? Would he ever be able to block the memory of the way she had felt under his hands? God, he hoped so. In spite of the heat, Nick shivered when he remembered Katherine speaking about leaving. The thought chilled him to the core.

She'd looked terrified. Why? He knew there was a closeness between them, that it had been growing ever so slowly. Their talks at night had built something between them, a closeness that hadn't depended only on physical proximity. But he'd frightened her. Could she be that innocent? No, she'd been engaged.

Nick couldn't figure her out. All he knew was that she had to be here when he came up, that he needed her face in front of him, her words in his ears, her presence. He shivered again. If she left... No, he couldn't even think of it. He had to leave her alone, had to give her distance. He had to keep her here.

This was new to him, this inability to understand a woman. They were usually so simple to deal with. He stared at the door. He couldn't go to the bed tonight. It would be impossible. He moved abruptly to the couch, threw himself down on the pillows and rested his head on one of the arms. He literally ached with the need to hold a woman, to fill and be filled. He'd ignored that need for a long time, but now it came back with a sickening intensity.

Rolling onto his side, he faced the darkened room. Ever so slowly, sleep crept up on him, and Nick grasped at it as an escape. But it brought no relief. His dream was so real that it almost seemed as if he were living it, as if he were going to make love to Katherine.

She stood before him, the blackness of the night sky behind her, the sound of distant waves drifting on the warm air. He wanted her. And she knew it. Across a distance of ten feet, they faced each other; then Nick took the first step toward her. He felt his feet sink in the damp silkiness of beach sand, and he realized he was on an island, and the only person with him was Katherine.

He moved closer, letting his gaze drift over her, her slender figure draped in something gauzy and white, that paradoxically covered yet exposed every part of her. A fire flared up, the flames licking through his body. Closer, closer, he stepped, until he could reach out and touch her.

How could fire surround him, yet not consume him? He marveled at it. The fire was fed by the knowledge that he would make love to Katherine, slowly, carefully, exquisitely, until they both cried out for release. He wanted to teach her, to find her mysteries and make them his. With a flick of his hand, her covering was gone, and her moon-bathed nakedness drew a flaming cord of desire through him that scorched him. His hands made contact with her shoulders, then trailed over the creamy softness downward to her breasts, which swelled with anticipation, her nipples tightening as his fingers circled them.

How did he know Katherine had never had a man before? That she'd never given herself fully to a man? He knew quite simply that he wanted to be her man. He wanted that desperately. As he drew her to him, his senses whirled with the knowledge that he could possess her, and he vowed to show her how lovemaking should be. The teasing, the caressing, the tantalizing pleasures, the searing paths taken by lips and fingers, the pleasure and the joy. The fire. With eternity before them, he would never run out of time. And he'd make sure that she would never be left behind in their passion.

Nick guided her down to the sand, the waves crashing against the shore, then hovered above her, learning her through his fingertips, exploring every inch of her, finding her just as he'd imagined she would be. And she touched him, deftly, surely, until he could hear his own moans echoing over the sounds of the ocean.

The blood pounded in his veins until he thought he would explode as her hands worked their magic. Had he thought he'd be the teacher, the one to give everything? No, Katherine made his body respond in every way, claiming a part of him he'd never realized existed. Maybe it hadn't existed with any other woman. Only with this woman.

He had no patience left. Urgency robbed him of the ability to wait. Katherine was there, under his hands, under him, opening to him, inviting him. But when he would have filled her, when he would have taken that last step to join himself to her, she was gone. With bone chilling swiftness, release was snatched from him in one horrible, irrevocable moment. The dream was gone.

Nick woke with a start, soaked with sweat, and his rapid breathing echoing all around him. He was on his stomach, his face pressed into the rough fabric of the couch. Damn it all! He turned onto his side quickly, his body full and swollen. He sat up quickly with a ragged intake of air, ran an unsteady hand over his flushed face, and stood.

A dream. Nothing more. Katherine wasn't there to ease his body or his spirit. And he couldn't go to her.

Friends, damn it, friends. He didn't feel like her friend now. He exhaled, then crossed to the door. But when he went out into the hall, he didn't cross to the bedroom. He made a sharp right, hurried through the house and out the front door. Once he reached the night air, he looked around, then strode down the porch, onto the gravel and off into the shadows.

"Valdez!" Kate called out as the gate opened and the giant of a man strode into the compound. His shirt was blotched with dampness from the ride out from the village, and his bald head was hidden under a well-worn straw hat. He lifted one hand in greeting; the other held the reins of the horse behind him.

"Katreen!" he returned, using the name Sorrella had coined for Kate.

Kate hurried across the gravel toward him, moving quickly despite the heat. She was so glad he had come. "I was hoping you would come today. I was about to call Rosa," Kate said in dialect.

He led the packhorses in through the gate so he and Sorrella could unload them at the back of the house. "The supplies came, so I brought them with the mail."

"Thank you." Kate smiled as she moved to let the sweaty animals pass. "How is Rosa?"

"Good, good," the man said, nodding. "Very good. The baby will show soon." He grinned with obvious pleasure. "A strong boy."

"A pretty female," Kate teased.

This exchange had become a pattern between them, and he looked at her with a mock scowl. "First a strong son, then a daughter."

"And you will take what God gives you, won't you?" she asked with a smile.

He looked down at her, and his face softened in a matching smile. *"Sim.* As long as Rosa is with me and the child."

Kate still felt pain at the thought that this strong man had lost two other wives. Rosa was even more special to him because of that. "Yes, you and your family. What did you bring today?"

"Food, mail." He handed Kate the reins of the horses as he went back to secure the gate. When he turned back to her, he asked, "Is he gone?"

She handed him the damp leather reins. "Nick left yesterday morning with Alfredo."

"I wanted to see him," Valdez said as he swatted the rump of the nearest horse to get it moving in the direction of the house.

Kate fell in step beside him, squinting as the sun beat down harshly, the waves of intense heat almost blinding. "He only stayed up here for a day this time," she said as they approached the porch steps. "We finally figured out something in the riddle, and he was anxious to get back down." She couldn't talk about the single day Nick had spent at the compound.

Long periods of not talking had grated on her nerves. There had been no night in the large bed watching the shifting shadows, getting to know each other better. Nick had made sure they were seldom alone, and when the second night came, he'd disappeared into the den. When he left, she'd watched him go, and on top of the usual sense of loneliness when he disappeared from sight, she'd felt a mixture of frustration and relief. She didn't want to be cut off from him, just to keep things on a safe footing. But that was what had happened. She'd been cut off.

Valdez tied the horses to the porch railing, then took the two steps in one long stride and grabbed for the screen door. "Sorrella!"

He stayed only long enough to unload the supplies and get something to eat. When he was ready for the return to the village, Kate thought about the days ahead and acted impulsively.

"Valdez?"

He looked at her as he stood on the porch, drinking the last of a cool drink, the hat pressed on his head. *"Sim?"*

"Could I go back with you for a day? I really want to see Rosa, to talk to her and visit."

He looked taken aback. "A visit?"

"Just for a day or so, until you could bring me back up here. I could ride one of the packhorses back."

"They are not for riding, Katreen. They are for carrying loads."

"Could we take the jeep?"

He shook his head. "No, fuel is too scarce for a double trip."

Kate didn't stop to wonder why it was so important to get to the village. "I could ride double with you."

Valdez looked uncertain; then his broad shoulders moved. "If you want, but I cannot bring you back for two days. I have work to do on the airplane."

Kate didn't have to think for more than a moment. "Thanks. I'll get some clothes and be ready in five minutes."

The trip to the village took over three hours, and the rump of the horse was so uncomfortable that Kate found herself longing for the jeep. She tried to move with the swaying gait, but the effort of staying on the horse by holding on to Valdez or the saddle wearied her. By the time she saw the village nearing, her whole body ached, and her arms stung from the constant slapping of the vines and branches that hung out from the sides of the trail.

"We are here," Valdez announced, nudging the horse to a faster gait as the trail became better.

As they approached the village Kate took in many more things than she had noticed the first time. Rich color flourished all around, on houses, in clothing, in the blossoms that spilled everywhere. A heady mingling of natural fragrances hung in the hot afternoon air, mixing with the spicy odor of cooking food. Shimmering rays of sunlight splashed over the cluster of houses, and the villagers rested in whatever shade they could find.

As Valdez rode slowly along the path, the villagers looked up, obviously puzzled by Kate's presence. She watched them, and her smile of greeting came easily, despite the heat and her discomfort. One by one the dark-skinned villagers hesitated, then nodded, touching their fingers to their chins in what Kate guessed was part of their greeting. When his house came into view, Valdez urged the horse to hurry, until he stopped it at the end of the walkway. There he shouted at the top of his lungs, "Rosa!"

He reached back to catch Kate by the arm and, without any warning, tugged her forward so she slid down the side of the horse and hit the ground solidly. He slid off at the same time that Rosa burst out of the house. When she saw Valdez, she broke into a huge grin, and she hurried down the walkway. As she looked past him and saw Kate at his side, she stopped on the rough walkway. She blinked as if she couldn't quite believe her eyes; then, with a squeal of delight, she ran to greet them with remarkable speed, considering the advanced state of her pregnancy. "Katreen! Katreen!"

Kate barely had time to smile and hold out her arms before Rosa had her caught in an intense hug. Breathless, Kate returned the embrace, then moved back a bit to smile down at the girl. "It's good to see you, Rosa, so good."

Rosa looked to Valdez. "Thank you for bringing my friend."

Valdez nodded indulgently and walked off with the horses.

Kate's stay extended past two days when Valdez had to fly to Manaus. Kate offered to stay with Rosa until he got back, and she was secretly thankful not to have to go back to the compound and spend her days in nerve-racking waiting for Nick to come back. Instead she kept busy, getting to know Rosa better, exploring the village, meeting the people and learning their ways. Strangely, she seldom felt like an outsider. Her ability to speak their language and her status as Rosa's friend made her approachable from the first, and she enjoyed spending the evening sitting in the small two-room ouse, visiting with the women and children who lived earby.

The feelings she had begun to develop for Sorrella, Aledo, Valdez and Rosa spread out to encompass the others. Kate genuinely liked them.

Valdez flew back early in the morning of the fourth day, ame to the house, then made a trip back to the hangar with ne packhorses to load them. Kate and Rosa were at the tiny ooden table in the main room, sharing cool drinks, when aldez came back, his skin gleaming with sweat. He wiped t his damp face with the back of his hand as he entered the ouse, his bulk dwarfing the low-ceilinged space with its hite walls and rough flooring covered by hemp mats. He ossed his hat onto the small sofa by the door, then crossed o the dining table near the low rear window, where the omen were sitting.

Kate smiled at Valdez. "You look so hot," she said.

He shook his bald head and touched Rosa on the shoulder. "Not too bad." He looked down at his wife. "Is it all ight with you?"

"*Sim*. I am fine."

"And how is my son?"

Rosa smiled. "He is fine." She looked at Kate. "He says hat he wants a boy child, but I think he will be happy with a female."

"So do I." Kate smiled.

"A son is good," Valdez said, falling into the pattern of easing as he patted Rosa gently on the shoulder. He glanced t Kate. "We will go back in an hour. The horses are oaded."

Kate nodded, shocked at the strength of her reluctance to leave. She looked into the ceramic cup on the table in front of her and slowly stirred her drink of mashed fruit and cool water. The pulp swirled with the motion of the spoon. "I'll be ready." She took a sip of the soothing fruit drink. "I hate to leave so soon."

"You will be back," Rosa said.

Kate wondered if she *would* be back, or if the return visit would just be a short stop on her way back to Manaus before flying home. She had never meant to get involved here on an emotional level. She needed to walk away without looking back, just as she had planned to from the first. This land wasn't hers, no more than the people were, no more than Nick could ever be.

I need to get back to school, she told herself. The thought had no sooner formed than she questioned it. The safety of school seemed almost a dream, a dream that she was beginning to cling to more and more. She took a deep drink. Was that safety just a dream? Could she go back to the compound and do what had to be done, then go back to her "real" life?

The compound. Nick. How could part of her yearn for his safe return from the valley, while another part of her knew that his return would only open the door to more uncertainty?

Kate took another drink, then looked up when Valdez led them to walk into the small bedroom at the back of the house. Rosa shifted to reach for a book that she kept on a side shelf.

"Please read before you go back to the valley, Katreen," the girl said softly as she opened the well-used children's primer. The elderly schoolteachers had used very simple, easy-to-understand stories to teach the children of the village, just as children were taught everywhere.

Rosa smoothed the pages before passing it across the table to Kate. "It might be long before you come again."

Kate nodded, feeling the sting of tears at the back of her eyes. She looked down at the book and began to read where they had left off the day before. "The moon has no light of its own. It shows only the light of the sun coming from the other side of the earth. Color and shape are different in moonlight than in sunlight . . ."

At the top of the trail Nick broke from the jungle and into the heat of the afternoon. Weariness made his steps heavy and slow. His horse trailed behind on the narrow path, led by a single rein, froth at its mouth where the bit rested, its coat rough from sweat, and its head low after five days of constant work. The animal stumbled momentarily, then scrambled to get its footing again and righted itself.

When they came to the compound, Alfredo called out to Nick from the rear, "I will go to my house."

"Fine," Nick said over his shoulder. "Take care of the horses. I'm going home."

Alfredo came up to take the rein of the horse from Nick. "I will see you later."

As Alfredo headed off to one side, Nick went on. Home. He moved faster, his feet awkward from weariness, yet the pleasure of being close to the end gave him extra strength. His eyes searched the compound for Katherine. He needed to see her, as surely as his body needed a cool drink. He didn't analyze the need; he simply experienced it. "Katherine!" he called.

He heard the front door open and shut. Footsteps sounded, running along the porch. With as much speed as he could muster, he headed for the side of the house and stepped up onto the porch, but he stopped in his tracks. He felt the smile on his face freeze when he realized it was Sorrella coming toward him.

"Senhor Nicholas!"

He stood very still, looking past the lanky woman, but no one came up behind her. "Alfredo is with the horses, then he's going to your house," he said. "Where's Katherine?"

Sorrella stopped long enough to say, "Gone with Valdez," before hurrying past Nick to head toward the back of the compound.

Gone! The world froze, and Nick had to try to speak twice before the housekeeper's name came out in a sharp gasp. "Sorrella!"

She stopped and turned back to squint into the glare. "*Sim?*"

"She went with Valdez?"

"*Sim.*"

For four days he had refused to think of the possibility that Katherine would leave, four days when he had forced himself to focus on hacking through jungle to try to find more caves. But now reality hit him in a hard jolt. His heart caught in his chest, and fresh sweat broke out on his sticky skin. "Katherine left?" He could barely manage the words.

Sorrella bobbed her head. "With Valdez."

He licked his lips and tasted the sharp saltiness of sweat. "Why?"

Sorrella was impatient to be gone, and her answer reflected her feelings. "Katreen wanted to go with Valdez."

"Why?" he repeated in a voice growing increasingly hoarse from tension.

Sorrella shrugged with impatience. "She went. Can I go to Alfredo?"

Nick found his thought process blurring. "Yes, go," he murmured.

As she hurried off, Nick had to close his eyes and put out a hand to touch the wall in an effort to fight a sudden wave of dizziness. For a second his head swam, and a strange ache filled him. He tried to focus, but his mind refused to settle into any rational pattern.

He drew a deep breath in an attempt to steady a world that had begun to tip precariously out of balance. *Gone.* The single word cut to his soul. Why had she left? He didn't understand. *I promised her, I assured her...* He felt bombarded from all sides, and he couldn't deal with it.

Nick covered his eyes with both hands and pressed until bright colors exploded behind his lids. *Enough.* Later he would be able to think this through. He turned, walked slowly along the porch, pulled the door open and stepped into a house filled with painfully complete silence. As he trudged through to the bedroom he found himself humming tunelessly just to break the emptiness that surrounded him.

An hour later he walked into the living room. He had thought warm water, clean clothes, a cold drink and a bit of time would help him put things in perspective, but he'd been wrong. All that had come was a building anger tinged with confusion.

He crossed to the screen door to look out at the compound, bathed in the glow of the late-afternoon sun. He wished he understood what had happened. All he knew was that now he had to start all over again, and he didn't know where to begin this time. All because of Katherine.

A kiss. *God, if I had done what I wanted to do with her that night, she probably would have shot me dead,* he thought with angry irony.

He stopped those thoughts. *I tried just to be friends before I went back down. I tried, damn it, I tried,* he insisted. He swallowed hard and tucked his cotton shirt into the waistband of his jeans, then pushed the door open and stepped out onto the porch.

The door snapped shut behind him, and he crossed to lean one shoulder against the porch post and squint into the clear sky. There had to be others who could do Katherine's work, who could pick up where she had left off. He frowned at the glare of the setting sun on the distant trees. Plenty of people were capable of helping him with the puzzle.

He frowned. Hadn't he wasted weeks hunting down people and trying to get someone to come here and help? The obvious couldn't be avoided. He had to go after Katherine and talk her into coming back. He had no idea what he would say to her, and that didn't sit well, but he had no choice.

He would have gone inside to call Valdez on the radio, but a sound from outside the compound fence kept him in place. He looked toward the vine-covered barrier and heard distant noises growing clearer. Nick listened to a rustling, the soft whinny of a horse, then footsteps on the gravel. Someone was coming. In two steps he was off the porch and crossing the cleared gravel area. He got to within five feet of the gate as it opened, then stopped in midstride.

Katherine stood in the opening, one hand poised to brush at her feathery hair where it clung damply in tiny curls to her flushed face. Disorientation robbed Nick of the ability to do more than stare while his mind raced. Was this wishful thinking—an apparition? Or hadn't Katherine gone? Was this a trick, an ugly joke? Or had she changed her mind?

"Katherine," he whispered. "You're here."

"Yes, I'm here," she said in a voice that seemed to echo through Nick. "It took longer to get here from the village than I thought it would." She brushed a hand across her face. "It must be the uphill climb that takes so much more time. I'll take the jeep ride anytime instead of a horse."

He didn't know why she'd come back. And he didn't care. All that counted was that she was here. A staggering sense of relief filled him, and as a monumental weight slid off his shoulders, he took two steps and almost reached out for her, but he stopped. Not again, he warned himself. Not again.

Unexpectedly, it was Katherine who reached for him and hugged him so tightly that it almost took his breath away. And it felt right. Oh, God, so right. And she was doing it, initiating it. He allowed himself only to loosely circle her shoulders and stand very still.

"You made it back all right," she breathed, her words muffled by his shirt.

"Yes, I made it back," he echoed. "And so did you."

Valdez came up behind them, leading the horses. "Good to see you, brother," the big man said with a grin.

Nick nodded, his chin brushing across the damp silkiness of Katherine's hair. "Yes, good to see both of you."

Katherine leaned back to look up at him, and without warning, she stood on her tiptoes to kiss him. Before he realized what she'd done, she was stepping back. He didn't want it to end just like that, to lose the feel of her softness and gentleness against him; he wanted more than a fleeting taste of her on his lips.

Just when he thought he knew what to do with her, she did something unexpected. His hands all but ached with the need to stroke the warmth of her cheek, to ruffle her hair, so he pushed them into the pockets of his jeans.

"I missed you," he said, his gaze holding hers as the simple truth came out. He tried to speak lightly, but each word exposed more of the truth. "I hated coming home to an empty house."

Katherine moved aside to let Valdez lead the horses inside, but her amber eyes never left Nick's face. "Sorrella was here, wasn't she?"

He nodded, watching Katherine over the backs of the horses as the large animals walked between them. "For a second, then she went to see Alfredo."

"Is Alfredo all right?"

"Yes, he is." The horses were gone, and nothing separated them now. "He's tired and dirty. You were in the village?"

"I went to visit Rosa. I didn't think about you coming up so soon, or I would have come back earlier. The next time, I'll be here."

The next time, but what about the next and the next? The question rang in his mind. *What about when this is done, and you're really gone—gone for good?* His hands curled into fists in his pockets. "You saw Rosa?"

"Yes." She stood very still, and the shadows of the approaching night veiled her eyes.

"I thought…" No, enough of that. He wouldn't voice his stupid fears to her. "I was worried when you weren't here." What an understatement.

She tugged at her shirt, where it stuck to her damp skin. "I'm sorry. I thought Sorrella would explain."

"No problem. Everything's fine." He watched her, inordinately aware of the way both his logic and his feelings seemed to be scrambled. He couldn't deal with what she made him feel, and he didn't know how to stop the world long enough to make sense of anything. He hated being out of control of a situation, yet he faced the fact that he held little, if any, control right now.

He forced himself to look away from Katherine and speak to Valdez, who was standing nearby with the horses. "I'm glad you're here, brother." An idea came, a way of getting away from Katherine long enough to figure out what to do. "I was going to call you on the radio to arrange a trip to

Mexico City. I've got business to take care of there." After all, he could always find business there.

"My timing is good?" The bald man smiled.

"Perfect."

"When do you want to go?"

"As soon as we can. Tomorrow morning?" He looked at Katherine. "I need to be in Mexico City for meetings," he said, making up a lie as he went along. He rationalized it by reasoning that if he could get away, he would come to his senses. "You can take a vacation. You can fly directly home from Manaus, then meet me back there in a week." He narrowed his eyes to blur her image in front of him. "We need a break."

Kate had never experienced such relief and confusion all mixed up together. He was back safely, yet she didn't know where to go from here.

She looked at Nick and felt all the peace she had known during her stay in the village slowly drift out of reach.

Why was he looking at her like that, as if he wanted to get away from here—away from her? Mexico City? She could go home? He was offering her time to see her family and friends. The very thing she'd said she wanted was being handed to her, and she didn't know what to say beyond, "All right."

"You'll meet me in a week in Manaus?" Nick asked, each word clipped and direct.

Home. She could go back, but she suddenly found that she didn't want to. She knew exactly where she wanted to go. "No, I'll go with you to Mexico City. I have friends there."

Nick looked taken aback. "Who?"

"A couple who do translations for the foreign service, Jack and Mary Walker. I grew up with Jack. He and his wife work in Mexico City. I haven't seen them since they got transferred there."

Nick hesitated, as if he wanted to say or do something more, but instead he nodded, then looked at Valdez. "We'll drive down in the morning, then fly to Manaus."

What on earth had he gotten himself into? he wondered.

Chapter 10

We're doing fine," Andrew Benson said to Nick's back. "I don't understand why you even called me down here." The stockily built dark-haired man pushed papers into his briefcase. "Al Green in L.A. had the deal all sewn up."

Nick stared out the hotel window and down five stories to Mexico City, to early evening streets alive with people, flashing lights and cars snaking along the broad boulevards. I didn't want to be alone, came the silent answer. But he couldn't say that—not to Andrew. "I needed to talk to you," Nick said softly.

"Why now? You called a month ago and said you'd be out of touch for the next few months. Before that you didn't do much in the business anyway—not since you hurt yourself in Brazil." Andrew exhaled a sigh. "Stupid bet. I never thought anyone would get hurt."

"It was my fault, and I recovered," Nick muttered.

"I should never have pushed you to do it," Andrew countered. "It was a stupid bet."

"You didn't push me, and it's over and done."

"I don't think so. You can't seem to let go of that valle
Although I can't imagine why you keep going back. If it wa
me, I'd be more than willing to get out of that hellhole an
never go back again."

There was no way Nick could ever explain his need to g
back to Andrew. Telling him that he was trying to unde
stand the culture was as close to the truth as he could come

With a sharp shrug, Nick buttoned the front of his su
jacket and gazed across the city to the distant hills and a sk
splashed with the last rays of the setting sun. As beautifu
as the approaching night seemed, Nick took in little of it
"The valley has its appeal."

"Are you coming back to the New York office?"

"No, not until after I've finished..." He stopped him
self. "I've got things to do, then I'll be back."

"You're going back to the wilds again, aren't you?"

"Yes. For a while."

He heard Andrew shift behind him, then the man spoke
"I hardly know you anymore, you've changed so much. I
one year you've turned into some sort of recluse, taking of
to that jungle of yours, and you've..." His words trailed off.
A chair moved. "What's going on with you, Nick?"

He hardly knew how to answer that question. He could
hardly say, I'm trying to figure out how to be a friend to a
beautiful woman who doesn't want any more than that from
me. What was going on with him? He should have backed
out when Katherine insisted on coming here with him. Why
hadn't she gone home, back to the college, and let him
breathe without her around? He'd felt suffocated by her
during the trip here, unable to think clearly with her so
close—and so beautiful.

Rosa and Katherine had visited for a few minutes in the
tiny mud-walled house, their heads together, sorting through
tiny baby clothes and giggling like schoolgirls over the bas-
ket that would be the baby's bed. In a strange shifting of
roles, Nick had felt like the outsider, like the one who didn't
quite belong.

He touched the pane with the tips of his fingers and watched the people far below. A change of scenery hadn't altered anything else. Even though Katherine was seldom in the connecting suite, he couldn't stop thinking about her.

"I've got a problem," he admitted, a bit surprised to be saying anything like that to Andrew. He'd known the man since college and worked with him for over ten years, yet he realized that they'd never been very close. They'd had more of a drinking partnership and an understanding than a real friendship. They'd lived their own lives, gone their own ways, but stayed attached by business and nights when drinks had been too prevalent. Like the night of the bet.

Nick pushed that thought aside. What he knew for a certainty was that Andrew did everything that Nick didn't want to bother doing in the business, and he did it well. The arrangement had been very satisfactory. This was one relationship in his life that was clear-cut. "Have you got time to talk, Andrew?"

"If you look at me, I might," the blue-eyed man said.

Nick turned to the other man. The long flight down from New York had left him short on patience. Nick knew that and spoke quickly. "I'll be honest with you, I don't know who else to talk to."

"Is that why you called me down here?" Andrew watched him with open curiosity. "This had better be worth the cost of the airplane ticket."

"That's the company's problem. Don't worry about it," Nick said with a wry smile. The call to Andrew had been impulsive, the same way the idea of coming here had been. He tugged at the cuff of his pale blue shirt, a nervous action meant to hide the scar on his wrist, and took a deep breath. He looked right at Andrew. "How long have you been married?"

The stocky man looked surprised. "What?"

"Married. How long have you been with Valerie?"

He frowned. "Eight years, six married."

"Are you friends?"

"Don't you think we should have a drink?" Andrew asked with an uncertain smile.

"No. Just answer the question."

Andrew sat down in an overstuffed chair and settled back with a sigh. "Sure. Of course we're friends."

"Were you friends before you went to bed with her?"

"I don't know."

Nick stifled his frustration with the man's answers. "Do you think it's possible to be friends with a woman you're attracted to? Platonic friends?"

Andrew hesitated. "I suppose so, but to tell you the truth, I wasn't thinking about friendship when I first met Valerie."

This wasn't getting Nick anywhere. He didn't really even know what he was getting at. Katherine. Would his thoughts always come back to her?

"Did you bring me all the way down here to talk about this?" Andrew asked.

"No, I was just curious," Nick said softly.

"Then why *did* you call me down here? That deal you claim to be concerned about doesn't amount to a hill of beans."

"If I told you I wanted you down here so we could go out to dinner tonight and do some serious drinking, would you believe me?"

"No."

"It's true." No smile went with his words. He couldn't spend another night alone in this room, seeing Katherine come back only long enough to get ready to go out for the evening with her friends. Being back in the real world had dispersed the closeness he'd come to share with her, just as he had wanted it to, yet a part of him hated the reality.

"You couldn't find some gorgeous woman to keep you company?" Andrew smiled.

Oh, he'd found a gorgeous woman, all right. He turned his back on Andrew and pressed his palms flat on the cool glass. For three days he had thought about the way Katherine had worked her way into his life. Nights in this room had made the truth difficult to hide from. Desire shouldn't have been born so easily, yet he desired Katherine in every way imaginable—as a friend, as a confidante, as a lover....

He stopped that train of thought immediately. How easy it would be to let his need for Katherine grow. If he only knew what frightened her, why she pulled back at the suggestion of anything more than friendship. Her ex-fiancé? Could things have been that bad between them?

"So that's it?" Andrew said behind him. "A woman?"

Nick turned, about to deny it, but a noise in the connecting suite stopped him from speaking. Katherine had returned. He had hoped to leave before she came back. He didn't ever want her to know that his real business in Mexico City had been to divert his attention from her.

"Well? Is it a woman complicating your life, Nick?" Andrew prodded, watching Nick from the comfort of his chair.

Nick stood very still, his breathing suspended as a memory came in a flash. *Nicholas, life can get complicated,* his mother had said somewhere deep in his past. They had been at the dinner table, just his father, his mother and him. The memory deepened. His mother and father, their hands joined. *But if you're lucky, you'll have one person in the world who believes in you and loves you no matter what you do.*

Where had that memory come from? He knew now that he'd never looked directly at those last years, but now he remembered them clearly. The idealistic words, the loving words.

Andrew spoke again, and Nick shook his head to try to clear it.

"What did you say?" He forced himself to look right at his friend and past the memories.

"Women can make complications," Andrew said with a half-smile.

"Life's complicated," he managed, his mind dealing with the past, but trying to focus on the present. And that pres-

ent held Katherine. It always came back to her. "We need
to get going to make our dinner reservations."

A soft knock on the connecting door drew his attention,
and he took a deep breath before turning to stride across the
thick beige carpeting. He needed to get out of here. He'd tell
Katherine where he was going, then make his escape.

He opened the door, and then Katherine stood in front of
him, barefoot, all in white, from her linen slacks to her loose
white pullover. The only color came from her deep eyes and
the richness of her short hair.

She smiled, a gentle expression. "Hi."

His response seemed trite and impersonal, but he didn't
know what else to say. "How are you doing?"

"Fine, just fine," she said in that soft, husky voice.

"Have you been enjoying seeing your friends?"

She held the doorknob, her slender fingers curling over
the brass. "Very much. How about you? Is business going
well?"

He nodded and lied. "Yes."

She glanced past him at Andrew, who had stood up and
faced the door. "Oh, I'm sorry. I didn't know you weren't
alone."

"Katherine..." The other man came forward while Nick
talked. "This is Andrew Benson. Andrew—Katherine
Harding. She's a linguist helping me with some work at the
valley."

Katherine extended a slender hand and smiled. "Nice to
meet you. I think you're the first friend of Nick's I've met."
She shook her head. "No, that's not right. I've met his
friends at the compound."

Andrew cast Nick a long look after shaking Katherine's
hand. "A linguist? I thought you'd finally learned the language down there?"

"I've never really understood it that well, and Katherine
picked it up immediately." He stopped any more questions
by talking directly to Katherine. "We were just about to go
to dinner." He couldn't stop the words that spilled out before he had time to consider them. "Why don't you come

with us? We can easily change the reservation and make it for three.''

She moved back half a step. "I don't think so. I'm really tired. I was going to go to bed early. But you have a nice time.''

His reaction should have been relief, yet it settled in as bone-deep disappointment. He flashed what he hoped was a casual smile. "I understand.''

"Nice to meet you." Andrew smiled at Katherine, then looked at Nick. "I'll wait for you down in the bar.''

"All right." Nick waited until the outer door closed behind Andrew to ask, "Are you sure you won't come with us?''

Katherine studied him intently from under her lush lashes, then asked something that rocked him. "He's the one you made the bet with, isn't he?''

He stood straight, tugging at the cuffs of his jacket. "How did you know that?''

"He seemed to know about the valley." She shifted from foot to foot. "You don't talk to just anyone about it.''

That was true, but how had she known it? "You're right." He broke off that line of conversation. "Are you going to see your friends tomorrow?''

"I was planning on going out to their house at the beach. Would you like to come?''

Her question took him aback. "No, thank you.''

"I know they're intellectuals and all, but they're really nice people. Although you might be bored." She looked uncertain. "I'm not, but ...''

"It's not that. I never told you that my mother was a teacher, did I?''

Katherine shook her head. "No, you never did.''

It seemed to be a night for Nick to retrieve memories from his past. "Not in classrooms, but she worked with the blind doing what they called 'mobile orientation.' She took people who were recently blinded and helped them learn to function in the sighted world." His voice softened on a chuckle. "I remember her walking around the house with a blindfold on. 'How can I tell what it's like without sight if I don't experience it myself?' she asked me. I put on the blindfold once and walked into a wall.''

Katherine smiled at him. ''How old were you?''

''Five or six. It was when we lived in New York State, just outside of Albany. My father was in politics, and my mother was involved with anyone who needed help.'' Nick shrugged. ''I had a horrible bump on my head for days after walking into that wall. 'That's from being blind,' I told a friend, and my mother heard me. She was so angry. I didn't understand why until she told me it frightened her to think of something happening to me, of me really being blind.''

Nick stopped himself. ''This wasn't what I wanted to talk to you about.''

Kate stared at Nick, barely hearing his last statement. His mother had understood what she was feeling now. It also frightened Kate to think of something happening to Nick. It terrified her. ''You took risks even then, didn't you?'' she heard herself asking, and her hand tightened on the doorknob.

Nick blinked at her. ''Risks?''

''I bet you jumped out of tree houses without using a ladder.'' Why had she said that? She didn't even know how often she'd sat in her own tree house, looking over the side, wondering if she should jump, but in the end she always took the ladder.

He frowned at her. ''I never had a tree house, but I guess I would have jumped. At least once, to see what it felt like.''

''I know you would have.'' And she did know. She understood.

''That frightens you?''

''Yes, of course. You could break your leg, or...''

''Or pretend you're flying,'' he finished with a crooked smile. She didn't return the smile, and Nick sobered completely. ''I frighten you, don't I?'' he asked softly.

Kate felt the heat rise in her face. ''Not you,'' she said truthfully. ''Your whole idea of life.''

''Why?''

She shrugged sharply. ''That's what I've been trying to figure out.''

''And?''

''You can risk your life, then turn around and do it again. You almost died in that valley, yet you go back down over and over again. It's like you come from a place I can't begin to understand.''

''You were from the same place as your ex-fiancé?''

''Of course. Mike and I had a lot in common.''

''So what happened?''

She frowned and looked down at her feet. ''Nothing much, really. I told you about Chicago.''

''Chicago was enough to break up your plans to get married?''

''It turned out that we didn't want the same things after all.'' And he'd never really touched her, physically or emotionally. She knew that now. That was why she'd been able to let him go.

''What did you want that he couldn't give you?''

She took a deep breath. No matter how much she wanted to, she couldn't throw caution to the wind and say, ''Nothing, he just wasn't a dark-haired man with gray eyes and a presence that takes my breath away.'' She shifted a bit nervously. ''I...I suppose I wanted a man who was kind, gentle and committed, and shared my values and my goals in life.''

''Boy, you don't come easy, do you?''

She didn't like this discussion at all. ''No.''

He realized he'd been talking just to talk. What he really wanted was to go back to the valley, and he wanted to go back now. This trip hadn't worked. He had been foolish to think it would, and all he'd succeeded in doing was to lose precious time on the project. Abruptly he said, ''We need to head back to the valley.''

Kate had felt as if she were marking time ever since coming to Mexico City, and his suggestion was exactly what she wanted to hear. ''When?''

''Tomorrow morning, early. Is that all right with you?''

"Yes." More than all right. "You never even told me if you found anything on the last trip."

"A cave with two sets of figures."

"And you didn't tell me?" she gasped. "Why?"

Nick crossed his arms on his chest. "Katherine, it was time to take a break. Believe me. Sometimes you need to step back to get a clearer picture of what's happening. A little patience can be a great attribute."

"But you had another piece of the puzzle in your hand and you didn't show me! I don't understand."

"It's still there, waiting for when we get back."

"Then let's get back as soon as we can."

"Impatient?"

"I sure am. I've never been able to stand suspense."

She looked at Nick, his hair long enough to curl at the collar of his shirt, his eyes the shade of morning fog. Shock coursed through her when she realized that she wasn't well-suited to being close to a man she could let herself love. Her whole face must have shown the shock she felt at the real-ization.

"What's wrong?" Nick asked softly.

Kate pressed a hand to her throat, as if she could still her thoughts with that touch. Love? No. But she was getting close, so close. And she had to stop it. How close was she? "Nothing," she managed. "I was just thinking about . . . about the new clues."

"You are coming back, aren't you?" he asked in a low voice.

Had he kept the news of the clues to himself to use for bait if he needed it at the last minute? "Did you think I wouldn't?"

"I wasn't sure."

She swallowed hard. "I . . . I'll be there until the work is done."

Nick lifted his hand as if to touch her, but he drew back before he could make contact. "Thank you. We'll head back first thing in the morning."

Chapter 11

Nick and Kate had been back from Mexico City for two weeks—two weeks of on-and-off rains, of Nick going below, two weeks of struggling to make another part of the puzzle fall into place. He had found three more caves, two on the western wall, one far beyond, to the north, but none of the writings he found seemed to fit with any of those they already had. Kate worked furiously from morning until night, whether Nick was there or not. She didn't want to stay any longer than she had to, not when just the sight of Nick could quicken her heart and confuse her reasoning.

Now Nick was away again, and so far he'd been gone six days, longer than he'd ever stayed below before. And today Kate was completely alone in the compound. At midday she sat on the porch step, watching the gate, listening for any sound of Nick and Alfredo approaching. Sorrella had left for the village with Valdez to see Rosa, promising to make the journey there and back in one day. The loneliness felt almost tangible to Kate.

"I'll be fine, Sorrella," she'd promised early that morning. "Go and see Rosa. Give her my love."

Now, restless, she stood and, despite the oppressive heat, circled the house until she found herself by the back gate. She stared at the metal barrier. Where was Nick? Six days. Too long. She knew it was too long.

She reached out and touched the gate, fingering the lock. She listened. Nothing.

One look. If she could look out onto the trail, she might see Nick and Alfredo. She undid the lock, tugged at the gate and looked out at the jungle. The path looked dry. Trees arched overhead, and fern fronds swooped across her view. Kate looked down the path until it curved out of sight, but she didn't see anything.

Cautiously, she stepped outside the fence and pulled the gate almost closed behind her. She stood very still and listened. Still nothing. She moved a few steps farther from the gate, and the vibrant green jungle surrounded her. She inhaled the sweetness that permeated the air. The drenching rains of the day before had washed away everything dusty and dry and left a lushness that was almost painful to the eye.

Kate walked slowly along the three-foot-wide path. After the confines of the compound, the outside world seemed light and fresh. She watched a bird with multicolored plumage dip low, then disappear into a towering tree. Her sandals made little sound on the soft ground. Farther down the path she heard a sound and stopped. Her gaze went to the source of the noise not more than ten feet in front of her—a tiny animal that looked like a squirrel, except that it lacked a bushy tail. It saw her at that same moment and froze.

Kate stood motionless, watching the tiny creature scrutinize her, then move in a flash to disappear into the jungle.

A sudden breeze scurried through the trees, rustling the leaves, brushing over Kate's skin and leaving a pleasant tingling in its wake. Then, without warning, a rush of wind tore through the jungle and the rains came again. They never began with a sprinkle, but with an instant outpouring that could only have been matched by a huge bucket being turned upside down. And they were worse than ever this time, coming down so forcefully that the contact hurt Kate. She had never thought that rain could be painful, yet it stung her face and arms and made her close her eyes to mere slits.

She looked around, all sense of direction snatched away by the gray walls of water. Which way should she go? Had she been facing the compound or away from it when the storm started? Away. She knew she had been looking down the path away from the compound.

She turned and hurried back along the path that was fast becoming a river. She broke into a run, fronds whipping at her, the rain blinding her, streaming from her hair and down her face.

How far had she come from the compound? The curve in the path. She remembered that and kept going. Only a bit farther, a few steps.

She tried to look ahead and had to lift her head, exposing her face to the force of the storm and the needlelike rain lancing from the skies. Through the gray dimness ahead Kate saw something dark. The fence. She lurched toward it and put out a hand to keep from falling into the gate.

Her hand got tangled in the vines. She felt the puncture of thorns and jerked back to rub her hand flat on her soaked shorts. With her other hand she pushed back the gate, stumbled inside, righted herself and swung the gate shut. After forcing the lock into place, she turned and ran for the protection of the house.

When she reached the porch she took the steps quickly until she got under the shelter of the roof, where she stopped to catch her breath. She had never seen rain like it—a literal wall of water. She clutched at her middle, trying to get enough air into her lungs, then pushed at her plastered hair. A stinging in her hand stopped her, and she drew it down to look at tiny spots of blood in the center of her palm.

Gingerly she touched the wounds, but felt little beyond a vague burning. Nick had told her about the vines, but so far she didn't feel too bad. A screech cut through the torrential downpour, drawing her attention, and Kate stared out into the rain. An animal. She'd heard that sound often enough in the past weeks. She shivered and turned to go into the house.

Sorrella couldn't come back from the village now, and Nick and Alfredo certainly couldn't come up in the storm. She really was alone now. She walked slowly back to the bathroom, where she stripped off her clothes and tossed the sodden pile on the floor, then reached for a towel to dry her hair. Moments later she slipped her white terry-cloth robe over her bare skin, walked into the bedroom and got onto the bed, to sit cross-legged on top of the blanket. She trembled when an animal screamed again, then absentmindedly rubbed at the tingling in the middle of her palm.

Kate couldn't remember a night so hot. She knew she was in bed, but she couldn't remember what bed. Her eyes didn't want to open, and when she finally forced her lids up she saw nothing, just darkness. She didn't know what was going on. The heat was unbearable. Her whole body throbbed with each heartbeat; then she felt pain and closed her eyes again. It ran from her hand up her arm, then into her shoulder to radiate into the back of her head.

Touch it and see what's wrong, she told herself, but her body refused to obey her command. Touch it. Touch it! The pain grew, but Kate didn't feel as if she were waking up. She seemed suspended somewhere in a strange gray land where reality was excluded. Yet she felt everything, including the heat. Nick would know what was wrong.

"Nick..." she mumbled, her lips thick and unresponsive. "I... I'm hot... so hot."

"Shh." She heard his voice as if from a great distance; then something cool touched her cheek. "Don't move. Keep your hand still."

That seemed a stupid thing to say, since she couldn't move her hand even if she wanted to. "Nick... it's hot."

"I know, Katherine, I know." The coolness moved to her forehead and felt so good that she could have cried.

"Thank you," she whispered.

"This will only hurt a bit," he said, his voice floating over her.

She felt the coolness shift to her wrist, to the center of the throbbing; then a sharp prick at her inner elbow made her gasp.

"No..." She choked and knew that she was crying.

The coolness came back to her forehead again. "I'm sorry, so sorry. I'd never hurt you if I didn't have to, Katherine. Never."

The throbbing in her hand grew with each passing second. "My hand ... what ... ?"

"Shh, lie still. I'll be here. I won't leave you."

The coolness was gentle, so gentle. She moved toward it and felt someone lift her until she was cradled in comfort and softness.

"Let her be all right," she heard Nick saying softly. "Please, don't let anything happen to Katherine."

Kate snuggled into the comfort of Nick's arms. How could anything happen to her when Nick was holding her like this? She felt safe, really safe. Nick rocked her gently back and forth, and a kiss brushed her cheek. She buried her face in the heat of his chest. "Thank you." She sighed.

Kate drifted up from a gray hole, finally realizing that she was waking up, not floating. When had she fallen asleep? She lay very still. She could remember sitting on the bed, the storm ... Nick. Slowly she opened her eyes to a bedroom filled with soft light, morning light.

Silence, the softness of the bed, the coolness of sheets on bare skin. She turned her head slightly and saw Nick. He was sitting in a wicker chair by the bed, slumped down, with his chin on his chest. He was fast asleep, his hair mussed, his jaw darkened by the shadow of a beard. His clothes looked as if he'd slept in them.

Clothes. That brought Kate instantly wide awake. The sheet. She moved slightly and felt the cotton shift across her bare breasts, a tantalizingly light weight on her nipples.

Why? She tried to remember. The storm. Hadn't she put on her robe when she stripped off her wet clothes? She closed her eyes for a moment, then tried to lift her hand to touch her face.

Something was wrong. Her hand felt heavy and stiff.

Concentrating, she managed to lift it high enough to look at it, and she gasped. Her hand looked twice the size it should be, the palm bright red surrounding a center of dead white. As soon as she moved it, she felt the throbbing. She vaguely remembered it hurting earlier, but it had been dark then, and Nick...

"Katherine."

She heard his voice and, letting her hand drop heavily to her side, she looked to the right and saw Nick pushing himself up, shaking his head as if to clear it of sleep. "You're awake," he said.

"Nick, what...?"

He stood quickly and came to sit on the edge of the bed. Cautiously he reached to touch her cheek with the tips of his fingers. "Shh. Lie still. You're going to be fine, but..."

"I remember the storm, the rain, but my hand...?"

"You touched the vines somehow." Nick gently smoothed her hair back from her face. "Thank goodness Alfredo and I had gotten most of the way back before it started raining, and we were able to give you the antidote in time. I didn't know when you'd hurt yourself. I hoped..." He sighed deeply, and his hand stilled on her cheek. "You'll be fine."

The vines? She remembered. "I fell against them in the storm."

"What were you doing out in the storm?"

"Looking for you." That sounded strange. She licked her dry lips. "You... you were gone so long."

His eyes narrowed. "We had a rough trip."

Kate wanted to ask about new clues, but her strength seemed to be ebbing quickly. She could hardly think at all, and sleep pulled at her, its tug stronger than her ability to keep her eyes open. "You're safe," she mumbled as her eyes fluttered shut.

"Yes, and so are you," he said softly.

"Yes . . . so am I," she whispered just before she fell into a soft gray cloud of slumber.

"You didn't get anything from the stuff I brought up the night of the storm?" Nick asked from where he sat in the chair by the bed.

The writing in the notebook resting on her knees blurred in front of Kate. With a shake of her head she scooted back on the bed, sitting cross-legged and tossing the notebook onto the sheets by her side. "Just what I told you." She tugged at the blouse she wore with her blue shorts. "A bed, I think, a high bed. Maybe it says that pigs are sweet." She laughed softly, a bit nervously, and rubbed her hands on her bare legs. "Maybe the fever scrambled my brains."

"You were awfully hot," Nick said in a low voice.

"I remember being hot and the pain . . ." Her voice trailed off, and she shivered slightly.

Nick exhaled. "Sweet pigs?"

"I would bet it's about a high bed and not pigs."

"So would I."

Kate cast Nick a sidelong look and caught him studying her from under dark lashes. The pale bracelet scar at his wrist seemed more evident with his deeper tan. "Maybe the word with sweet is air. I'm not sure."

"It can't be much longer before we have all the pieces. That last chunk came from a cave well past the others. Alfredo and I stayed in it during the worst of the storm. Santeen mentioned something about another cave farther north, but we couldn't keep going." He slumped lower in the chair. "I think Santeen is right about the valley configuration. It must go to the north quite a way. Maybe that's how the bandits stumbled into the valley in the first place. They might not have known they were in a valley until it was too late and they were lost."

Nick watched Katherine lean back against the headboard. She brought her knees up to her breasts, then circled them with her arms and rested her forehead on them.

Almost a week of rest and being fussed over by Sorrella had brought Katherine's strength back quickly, putting healthy color in her cheeks and returning the clearness to her amber eyes. But during that week Nick hadn't been able to make himself go back down into the valley. He had stayed at the top, watching over her while she healed, as well as struggled to make another part of the puzzle fall into place. He came into bed after she fell asleep each night, and he made sure he was up before she woke in the morning. But during the night he lay by her side while she slept, inordinately aware of the soft rhythm of her breathing just inches away from him.

It seemed impossible for him to banish the vision of how he'd found her when he first got back. He knew he would never forget the jarring fear that had shot through him when he found her unconscious on the bed, a fear that didn't begin to subside until he had settled her under the covers and given her an injection of the antidote, and she'd finally opened her eyes.

That time had seemed like an eternity. She'd stirred, and he'd given in to his need to hold her, to gather her against his chest and simply rock her until she stilled and slept peacefully.

He stood abruptly, the memories of her naked in his arms drawing up a cord in him that left him tight and uncomfortable. "It's late," he said without looking back on his way to the door. "Time for bed."

Kate watched Nick leave.

Had he held her while she had fever? She didn't really know. Had he comforted her, rocking her, easing her pain? Maybe it had been a dream. She could feel a distance between them, the same void that had been evident in Mexico City.

Kate pushed those thoughts aside and made herself get ready for bed. In ten minutes, in the darkened room, she snuggled down under the sheet, and her last thought before she drifted off to sleep was that she should talk to Nick about when he planned to go back down into the valley again.

Instead of a dreamless night, as the others had been since her accident, she began to dream immediately. But she couldn't quite grasp any of her dreams; they flew past, leaving only feelings in their wake.

Nick stayed up until midnight, then changed and went into the darkened bedroom, carefully getting in on his side of the bed. Katherine shifted as he settled; then he heard her sigh softly.

He wondered how she could have worked her way so completely into his life and his thoughts. When he should be concentrating on the puzzle, all he could think of was the way she smiled, or the way she still insisted on wearing her sandals until the last moment before she got into bed. And lying next to her was becoming almost impossible.

He turned away from her and closed his eyes.

Kate's dreams all melted together into a single dream of a stormy night with her looking for Nick. She was running, running, the jungle whipping at her, her lungs about to burst; then the rain came, cold and hard. She tried to get back to the house. Through the rain she saw the lights and ran for them, but Nick was nowhere around.

Kate stood on the porch, alone, scared. She knew Nick was gone. Really gone. She'd known this would happen. That there would be a day when he would no longer exist for her. When he'd be gone. And that knowledge hurt—it hurt more than she had thought possible. Love shouldn't hurt so much. Love? No, but close, so close.

And the pain grew. It spread in her, tearing at her, and she felt the scream come a split second before it echoed in her ears. "Nick! Nick!"

Nick jerked out of a restless sleep, his eyes opening to a room shadowed with the grayness of the morning light.

"Nick!" Katherine screamed into the stillness, and he scrambled across the space that separated them. He reached for her, gathering her into his arms. "Katherine," he soothed as she shuddered against his bare chest. "It's all right, it's all right."

"Please, don't go, don't go," she sobbed, and the anguish in her voice tore at him. "Please," she gasped. "Please, don't leave."

"I'm not leaving," he promised as he buried his face in her hair. "Not yet. Now now."

What he knew should have been an act of compassion on his part wasn't, not with Katherine in his arms like this, all softness and heat. He felt no gradual building of awareness, only a white-hot explosion of passion that almost staggered him. He wanted Katherine. It was that simple. And he'd been long enough denying what his body had sensed almost from the first.

The idea of making love with Katherine, an idea he'd so neatly avoided examining closely since coming back from Mexico City, came to life in him. When she moved closer, he steeled himself and tried to ignore the way his world centered on her at that moment, the way his body responded completely and uncontrollably. Aching heat filled him, and he couldn't stop the low moan that tore from his throat.

"Nick," she whispered, the ripple of her breath running over his skin.

She needed comfort. She needed... *Enough.* He only knew what *he* needed. He had never thought of himself being particularly noble, and he knew right now that he wasn't feeling noble at all.

Kate felt secure in Nick's arms as he eased her back into softness—safe and secure. His lips found hers, and she trembled. This is a dream, she told herself. I can do anything I want and not get hurt.

Nick seemed to be above her when he spoke. "I was so afraid I'd lose you from the fever."

He was afraid. Somehow that pleased her. Now he'll understand how I feel, she thought. How afraid I am of losing him.

"I've wanted to touch you like this for so long," he whispered just above her.

And then he did touch her. "All those nights with you in my bed . . ." *His bed.* That was where she was. The dream began to come into focus for her at the same moment that a finger lightly outlined her lips, then trailed along her jawline to her shoulder. Bare skin on bare skin. Rasping, yet gentle. Kate felt her breath catch. His finger wandered slowly along her collarbone to the pulse at the base of her throat, then downward.

Her nightgown slipped off her shoulder until her breast was exposed to Nick's touch, until his finger traced the fullness there and his hand covered her, supported her, kneaded her, until she felt her soul clench. The response shot through her, claiming her more completely than anything else she had ever experienced in her life. In that instant she became fully aware that she wasn't dreaming. She wasn't safe, she could be hurt, yet she felt a pleasure that knew no bounds.

It took courage to open her eyes, to look up at Nick above her in the soft light of dawn that filtered into the room.

His hand stilled on her when their eyes met. He looked as dazed as she felt, as shocked by the strength of their mutual passion as she was. For a long moment they didn't move. Time stood still, tempting Kate with the illusion of safety for that single frozen heartbeat. Then Nick's fingers moved with exquisite slowness, capturing one sensitive nipple, making it swell and peak, and time began to race.

When Nick dipped his head until his lips took over from his fingers, Kate moaned deeply in her throat, a sound of pleasure so pure that no words could suffice to express it. This felt right. It felt as if it had been a lifetime in coming.

"Katherine?" he murmured, his uneven breathing hot on her damp skin, tightening every nerve ending in her body. His lips trailed fire into the valley between her swelling breasts, then dipped lower to the fluttery movement of her diaphragm at the edge of the light material of her nightgown. She buried her fingers in the rich thickness of his hair and arched toward him.

Logic was blocked, and all Kate knew was her all-consuming need for the man beside her. Did other women react this fiercely, this swiftly, to the touch of a man? She had never felt this way with Michael. Never had she been so aware of her own womanhood as she was at this moment.

Nick lifted his head and looked at her. Hesitantly, Kate touched his face, her fingers sensitive to the slight bristle of a new beard. The fire in his eyes sent awareness slicing through her, and her body shook with a spontaneous tremor. Passion? Desire? No, those words didn't seem adequate to describe what she felt at that moment.

Morning light softened lines and angles, but nothing could soften the reality of the moment, and Kate wondered how they had waited so long. She feared this, yet welcomed it. She knew she shouldn't, yet she did.

Caution had no place in that bed. Kate tugged Nick to her so she could touch his lips with hers. Hunger filled her as surely as the heat and softness that radiated from his body to hers. All she had time to do was breathe, "Yes, Nick, yes," before he came to her.

His mouth claimed hers, and a hundred thousand pleasures that she'd never even guessed existed surged around and through her. Only Nick existed for her, and she knew he would never be erased from her mind, or from her heart. She tasted him, trying to draw him into her being, to lock that taste deep inside her.

So this is what real love feels like, she thought without shock. Love. She couldn't say the word, but she felt it. How simple to slip from almost loving into really feeling it. Kate opened her mouth, welcoming Nick's invasion. Needing it. Wanting it. Loving it.

Nick felt her submission, and with it came an urgent need for him to know everything about her, every part of her, every inch of her being. Yet he doubted that a thousand years would be enough time for him to know all her mysteries. He stroked her skin, pushing aside the last of her clothing as he went, and he claimed her breast again, inordinately pleased that he was the one to hear her moan of pleasure.

Kate didn't even notice that her nightgown was gone, or that Nick was by her side, his hard nakedness pressing a path of fire along her skin. He never left her completely.

With the urgency of lovers denied their joy for a lifetime, they came to each other. Every touch brought new awareness with it, leaving deep bonding in its wake. Kate felt and knew Nick, the strength and power of him. She was joyful that her touch could make him tremble; she felt elated with power. She felt daring and anxious, impatient to know the full measure of joy to be found in loving this man. How miraculous that he had found her and brought her here.

New, all new. Everything. She'd never loved another man, she reasoned with unfailing logic, so how could she have known this heady magic in a man's touch, in a man's desire for her?

Nick moved, and the strength of his arms supported him, holding him above Katherine. Passion made her skin glow, her lips part, her delicate nostrils flare. He wanted to give her all the pleasure he could, to sustain it and extend it, but he felt bereft of patience. The wait had been too long, too hard. Those nights by her side without letting himself reach out for her had taken their toll; his need had been too long denied.

"Now, Katherine, I want you now," he moaned as he looked down into golden eyes that were heavy with the passion he knew was in his own.

"Yes...yes," she breathed. "Please."

"Don't be afraid," he heard himself saying, afraid himself of hurting something so precious, so beautiful.

"I'm not," Kate replied. And she wasn't. She reached for him, drawing him down to her, opening herself to him, and she felt him against her. She felt frantic with need and wildly free, and her hips rose to meet him.

She felt pressure, heat. Then he filled her, and she uttered his name in wonder. Love. And she wanted more, so much more. His groan echoed through her as she wrapped her legs around him, and they lay motionless for only a moment before a rhythm began, a perfect match.

Kate held on to Nick, her fingers pressing into the strength of his shoulders, her body instinctively knowing what to do. She felt herself spinning out of control in the most delicious way, getting closer and closer to the point where two unique people became one. Where spirits melded so there was no separation. And she approached it through a web of pleasure where emotions were incredibly sharp, yet so diffused that they were around her and in her.

Faster and faster she approached the crest of sensation, until there was nothing but flames and joy, then an explosion that took Kate and Nick to a place she had never known existed before, to heights that were dizzying and joy that was overwhelming.

Then slowly, ever so slowly, Kate felt herself begin the downward spiral, and she clung to Nick, trying to fully absorb the shattering experience.

Katherine felt light and delicate, bathed in a wonderful sweet dampness. Nick held her to his side, the dregs of desire still in him, the ashes still flickering with life.

He held her, and neither one spoke.

Kate held the knowledge of her love inside her in much the way that she held on to Nick. Soon there would be time to talk, to share the secret. Soon things would be right. No, perfect. For now, she simply let her body fall into a deliciously sated state where pleasure still tingled through her. The light of the new day filled the room. Dawn. The dawn of so much. Kate spread her hand on the firm muscles of Nick's stomach and closed her eyes.

That gentle peacefulness barely had time to settle over the room before a sharp knock on the bedroom door shattered it.

Sorrella called, "Senhor Nicholas! Hurry! Quick! It is Valdez!"

"Damn lousy timing!" Nick muttered with a grin, then gave Kate a quick, fierce kiss before rolling away from her to get out of bed.

She pushed herself up on her elbows, the sheet clutched to her breasts, and watched him go over to the dresser, his lean body clearly defined in the light of morning. Her breath caught in her chest, and desire for the man came back with amazing strength.

"Just a minute," he called to Sorrella as he stepped into his pants. Then, sparing just a quick glance for Kate, he went to the door and opened it. "What's going on, Sorrella?"

"Valdez, he says to come right now."

"Be right back," Nick tossed over his shoulder as he hurried out of the room after Sorrella.

Kate had time to do little more than scoot back against the headboard and smooth the sheet before she heard Nick running back down the hall toward the bedroom.

He raced into the room, tension etching deep lines on his face. "Valdez said that some men hit a village farther down the line a few days back asking questions about the valley." He rummaged in a drawer and turned with a clean work shirt in his hand. "They tried to hire some locals to bring them here."

Kate couldn't figure out what he was talking about. All she could think of was what had just happened between the two of them. "I don't understand."

"Remember when I told you about the treasure that got sold on the black market, the items that showed up recently in Manaus?" Nick asked as he stood over her while he put on the shirt.

She nodded. "Yes, I remember."

"That's who the men have to be—black-market dealers."

Her heart began to race, and she sat up straighter. "And they're looking for the valley?"

"Yes."

"Where are they now?"

"Valdez doesn't know, except that they have to be close." Nick quickly buttoned the shirt and rolled back the sleeves. "Rondo's been out looking for them, but so far, nothing."

"Nick, they're just dealers, looking to make money."

"And they'll do anything to get it. I've heard about their kind, out for profit at any cost. They don't work inside the law. They don't worry about rules or decency."

"They can't get here."

"They can and they will. It's just a matter of time. What worries me is Alfredo being down in the valley." He tucked in the shirt with quick strokes. At her questioning look he said, "He went back yesterday to make his yearly visit. If the invaders find him off by himself..."

"How could they possibly get past Santeen and the others?"

"If they were sober, no one could get by. But on Alfredo's yearly visit they drink for days on end." Nick ran his fingers through his tousled hair. "If the tribe is alert, they could kill the intruders, but if the intruders have guns, they could massacre the Indians... Alfredo included."

His expression grew grim. "My only hope is that since Alfredo just got there, they'll still be relatively sober. And he knows the land like the back of his hand. He could hide down there forever without being seen... if he has warning."

He rammed his hands into his pockets. "Those men might stumble onto something, make some blind, stupid guess and find everything."

Kate couldn't begin to take everything in. "We have to do something for Alfredo and his people."

Nick studied her from under lowered lashes. "We?"

"*We*. I think it's time for me to see this valley. We can go right now."

"*We* aren't going anywhere. *I'm* going."

"You can't go down alone, and Valdez can't leave Rosa." As his face set with stubborn determination, Kate scrambled to her knees, somehow managing to keep the sheet in front of her. She spoke impulsively as she looked up at him. "If you don't take me, I'll follow you, and I'll probably break my neck."

"The Indians would find you in a second."

"Either way, you wouldn't have your translator anymore."

Kate expected an explosion of anger, not a crooked smile. "So it's threats, is it?"

"No, promises."

With a naturalness that seemed as old as time itself, Nick pulled Kate to him in a strong, smothering hug. With her head cradled to his chest, his voice echoed in her ears. "You aren't strong enough."

"I'm fine."

"It sounds like folly to me."

"I don't care. I'm going this time. I'm not going to stay up here and be scared to death about what could be happening to you . . . to everyone down there."

He moved back to gently frame her face with his hands. "I had no idea what I was getting into when I asked you to come here."

Her whole world centered on Nick at that moment, narrowing until nothing else mattered. "And I had no idea what I was getting into by accepting," she admitted softly. And I had no idea I could love you so much, she added silently.

He stroked a line along her cheekbones. "Determined to come?"

"Yes," she said. She wasn't about to wait at the top to find out if he lived or died. "I'm coming."

Nick wasn't the man she wanted to love. He wasn't that man at all. She stopped herself short. That wasn't entirely true. He had almost made her heart stop when they were together, but she couldn't live with the knowledge that he could put himself in danger on a whim, that he might be gone before she could fully love him. She couldn't.

Sorrella called from another part of the house. "Senhor Nicholas, Valdez calls on the radio again!"

Nick called, "I'll be right there."

"I'm going with you," Kate said.

"You don't know what it's like down there, Katherine."
He held her shoulders. "It can make you sick. You can't
breathe. And Santeen..."

"I'm coming," she said. She wasn't going to be left behind.

"All right," he said and touched her cheek. "Half an
hour, and we'll leave."

Chapter 12

Kate gripped her horse's leather reins, leading the small bay mare along a winding path that hugged the craggy valley wall to her left. Her neck ached from keeping her head down to watch her footing on the steeply angled trail. Her light cotton shirt and jeans were damp and uncomfortable against her flushed skin. The closer they got to the valley floor, the more intense the atmosphere became, with dimmer light and thicker mists.

As they came to another in a series of switchbacks, Kate glanced ahead at Nick. His horse followed him surefootedly, carrying bulging saddlebags and a sleeping roll. But she could see past them to Nick. That was all that counted. She could see the dark sweat stains on his blue work shirt, and the way his hair curled damply against his dark skin. The memories of the early morning hours stayed with her with each step she took.

But her surroundings couldn't be ignored. Nick had often told her how miserable it was down here, and he hadn't been exaggerating. Yet in spite of the discomfort, in spite of the heat and oppressive humidity, the natural beauty was awesome. The lushness of the upper jungle was magnified a hundred times down here. Trees soared upward and out of sight, their leaves perpetually shiny from the drifting mists, their knotted trunks partially obscured by layers of lush creepers and vines. Brilliant blossoms braided through the trees, making their way upward, the way everything seemed to down here.

And over everything were the mists and the ever-present rushing of the waterfalls. Microscopic drops of water hung in the hot air, and the echoes of the crashing water were everywhere.

Kate and Nick had left within an hour of Valdez's call, following a path northward through the jungle until they found the valley entrance and started their descent. They were still climbing down, switching back and forth, their progress effectively hidden by a jungle so thick that it blocked out everything more than ten feet in any direction. Cautiously Kate followed Nick, letting her horse have its head to feel its way downward.

Her impulsive decision to go along had frightened her a bit at first, but now she knew she had done the right thing. Better to be here than up at the top, remembering and worrying. She inhaled the heavy air, filled with the smell of earth, vegetation and dampness, and scanned their surroundings, blinking at the mists that turned her hair into a sleek cap. She had never dreamed that the valley could be like this. Imagination had failed her completely.

Gradually the greens began to fade into a dull grayness, as if everything vital had climbed upward from the spongy bottom, away from the layers of decomposing vegetation. The trees formed a canopy above them, vines twining densely from one to the other to completely shut out the last remnants of sky, turning the day to dusk, bathing them in a cathedral-like gloom.

Finally Nick stopped, and Kate looked up to find him turning to her, his features a blur in the low light. "From here on the path is single file. The horses have to follow. Keep your hands close to your side, and don't talk unless it's necessary. Sound carries down here for remarkable distances, despite the sound of the falls. If the Indians are sober, they'll find us soon enough."

Kate nodded her understanding and asked in a low voice, "Where is Alfredo?"

"To the northwest, probably. He was going to spend most of his time with Santeen, but he was also going to see about those caves farther up the valley."

"Can we ride?"

Nick shook his head, swiping at the moisture that trickled down his temple from the curls that clung to his flushed skin. "Not for a while." He turned to start down again, and it was then that Kate realized they had reached the bottomland. They were walking in boot-deep vegetation, all of it in various states of decay, past deathly gray root systems that clutched at the naked tree trunks, and through mists that brushed lightly across the skin.

A crude path had been hacked through the mass where nothing green survived without the sun, and where no new growth germinated without dying immediately from lack of light. How could people survive if plants couldn't? Kate wondered. She stayed as close to the back of Nick's horse as she could, walking in a straight line.

They paused after a few hours to eat some spicy meat turnovers. After they washed the food down with tepid water from Nick's canteen, he had unexpectedly reached for Kate, hugging her tightly for just a moment. Then, without a word, he'd headed off, leading the way deeper into the valley.

Kate's legs began to ache, and her neck tightened from ducking to avoid getting caught in the vines overhead. No words were spoken. She nervously took in her surroundings, straining to see into the hazy dimness, and she shivered. Her only constant down here was Nick, as much a focal point now as when they had made love hours earlier.

Finally she realized that they were climbing. Her calves began to ache, her back muscles tightened, and she gave up trying to keep her face free of moisture. There was no way to avoid the saturating effect of the mists.

The horses followed docilely behind the two people, and Kate made herself keep up with the pace Nick set. She didn't want to hold him back in any way at all. She pushed herself, ignoring the pain in her side and the burning of her lungs. Suddenly she sensed a change around her. At first she couldn't place it; then she realized that her horse was holding back a bit, and she heard a soft sound that was barely audible over the rushing water. She stopped. "Nick?" she called softly.

He turned, looking back to where she stood by her horse. His face was smeared with sweat, his hair curling crazily, and his voice was low and impatient. "What is it?"

"I thought I heard something, a whistle, maybe. Could it be Alfredo?"

Nick laid a finger on his lips. There was nothing at first; then the sound came, a soft, toneless whistle. "They found us," he breathed as he drew his hand back. "Keep up with me, no matter what happens, and don't stop until I tell you to."

"But . . . ?"

"Do as I say," Nick said. "Please."

Kate nodded immediately, and Nick started off again. The pace was faster now, and she had to struggle to keep up. They passed mammoth trees, then changed direction slightly, wading through piles of rotting leaves that oozed around their boots. The cloying odor of decay seemed to be everywhere.

They merged with another crude pathway, a wider one, this time. Nick kept going, apparently heading toward the whistling. The jungle began to thin, and the sound came in short bursts, making the hairs at the back of Kate's neck prickle uncomfortably. They were being watched.

Nick stopped. He came back to Kate, tied the reins of her horse to the back of his saddle and took her by the hand. He pulled her up to the front with him, then took his horse's reins with his other hand and started off again, with Kate held firmly at his side. She wanted to ask what was happening, but his intently grim expression stopped any questions she might have had.

She simply held tightly to him, to his strength, thankful for the contact while she searched the land around them with her eyes. For a short time the whistling stopped; then it began again, only louder and more shrill. Nick stopped. He kept his hold on Kate as he looked around at the tangled curtain of vegetation. He seemed to her to be waiting for something.

The whistling stopped. Kate turned to look at Nick and caught movement out of the corner of her eye. She turned toward it and barely stifled a gasp when a single man stepped out of the jungle not more than ten feet down the trail.

Tall and skinny, with dark skin pulled tightly over prominent ribs, enlarged joints and a grossly protruding belly, the stranger came silently forward. His only covering consisted of a loincloth, along with several strands of wooden beads that hung around his neck. His long black hair had been braided into thin tendrils that framed his heavily creased face. His tiny black eyes stared at Kate and Nick through the gloom, and she knew that she had finally met Santeen—the headman.

He came within three feet of them, stopped and nodded sharply, his tangled hair bouncing crazily around his face, which had been decorated with smears of orange clay.

"So, he comes," Santeen said in a guttural voice. He stared; then his lips parted in a moist, nearly toothless grin. "Time is long. Santeen is waiting."

Nick's hold on Kate had become numbing. "Santeen, I have come back to see you."

The small black eyes turned to Kate. Even in the poor light, the glitter of appraisal couldn't be hidden. "Female of son?"

"Yes, Santeen, son's female." His voice held deference. "Son's number-one female," Nick added with a trace of emphasis and put his arm around Kate's shoulders. He pulled her tightly against his side. "Number-one female," he repeated.

Kate stood very still, unable to look away from Santeen. He stared at her, then stepped closer. "Son takes female," Santeen mumbled and reached a filthy hand out to Kate, making contact with her chin.

Swallowing hard, Kate endured the poking of her cheek by the old man's sharp finger. She couldn't keep herself from flinching when he touched her shoulder and finally her middle. Eyes wide, she held her breath. There was no sign of kinship that she could find between Alfredo, Sorrella and this filthy man in front of her. It had been so easy to grow fond of the mother and son, to feel a tie with Rosa, to share the joy over the baby that was soon to come. Foolishly, Kate had believed that they were what the bottomland Indians would be. How wrong she had been.

She stared at Santeen. The man was in his original state, untouched by so-called "civilization."

He jabbed Kate sharply in the stomach again. "Son is wise to take a female," he mumbled.

Nick couldn't ease his hold on Katherine. His whole being tingled with the horror of what might happen. "Yes, it is good," he said, hating the tightness in his voice, yet unable to ease it. Why had he let her come? He should have forced her to stay at the compound.

"Cost much for female?" Santeen asked, his hand drawing back to scratch his bloated stomach.

Nick never looked away from Santeen, but he was struck by Katherine's vulnerability. He swallowed his fear. If anything happened to her... Torga's life had been snuffed out because of him. Could he endure it if something happened to Katherine? No. The answer was quite simple. "No, she cost little," he said, hoping that setting a low value on her would dissuade Santeen from feeling obliged to demonstrate his power. "Little cost for son."

"Little?" The tiny eyes glittered.

You don't want her! he wanted to scream at the toothless man. She's made for loving and cherishing, not for being anywhere near you. "We have come for Alfredo, firstborn of Sorrella. He is here to see Santeen."

The old man's eyes never left Kate as he jerked his head northward. "He works away from them."

Nick's stomach knotted. "Them? Who is them?"

Santeen's attention was diverted from Katherine by the question. He smiled slyly, as if cherishing a secret all his own. "Them and hands of fire."

"The Indians spotted the intruders already, and they're armed," Nick said quickly to Katherine in English, his fingers tightening on her shoulder to stop her sudden jerk. "I am going to the large water," he said in dialect to Santeen. "Would I be near 'them'?"

Santeen rubbed his belly. "Find Alfredo and go." He threw back his head and whistled, a long, piercing note. From the thick growth on either side, men emerged onto the trail. About twenty in all, they formed a semicircle around Kate, Nick and Santeen.

A show of strength. Santeen wasn't done yet. Katherine pressed closer to Nick. He could feel her trembling with painful clarity, and he killed an urge to run and keep running until she would be safe from any hurt. "I will find Alfredo and send the other men out of this place."

Santeen shook his head and turned to Katherine. His eyes glittered, a look that Nick had seen once before when Santeen had staked his claim on a horse Nick had brought down to carry supplies. A horse was easy to give, not really missed. He swallowed hard. Santeen saw no difference between an animal and a female. "I will send them out," Nick repeated, trying to draw Santeen's attention.

Santeen poked Katherine sharply in the shoulder, grazing Nick's hand with his broken nail. "Too thin, too thin."

"Yes, she is," Nick agreed tightly. "The men, I will get them out of here."

"I took his horse. It was no good. His female would be no good," Santeen muttered with a guttural laugh to the men standing silently nearby, blocking any avenue of escape. The others laughed, slowly shaking their heads from side to side, making their hair swing crazily back and forth.

You stupid old man, Nick thought with monumental relief. Stupid.

"Go," Santeen said and waved his men away. One by one they melted back into the jungle. "Get Alfredo," Santeen said, his eyes never leaving Katherine. Abruptly, with a wave of his hand, he started to walk away slowly, but Nick didn't breathe until Santeen had disappeared into the heavy growth farther down the trail.

Nick waited without moving, feeling Katherine holding her breath beside him. With a heavy sigh, he looked at her. Her eyes were huge in her pale face. What would he have done if Santeen had wanted her? He didn't have to think twice. Nothing would have kept him from saving her. His single-minded surety that he would have given his own life for her stunned him.

She's a beautiful woman, a woman who gave me more pleasure this morning than I've ever known, he thought. But would he die for her? He had never known anyone he would have died for before. His gaze swept the lines of her face, the pale lips partially opened, the flaring of her finely etched nostrils when she dared to take a breath. She meant more to him than life itself.

Was this love? He didn't know, but he did know that he'd never experienced this sensation with any other woman. He felt awkward and unsure. Soon he would sit down and figure out what this was all about. But not now. Now he had to finish what he had started a year ago.

Kate watched Nick as he let out a low, hissing breath. His skin seemed tinged with gray. She trembled. "What was that all about?"

"A show of strength. It's over."

"Santeen," Kate said softly. "It's hard to believe Sorrella and Alfredo have anything to do with him."

Nick let her go and nodded. "It sure is."

Kate looked around. "How can a person smell like that?"

"They use rancid grease to insulate their skin from the heat and insects. They use mud and clay for body decorations and to hold their hair back from their faces. Add that to drinking and sweating..." He shook his head. "It gets pretty lethal."

"How do you know they've been drinking? Santeen didn't act drunk."

"They know about the intruders, but they haven't done anything. If they had been stone-cold sober, they would have done something at the first sighting." He spoke softly as he scanned the jungle. "Let's get moving before he goes after the intruders to slaughter them."

Kate cringed. "You don't mean that."

"I do." He looked back at her, and Kate saw the truth in his eyes. "Those men deserve what they get."

"And you can't mean *that*, either."

"I have a hard time feeling compassion at times," Nick muttered.

Kate looked around at the still jungle. "I know, but—"

Nick cut her off. "No time to talk. We have to get moving."

Kate dug in. "You aren't going to help them?"

"I can't do a thing for them," Nick said, motioning her back to the horse. "We can ride now."

Kate reached for his arm and felt his muscles tense under her hold. "No, I'm not going to let Santeen slaughter those people. I can't just turn my back and go off like nothing's wrong."

Nick shook off her hold and reached to frame her face with his damp hands. He forced her to look directly into his eyes. "Listen to me, and listen well. Santeen almost took you a few minutes ago. He took a horse of mine when I first came down here, not because he wanted it, but because I had it. I found out later that he cut its throat. He never really wanted it at all. He just wanted to show me who's boss. Do you understand, Katherine?"

"I...I..."

"I won't let anything happen to you. I promise you that, but we have to get going. If Santeen drinks more and decides to show me that he can have whatever he wants..." Kate felt a tremor course through him, and it frightened her. "Get on your horse and stay right behind me."

"The men..." she gasped.

"...will have to take care of themselves. Our safety is all that's important to me right now." He searched her face. "*Now*, Katherine. Get on your horse. I don't want to get caught in the middle if those men happen to be close to here."

Her tongue touched her lips, which were salty with sweat. There was nothing she could do but nod. Nick let her go.

"If anything happens, get off your horse and run. Burrow into the ground cover and stay there until Alfredo or I come to get you. Understand?"

"Yes," she said simply.

Nick untied her horse's reins from his saddle and handed them to her. "Follow me closely," he said and turned away.

They both got onto their mounts and headed off. Kate kept her eyes straight ahead, nudging her horse to keep up with Nick's. The land seemed to be inclining upward, and the roar of the water grew louder. The air, already unbelievably damp and hot, became one with the heat in her body.

After a few minutes rays of pure sunlight cut through the jungle. Vines began to appear at eye level with leaves of yellow green. The light intensified, the ground changed rapidly from yellow to green, and the roots were gone. Runners hugged the ground, massive trunks took on deep color, and as the roar of water became deafening, Nick and Kate emerged into a clearing beside a large pool. And across the frothing green of the surface, Kate saw the falls.

She nudged her horse until it was even with Nick's and craned her head back to look up at the massive wall of water that fell hundreds of feet, giving the illusion of falling from the heavens. Her eyes followed it down to where it crashed into the pool, producing the mists that felt like gentle rain on her skin. The nearby foliage took on a deep, glistening green, and the sun's brilliance all but blinded her eyes. As Kate inhaled, the stench made her stomach lurch. She reached for Nick's arm. "Nick?" she called in a choked voice.

He turned, immediately aware of her problem. "Breathe through your mouth."

"What is it?" she asked.

"Side pools." He motioned to the right, about twenty feet beyond Kate. "They fill from the mist, but they have no drainage, and the water holds rotting vegetation."

Kate looked at the small, irregular bit of water covered with slime, dead insects, leaves and vines, all in varying states of decay. "Why doesn't the main pool look like that?" she asked, raising her voice to be heard over the roar of the falls.

"I haven't a clue. I suppose it must have some sort of drainage, but I've never looked into it. The mysteries of this place are staggering."

Kate didn't question that statement. This entire land staggered her.

Nick touched her arm and pointed past the water to the west. "Let's get going." He nudged his horse onward, and Kate followed.

The jungle thickened again, but not unpleasantly, as it had on the first leg of the trip. Here the sunlight filtered through softly, bathing the emerald-green land in a gentle glow. On occasion Nick used a large knife to clear headroom, but the way seemed easier, less steep, and with less hindrance from the land itself.

Kate's shoulders had begun to ache from controlling the horse, and when Nick stopped, she pulled her horse up behind his. He dismounted and motioned to her to do the same, and as she dropped onto the spongy ground, he whistled softly, a long, low note.

Kate looked around, trying to see the reason for stopping; then she saw movement. A single Indian came out of the trees ahead, his brown body shiny and decorated with dabs of mud and a small loincloth. Black hair fell around strong shoulders, and as he came closer, Nick smiled. "Alfredo, I was hoping it was you following us."

Alfredo? Yes. Kate stared, realizing that the boy had assimilated perfectly into the bottomland. He held one finger to his lips and hurried over.

He stopped a foot away and spoke in a low voice. "Have you seen Santeen?"

"Two hours back. He's out with his men." Nick watched Alfredo. "Did you know about the intruders?"

Alfredo actually smiled. "I saw them this day. The sun came up, and I saw them. They are ahead of here." He motioned north with one hand. "By trees. Those stupid Yardez brothers brought them out here and sent them down by themselves."

"The Yardez brothers?"

"From Mannan's village. They are very stupid." He chuckled at some joke that totally escaped Kate. "They did not know where to take them, but they wanted the money, so they sent them down by the trees. They fell into the pool by the Mother Falls, and they lost their packs."

"Alfredo," Kate interrupted, "Santeen will kill them."

Alfredo shook his head. "No."

"But..."

"The brothers came down when they heard the yells, and they were bitten by things in the water." His smile broadened as he talked. "Fools! They thought they could come here."

Kate tugged on Nick's arm. "Please, tell him..."

"He knows," Nick said, covering her hand with his. "He knows."

"Alfredo knows," the boy said, his smile never lessening.

Kate reverted to English. "Then he doesn't understand. We can't let the men be butchered."

Alfredo frowned at her. "Butchered? What is this?"

Kate tried to keep her voice reasonably calm as she spoke. "They will be killed."

"No, no. I heard them talking. They were like females, yelling and shouting. They will be out of the valley before Santeen decides to kill them."

"Are you sure?" Kate asked.

Alfredo stood straighter. "*Sim*, sure."

She all but collapsed against Nick. "Thank God."

Nick's hand tightened on hers. "I hope they know how lucky they were."

Alfredo looked around. "I must go to Santeen, but I need to tell you about a hole." He pointed north again, and Kate could see the freshness of newly cut trail that angled off to the west. "It is there, with many writings. The trail is made."

Nick hesitated. "I will not have time . . ."

"Go and see," Alfredo said.

Nick looked at Kate, then back to Alfredo. "If I go, will you come back when the sun disappears?"

"*Sim.*"

"We can camp by the small falls."

"When the sun goes." Alfredo nodded.

"You go and tell Santeen that the men are gone, then come to the falls."

Alfredo turned without another word, blending back into the jungle, as elusive as a flash of quicksilver.

Kate turned to mount her horse, but when she looked down, she found Nick beside her. He reached up to cover her hand on the saddle horn with his. "This could be the cave we've been looking for, Katherine."

"I hope so."

He rubbed the back of her hand with his thumb, a comfortingly intimate gesture. It made her wish she could hold on to the joy she'd felt between them at the beginning of this day, but it was gradually being diluted by their experiences in the valley. His thumb moved across her skin, and her memories sprang to life.

"Katherine, I never wanted you to come down here, much less have you spend the night. But we've come too far not to look at the new cave."

She looked into his eyes and didn't hesitate. "Yes, you're right. And we're wasting time."

"Thank you," Nick said softly, then touched his lips to the back of her hand before turning quickly to mount his own horse.

They headed onto the new trail. The noise of the falls began to fade, and filtered sunlight danced on broad leaves. The air became more uncomfortable, more humid. The afternoon sun was heavy in a sky that became more visible all the time. Then the jungle fell away, and a rough granite wall stood in front of the trail, a solid barrier that rose skyward.

After following Nick's instructions to tie her horse alongside his to a low tree limb, Kate followed Nick on foot along the wall on a path littered with runners that had just begun to wilt. Nick stopped and pointed ahead. "That must be it."

Kate hurried to his side and saw something that looked like little more than an irregular opening in the rock, a space barely large enough for one person to crawl through.

"Stay here," Nick ordered as he went to the hole and dropped to his knees, then eased himself into the opening hands first. After hearing nothing for several seconds, Kate stooped to look in. There was a flickering light about ten feet away through the thick darkness. "Come in, but keep low," Nick called in an eerily echoing voice.

Chapter 13

Kate dropped to her knees and slowly started into what seemed to be a low tunnel. The sides and roof were so close that they brushed her hair and shoulders as she crawled toward the light. Just when claustrophobia threatened, the tunnel widened and she emerged into a small cave. Her hands touched cold stone filmed with fine silt. Cautiously, she stood.

In the flickering light of a candle stub set on an outcropping of rock on the wall, she saw a space that looked as if it had been hand-chiseled to make a slanting arch overhead. She looked toward Nick, who had to stoop slightly, and saw that the candlelight cast shadows in the hollows of his cheeks and over his eyes.

She moved to him, speaking in a hushed whisper. "I never pictured the caves like this—like tombs."

"Wait until you see what's here with us." He took a small flashlight out of his hip pocket and played it over the floor at his feet. The light lingered just long enough for Kate to see bones laid in perfect order, the frame of a human being long gone from this world. "And this," Nick said, raising the beam to the wall over the skeleton's head. "More writings."

Kate moved carefully, avoiding any contact with the remains. "Alfredo was right. There are a lot of writings here. And they're more complete than the others." She touched the rough stone with the tip of her finger. "I need to write them down."

Nick shifted the light, then pulled a slip of paper and a pencil stub out of his pocket. He offered them to Kate, and she copied the marks while Nick held the light for her. Finally she handed him the finished copy. "This could be the final site," she said excitedly.

Nick snapped off the light, putting everything back in the safety of his pocket. "How do you know?"

"There's much more to this clue." She frowned at his shadowed face. "It's broken up, but it's clearer. It's about rain, and about parting. I'll have to work on the rest."

Nick motioned to the opening. "Let's get out of here and leave this poor fellow in peace."

Kate hesitated, her eyes drawn to the blurred outline of the skeleton; then she crossed to the opening. Quickly, she crawled out and straightened in air that seemed ten times more offensive than when she had gone into the cave. She brushed at her clothes and turned as Nick came out and straightened to his full height.

"The air in there was clean and fresh. How can that be?" she asked.

He swiped at the grime on his knees. "A vent hole that runs to the top land. It was lucky of the workmen to find it. The other caves had them, too. At least, two did." He started back to the horses, with Kate close behind.

"I don't know how you've managed to come down here so many times."

He stopped by his horse to look at her, his eyes pale in his tanned face. "You do what you have to do," he said simply and swung up into the saddle.

On the way to the small falls where they were going to camp, Kate kept her eyes on Nick. She trembled from the need to make physical contact with him, to touch his hand, to confirm their bond in this hostile place.

Could Nick let go of the need to risk everything? Could he ever lead a life that was safe? Kate had to believe that he could change, just as she knew she had changed since meeting him. She couldn't stand to love a man who didn't value his own life, who would put it on the line for anything. She couldn't endure the idea of a life spent never knowing when she would lose him.

That brought her up short. He'd never promised her anything. He'd never uttered a word about love, about commitment. She had been the one to feel those things.

Stop! Kate told herself, and she was thankful to see Alfredo come out of the jungle as the path swung north. He had a hurried conversation with Nick, then went on in front. They turned east and eventually emerged into a small clearing awash with the rays of the setting sun. A low waterfall to one side ran out of a gash in the valley wall. The rushing sound it made was soft, the air near it cleaner, yet still faintly touched by the odor of decay.

Nick called softly to Alfredo, "Go and see what is happening."

Alfredo nodded and slipped silently away as Nick dismounted. He turned to Kate as she jumped to the ground. "We'll stay here."

Kate looked around the clearing, at the tiny-leafed ground cover, at the huge ferns that rimmed the edges, and the slender trees whose lacy foliage half hid the sky. Pretty. It wasn't a term she'd ever thought she would use for this place. The greens seemed intense, the blooms brilliant and full, and the water looked clean. "Is the water good here?"

Nick shrugged. "You can use it to wash with, but don't drink it." He took the saddlebags off his horse. "It's warm, naturally heated from the sun."

"Thank God for the sun," Kate breathed, lifting her face to drink in its warmth and freshness. "I never thought I'd be so glad to see it again."

Nick spoke close to her right ear. "This place makes you appreciate a great many things."

Kate turned, finding him so close that she could hear every breath he took. Maybe here they could talk and she could understand what was happening. But she didn't have a chance to say anything before he brought everything back into a pragmatic focus.

He reached into his pocket and took out the paper with the new writings on it. "There's still enough light for you to work on this, isn't there?"

She took the paper, feeling the heat and dampness of his body trapped in it. "Yes, there's enough light." She felt her whole being readjust. It wasn't time to talk—not yet.

Late that night Kate lay on her back on the blanket, staring up at the veiled moon in the black sky. Nick lay nearby, separated from her by several feet and the piled saddles. His breathing had been deep and even for a long time. Alfredo sat at the edge of the clearing, with his back against a tree, his head bowed and resting on his bent knees. The sultry night was filled with jungle sounds and the rush of water falling into the pool. Kate watched the stars flicker to life as sleep evaded her.

She shifted, uncomfortable in her clothes despite the fact that she'd had a chance to bathe in the small pond while Nick and Alfredo talked earlier. She tugged at her blouse and went over the riddle again and again. Rain? Water? What could it be? Water was everywhere, in the valley and above. Sweet air? There wasn't any of that down here at all, so maybe that one clue eliminated the bottomland as the resting place of the treasure. A high bed? A place above the others? Could that hint at high land above the valley, or could it hint at the far end of the valley?

She closed her eyes tightly. Maybe the treasure had long since rotted away. She bit her lip, then rubbed her hands across her eyes. It could all be gone. She rolled onto her side and pulled her knees up to her stomach. If there was no treasure, what would Nick do? What would these people do? They'd never have what they needed to survive. There would never be another school nearby.

A school? The idea held great appeal for Kate. She opened her eyes and saw Nick lying with his back to her beyond the saddles. Quickly she rolled onto her other side to keep him out of her sight, so she could concentrate on relaxing. She counted each breath she took. Eventually she felt a lessening of her tension, and gradually she drifted into a light sleep.

She didn't know how long she dozed before the dream came. The tree house, herself, but this time it was in the jungle, high, over the water. Santeen burst into the dream, along with his men, their bodies splashed with brilliant colors. The girl watched them crashing through the jungle, then saw their prey—Nick.

The natives flew through the ugly gray land, impervious to the vines and roots that whipped at them, but Nick stumbled and fell constantly, his face and arms bloodied. He lunged out of the jungle, into the clearing by the great falls, passing under the tree house as if it didn't exist. Kate ached with the need to scream, to help him, but she couldn't move or make a sound.

The stench filled her nose, and her throat and mouth burned. Nick ran for the water, the Indians close behind, and as he stepped into the water, the Indians stopped.

Kate looked for him, but he was gone.

She looked back to the Indians by the pool and saw them on their knees, pointing to the large waterfall. She followed the direction of their outstretched hands and saw only a solid wall of water. No sign of Nick anywhere.

Tears stung her eyes. She didn't want Nick to disappear again. She loved him, and she could never let him go. She felt heavy and lost. Then the giant falls parted like a veil, and Nick was standing behind them on a stone ledge, untouched by the force of the water. Kate called out to him, but he didn't look at her.

She called and called until she felt someone grab her shoulders and shake her. In a flash everything was gone and she knew she was being pulled from both the dream and from sleep. In the light of the moon she blinked her eyes to find Nick over her, holding her shoulders, and his name died on her lips. It was like a replay of the other dream. Were her fears of losing him that great? She knew the answer. Yes.

"Shh, Katherine," he breathed close to her. "Quiet."

Alfredo came up behind him. "What is it?"

"Nothing, Alfredo," Nick said softly. "Go and make sure that Santeen was not disturbed."

Alfredo moved back to blend with the night, and Kate trembled. She reached for Nick and held him tightly, taking deep, gulping breaths. He hadn't gone from her; it had only been another dream, yet her sense of loss didn't diminish. It will be all right. It has to be, she told herself fiercely. *It has to be.*

"What is it?" Nick asked softly, his breath ruffling her hair where his chin rested.

It will be all right, she chanted in her head. The treasure will be found, and Nick will pay his debt. "A . . . a dream," she managed in a choked voice. "A dream," she whispered again, making herself move back from his hold.

He crouched beside her, rocking back on his heels. "Are you all right?"

The dream was still vivid in her mind. "The Indians were after you." She looked into his face, every feature precious to her. She pressed her hands to her thighs and shifted to sit up. She'd changed so much, reached for new things, and Nick was part of that change. But she still hadn't mastered the art of living with fear. She licked her lips nervously. "They were going to hurt you."

Nick laughed softly, a velvety sound on the night air. "That came from meeting Santeen today."

"It was a very vivid dream. You disappeared behind the water at the giant falls. You were hiding behind the water."

"I was hiding? How could I hide behind a waterfall?"

Kate gasped as the last piece of the puzzle fell neatly into place. "That's it, Nick, that's it!"

He touched her lip gently with one finger. "Shh, not so loud. I don't want Santeen coming down here to check on us."

Kate lowered her voice to an intense whisper, her hands clenched on her thighs. "A rising moon, the shadow of a tree, a bed above the others." Her hands began to tremble from excitement and joy. "The robbers were uneducated, but they had a leader. He was the one who thought up this game of leaving clues. He called the waterfalls rain. Behind the shadow on the rain, where the air comes sweet."

"Behind a waterfall?"

Kate nodded. "You've found caves on the southern wall, the eastern wall and the western wall. You never found one on the north wall."

"There isn't a north wall."

"But the valley jogs, doesn't it, the way it does here? A finger of land coming in at an angle?"

"Yes, I suppose so."

"Is there a waterfall in that direction?"

"Alfredo told me about one called Father Falls, near the place where the invaders came into the valley. I've never been near it."

"That has to be the place," she breathed. "The robbers came down that way first, then went back that way to hide the treasure."

Nick rocked back and forth as he concentrated. "There is a tale about the trees in that area." Nick slapped his thigh. "The trees! Alfredo told me that they're different there, tall and narrow, pointing to the sky."

"And their shadows would be obvious where they fall on the water." Kate leaned toward Nick. "The leader might have been crazy at the end, maybe even killing his men and leaving them in lesser caves they must have cut out of the walls themselves. He would save the best for himself, and he wouldn't let go of the treasure even in death."

"But where would his tomb be?"

"The moon rises in the east, behind the trees, and that would make a shadow on the waterfall. Behind the falls, there must be some sort of cave, a cave with a vent." She grinned, her joy staggering. "Behind the water there's a high bed where the air is sweet and the treasure is hidden."

Nick watched her intently. "That's it? No parchments, no maps, just another cave?"

"That's it, Nick. That has to be it." Relief, joy and unparalleled thankfulness rushed through Kate. She touched Nick's hand where it rested on his thigh. "Whatever you're after, that's where it is. You've done everything humanly possible. And now you've succeeded."

His moon-shaded features gave away nothing beyond the growing smile on his lips. "*We* did it, Katherine. We succeeded." The soft words echoed in the night.

"Yes, we did it," she echoed unsteadily.

When he reached for her, she went to him without a word, holding him, loving him with a single-mindedness that almost dazed her. An alien land surrounded them, but he was as familiar to her as if she had known him all her life. The rhythm of his heart matched hers. The scent of him filled her being, and she relished it.

"What would I ever have done without you, Katherine?" he whispered, and his voice echoed through her, uneven with intensity. "It's almost done," he said and drew back to look down into her face. The two of them kneeled together in the silent clearing.

"Thank you," he said and leaned toward her until his lips grazed hers. She felt the fleeting contact in every part of her being.

His hands framed her cheeks, his breath silky on her skin, his face so close to hers that his features blurred in front of her. "Oh, Nick . . ." she managed.

"I held you this morning, yet it seems an eternity ago now." His thumbs moved sensuously along her cheekbones, and he chuckled roughly. "I've got the sneaking suspicion that you're an addiction for me, an important addiction," he said, then bent again to taste her lips, his touch unsteady and searching.

"Important" didn't begin to describe how Kate felt about him. Important? She could survive more easily without air than without this man who touched her in a way she could barely begin to comprehend. She answered the kiss easily, simply, by opening her lips to him.

Kate felt her existence shift and soar. There was none of the gentle swelling of desire that had come with the dream that morning. In the same second that she felt him invade her mouth with his tongue, desire flared and exploded in her. She felt fragmented. Nick deepened the kiss, and his hands lowered to the buttons of her blouse.

One by one the buttons popped open, but the pace was too slow for Kate. She tugged at Nick's shirt, wanting to feel the smooth skin of his back and sides, to feel his chest against her breasts.

Nick took her lead, moving back to quickly stand and strip off his clothes. He tossed them to one side, but never took his eyes off Kate while she removed all hers. The tangled pile of jeans and shirts was pushed to one side, and she looked up at him, not ashamed to kneel in front of Nick in the moonlight. The heat of the jungle was nothing compared to the heat in Kate when Nick came back to face her through the sultry night with mere inches separating them.

He reached out and touched the spot between her breasts, and his finger trembled on her skin. "You almost make me hurt," he groaned.

She knew exactly what he meant. Pain, exquisite pain. When his hand shifted and touched the swelling fullness of her breast, she gasped and moved forward and into his open arms.

Nick held Katherine to him for a long moment, absorbing the way she fit against every angle of his body. Soft against hard, smooth against rough. They knelt together in the clearing, unmoving. Don't rush, don't rush, he told himself, Alfredo will be gone for hours. But his body wouldn't listen to reason when Katherine shifted and her hips moved against him, sending a bolt of pure passion into his loins.

He wanted to take her in a rush, in a searing, heady burs
of raw need, yet he wanted to give her so much more tha
just pleasure. He wanted to touch her, explore her and fin
her warmth. To bring her to a point where her needs wer
every bit as intense as his. He'd never felt like this with
woman before. He'd always been a lover who wanted to give
as much as receive, yet with Katherine he yearned to give he
a part of himself, something that would bind them togethe
more tightly than physical need and desire. And he didn'
want to hurt her.

God, he'd never forgive himself if he hurt her.

Kiss her slowly, and let it happen gently, he told himself
but when his mouth closed over hers and he felt the pres
sure of her hips yearning toward him, hardening him, cau
tion flew to the wind.

The fire spread through his loins, out of control. There
was only this place, this untamed jungle, but it was n
fiercer than what Katherine was doing to his reason, to hi
senses. His mouth urgently tasted her, gaining possession of
her tongue, swirling, falling, finding sweet delights that h
had tasted this morning, yet they felt flawlessly new. Thi
was glory, tempestuous, all-consuming glory.

They fell back onto the blankets together, the sounds of
the jungle all around, yet all Nick heard was their mingled
breathing, and all he felt was the racing of his heart. The
first time had been unbelievably exciting for him, yet even
that paled beside the reality of this moment with Katherine
under him, the invitation in her eyes a heady mixture of
passion and desire.

Nick could smell the wildness of the grass and jungle, but
the sweetness of the woman pinned beneath him was more
potent, more demanding. Passion raced through him, and
with unsteady hands he touched skin as delicate as fine silk,
exposed to the night and to him.

Her breasts were high and firm, their pinkness tempting,
their tips rising, hardening. And his hand went lower, ca
ressing the silken tautness of her stomach, the valley of her
navel. Soft, delicate, riveting. His mouth followed, nib-

ling, teasing, feeling the rippling answer to his demands. He skirted the downy thatch of golden hair, tasted the heat of her inner thighs, then rose again and found her.

Kate whimpered, her world spinning out of control, yet she was securely rooted with this man who showed her delights she'd never experienced before. She heard her own sounds, disjointed and soft, panic and pleasure mingling until Nick framed her hips with his hands and deepened his caress. Kate rose higher and higher, her body arching, her hands clenching until her nails bit into the softness of her palms.

But she didn't want to make this journey alone. "Nick," she gasped. "Please. I . . . I want you, please."

He didn't need another invitation. He moved to join her, sliding over her and finding her moist, hot center. Before Kate could absorb the pleasure of anticipation, he was in her, filling her, claiming her.

Nick felt her quiver and surround him, and he shuddered with an emotion that all but overwhelmed him. Passion? No, this wasn't passion. It went beyond that, yet he couldn't find a word that explained it. When he moved inside Katherine the sensation was so intense that he had to pause to absorb it.

But she wouldn't let him rest. She arched more firmly against him until her legs circled his hips, making his penetration deeper and more exciting for them both. He had her, all of her, and the power he felt swept over him like the wind, wild and full of wonder.

While the jungle throbbed with its own life, Nick found a new life. He lost himself in Katherine, whispering the wonder of her in her ears, telling her with his body how special she was, and she responded until he felt he had touched the secret core of her.

At the last minute before he hurled them both into ecstasy he looked down at her, at her flushed skin, her lips swollen from his kisses. His own pleasure washed over him at the same moment that she tasted heaven, and it was more

complete than he'd thought possible. He barely had time t
utter her name before he flew to the stars with her.

For a long time Kate welcomed Nick's weight over her, hi
ragged breathing in her ears. Then he shifted to his side
pulling her to him, and she cuddled against him, satisfac
tion leaving her sated and drowsy. But she had to ask Nic
one thing.

She spread her hand across his damp, hot chest. "Wil
you come back to the top with me and get Valdez? The
you, Alfredo and Valdez can come back down to look fo
the cave."

For a moment he was very still; then he raised himself o
one elbow to look down at her. His eyes were lost in shadow,
but Kate could see the tightness at his mouth. Gone was th
open gentleness, and she almost mourned its loss. "Ther
isn't time for that," he said.

"There isn't time to protect yourself, to make things
safer?" she asked.

Nick touched her, trailing his finger along her cheek, to
her throat, then down to her breasts. "I need to get this over
with. Alfredo can take you up to the top and—"

"Oh, no, you don't," she gasped. "I won't stay here or
go back up to the compound."

"You can't come," Nick said, sitting back to face her, his
nakedness of no concern to him. "I need to do this, Katherine. And I know that I need to do it alone. You're too
damned important for me to let you come. Alfredo will take
you back to the top."

She put more distance between them, hoping it would
make it easier to say what she needed to. "I can't do that.
I'm afraid of what you'll do to yourself."

"What are you . . . ?"

"You'll kill yourself for something like this treasure.
You'll put your life in jeopardy to do something that ten
other men could do as well and much more safely." She
licked her lips, unnerved to find the taste of Nick there.
"Please, let the others go with you. Let me go with you.

Don't go on alone." She hugged her arms around herself. "You could die!"

"I'm not going to die," he said and moved toward her, but she jerked farther back, afraid of one more touch.

"Do you know what, Nick?" she said through clenched teeth. "I almost hate you for doing this. You're so damned...hot-blooded, so impetuous, always going after the impossible!"

Nick shifted back until his eyes were pools of blackness in the night. "No, I'm paying a debt. Period!"

She reached for her clothes, awkwardly putting them back on without standing. "A debt?" she muttered as she snapped the waistband of her jeans. "Do you have to die yourself to pay it back?" She shook her head sharply as she buttoned her blouse with fingers that felt as if someone else was making them work. "Damn it, another day wouldn't hurt. You could wait..." She stopped when she saw the expression on his face. No, he couldn't wait. She knew it.

"I'm going," he said flatly.

Kate pushed herself to her feet, surprised that her legs would hold her up. "I know. And it doesn't matter that I want you to stay here or take me with you, does it?"

Nick sprang to his feet in one fluid motion. "It matters, but I can't do it." He stooped and picked up his jeans. Silently, he stepped into them, then looked right at her. "If I could, I'd go up with you right now, but I can't." He raked his fingers through his hair. "Don't make me choose." His voice was low and vibrant through the shadows. "And I'm not taking some damned army in to find the treasure! It's up to me, Katherine. I have to do it. I have to finish this myself. Do you think I have some damned death wish?"

"Don't you?" she asked flatly.

She saw his hands clench at his side. "I wish you understood, Katherine."

All she understood was that she'd lost him. She didn't belong here; she never had. And she hated him for that. He was bent on doing this, and everything else be damned. The urge to strike out, to beat her fists against him, to make him see how precious he was, how precious his life was, all but choked her. Finally her hand shot out before she could stop it. Nick didn't even try to avoid the blow. He simply stood there, let it sting across his face, then turned and walked away.

Kate watched, stunned, as Nick dropped down on his blanket, his back to her. Then she slowly sank down to her knees. "Go and do what you have to do," she whispered and held her hands tightly together to stop the tingling in her palm.

The pleasure she'd felt just moments ago had been replaced by pain that seemed to be tearing her into little pieces.

"We'll talk later," Nick said.

Kate shook her head no, but he never turned to see the motion. They wouldn't talk. Talking wouldn't help a bit.

Nick stretched out full length, his hands clasped behind his head. He knew the words that would change everything. Yet he couldn't say them. *I'll stay with you. I'll leave this all up to someone else.* He couldn't say them because then he'd be alive, yet quietly dying inside, because he hadn't finished this.

Stars glinted in the darkness overhead. Stars, hanging alone in space. Space. Infinite. Free. He blinked. He heard Katherine settling behind him, and he closed his eyes. She would understand when he finished with his debt. He'd make her understand. He'd changed. He wasn't the man who'd run the car off the road in Monte Carlo, or the man who'd made a drunken bet. He'd changed. But, no matter what, he had to see this through to the end.

He knew she saw it as folly, impetuous, hot-blooded, foolhardy. She didn't understand. It was the one thing he had to do. The only thing he *could* do.

Chapter 14

The valley to the north was ungiving. Nick trudged on alone; he had left his horse a mile back when the going got too rough. He swiped at the thick growth with his knife, trying to clear a path. He'd left the campsite before dawn, leaving Katherine asleep. He'd stood over her, watching, storing the memory of her gentled by sleep; then he'd headed out alone.

This was something he had to do by himself; he had to finish this on his own. Insects buzzed wildly around him, and the sound of water increased as the humidity grew to a misting rain. Just when he wondered if he could put one foot in front of the other one more time, he broke from the jungle and saw Father Falls.

The valley had grown shallow here, and the falls crashed from a spot near the top of what was apparently a finger of land jutting into the valley. Though they were no more than a hundred feet high, the falls were wider than any of the others and fed a broad expanse of water, more like a lake than a pond. No decaying life-forms marred the surface of the foaming, rippling blue. The air smelled only of dampness, earth and living things.

Nick took three steps to the side of the water. He stared at the blue-white beauty of it and knew he would never have found this without Katherine. Katherine. He had a flashing memory of her, of her softly yielding body under his. *"Stop it!"* he told himself sharply, and headed off again.

He went to the west, looking for the shortest course to the side of the falls. For three hours he cut and hacked his way around the lake, his hands beginning to sting and ache from blisters and cuts. A high bed, sweet air, shadows on the rain. He stopped to stare up at the trees, wishing he had come last night. He looked at the treetops, tops that reached almost to the heavens. But eighty years ago? Where would they have been? Where would their shadows have fallen on the rushing water?

He shrugged off his backpack, dropped it to the ground and sat on it, his arms around his bent knees. What had he heard about the trees here? He tried to remember. They were slow-growing, but that didn't help him figure out how many feet a year they grew. He frowned at the water, then at the trees, at their spearlike tops that pointed into the blueness of the sky.

His gaze went back to the water. Halfway up the fall, a definite line could be seen, a darker shade of blue, a band maybe twenty or thirty feet wide. He stood to stare at it. Darker? Why? Could there be something back there? A cave? He reached for his pack, pushed his arms through the straps and headed off.

The sun was straight up in the sky when Nick reached the granite promontory where the falls originated. He hacked at the thick growth of young plants and pushed through trees that grew so tightly together that he had to ease his body sideways between their trunks. Finally his hands touched the roughness of the wall, and he turned east, looking for something, but not knowing what it would be until he saw it.

Minutes passed, shifting into an hour, then another hour. He moved slowly, impeded by the jungle. God, let it be here, he prayed over and over again. His hands touched the granite walls, and then he stumbled when his hand touched nothing. He fell sideways, certain he would hit the wall, but he didn't. He plunged through the curtain of vines and leaves, then fell awkwardly onto a shelf that angled upward toward the falls.

He sat on the hard stone, the path in front blocked by years of debris, but he knew he'd found his goal. A natural ledge angled upward behind the falls.

The secret place.

He climbed again, pushing and shoving at the debris to clear a path, the water coming closer all the time. Finally, the falls were to his right, the water a rushing echo all around, shutting out all sounds, including his own breathing. It was strange to be behind so much water and not get wet, to walk in the shadows behind the veil of rain and be on solid ground. He kept climbing; then he looked up, took one last step and found himself in the largest cave he'd ever seen.

Behind the water there was a hollow space twenty feet high and maybe fifty feet wide, and at least fifty feet deep, going back into a tapered area that dropped away into the shadows. Nick steadied himself on the rough ground and saw what he'd been looking for all along.

On one wall a bed of stones had been fashioned, and there were bones lying on it. At the head, a gold fan inlaid with precious stones had been hung on the rough wall; along the sides and foot of the bed boxes of wood in various states of decomposition spilled treasure onto the stone floor.

Nick stared at the stunning display and slowly sank to the ground. Sitting on the cold stone, behind the wall of water, he looked at what he'd risked his life for. Gold, precious stones, silver. This is it, he told himself. This is what I've risked everything for. He blinked rapidly, then covered his face with his hands.

It should have felt better than this. It should have given him joy unbounded. Instead, he felt empty. For a flashing moment he thought of Katherine. She'd been right all along. He could have waited another day. Nothing was important enough to die for here. And he'd left her feeling hurt, fearing for his safety, and angry. He'd gone about this all wrong.

He lowered his hands, got up, crossed the uneven floor and slowly, with deliberate movements, began to inspect the treasure. The debt would be paid in full very soon now.

Kate stood alone at the window of her father's study, staring out at the campus, which was deserted for the Thanksgiving holiday. The moon made strange shadows as it cast its light through the leafless trees, and the old lecture hall across the way was blurred and softened by the night. The new construction beyond the older buildings glinted with moonlight caught on exposed metal and structural supports. Kate rubbed the back of her neck, her hair still only long enough to curl softly against her skin, and turned back to the room.

The overhead light drenched the space with warmth, touching the mellow wood of the desk and mantel with a rich glow. Kate was surrounded by the familiar, by the safe, by the things she had grown up with, yet she felt detached. Her eyes were shadowed, and her mouth felt tight. Despite her lingering tan, she looked at her reflection and saw a paleness there, her freckles vivid across her nose. She shrugged. She was a different person than the one who had gone off with Nick last summer.

She crossed the silent room and dropped into one of the leather chairs by the crackling fire. She felt the heat through her well-worn jeans and pale yellow sweater. But she didn't feel warm. Since the morning when she'd woken from a fitful sleep in the clearing, she had changed. Nick had been gone. There had been no goodbyes, no moment of separation. He had left while she slept. Alfredo had been the one to answer her call.

"Senhor Nicholas is gone," he had said in answer to her question.

"Where, Alfredo? Where?"

"Gone. He said he will find what he wants over there." He had lifted a hand to point northward. "He will get what he wants."

"Why didn't you go with him?" she had demanded nervously.

Alfredo had shaken his head, and his eyes had grown larger. "Alfredo could not go. He told me to stay with the female."

"He went alone," she'd said, hoping her fear didn't show. "Bring me my horse," she'd said as she began rolling up her blanket. "We'll go and help."

"No."

"What?"

Alfredo had held out a piece of paper. "Senhor Nicholas left this."

Kate reached for the paper and opened it to Nick's hurried scrawl. *Katherine: Alfredo can take you up safely, then come back to help. Don't worry about me. I'll survive. When I get back up we'll talk. Nick.*

While her eyes took in the words, Alfredo had said, "He told me to take Katreen back where it is safe."

Kate had looked into his clay-smeared face. Safe? How accurate that word had been. She had stayed in the clearing for an hour, sitting alone, then finally made herself leave with Alfredo. At the compound she'd had Sorrella contact Valdez, and when the bald man came early the next day, Kate had left the compound. She had known she couldn't stay. She'd had to go back to her own world.

Now she tucked her feet under her and, with her cheek pressed to the warmth of the leather, stared into the fire. Her father had been pleased to find her at the door two months ago. How simple it had been to tell him the project was over and done, completed successfully. Now all she had to do was prepare for her start on her degree in the spring.

There had been no calls and only one contact from Nick—a check signed by a secretary with Dantry International. Kate trusted that eventually Nick would become a memory, a stranger she remembered, but didn't yearn for.

She turned as the study doors opened. Her father strode into the room and turned on the television. "Kate, I just heard something you might be interested in," he said.

"What?" she asked.

"Shh," he said as he stood back. "It's the next story."

So suddenly that it took her breath away, Nick's image filled the screen.

"Nicholas Dantry is our guest this evening," the announcer said. The picture changed to show a dapper little man in a black suit facing Nick across a small desk.

"Mr. Dantry," the little man said to the camera, "has just returned from Brazil, where he made an announcement three weeks ago, through the Brazilian government, of a unique find in a valley near the Amazon. Little has been known of the nature of that find until now." He turned to Nick. "It's a pleasure to have you with us this evening, a real pleasure."

Nick nodded as the camera shifted back to him. "It's a pleasure for me to be here to talk about something that is very important to me."

"Yes, Mr. Dantry, why don't you fill our viewers in on your project and what's been happening in Brazil?"

Nick shifted, settling into his chair, looking completely in control. "It's true that I've been working in a valley in Brazil, but I would prefer not to pinpoint the location, in order to protect the area and the people who live there."

"Of course. What we are interested in is the nature of this find of yours. That and what is to be done with it?"

Nick began talking, telling the same story to the world that he had told to Kate months ago, about the robberies, the hidden treasure and the black-market dealers. Then he spoke of new things. A large waterfall, a cave behind it, and the treasures lying beside the raised deathbed. He finished with, "And the value of these pieces has been estimated and put in trust for the people of the valley. Next year the government is planning a movable exhibition of the best pieces to be shown around the world."

"Why are you giving out the information now?"

"The time is right. Everything is settled and in order."

Kate couldn't take her eyes off Nick, and she realized that what she felt for him hadn't lessened at all. She had heard the news, two weeks after her return, that he had found a "treasure." The reports had been little more than speculation, but she had known that Nick had gotten what he wanted.

Now he was on television talking about a cave hidden behind a waterfall, about a skeleton lying on a raised bed surrounded by wealth plundered by long-ago robbers. The moderator asked questions and Nick went on to talk about bringing the treasure out on horseback with the help of an Indian boy, about wealth that would preserve a culture and a people.

When the interviewer said something she didn't catch and Nick laughed, she tightened. His teeth flashed, his eyes crinkled at the corners, and Kate decided she'd had enough. She stood, turned off the television and looked at her father. "That's all in the past. I'm happy for him, but it doesn't have a lot to do with me now."

Jon shook his head. "I don't see why you aren't up there with him, sharing in this excitement and the honors."

Her father would never understand how much she had shared, how deep her joy for Nick went. Or how deep the pain was that had settled in her being. "It's all his, Dad. It's all for him."

"I've been waiting for you to tell me what happened down there."

She tensed. "Pardon me?"

"You never said much about what you did in Brazil. Why?"

"There wasn't much to say."

"I received a letter from Mr. Dantry yesterday."

Her hand curled into a fist. "You what?"

"Received a letter from the man. A short note, actually. He told me that he could never have completed his work without you." He looked questioningly at her. "You never told me that you were sick while you were down there."

She felt decidedly unsteady for a moment; then things settled back into place with a thud. "I . . . I got an infection, but it wasn't serious. Why didn't you tell me about this letter before?"

"I meant to, but I didn't have a chance. The letter was postmarked Mexico City. Didn't you know he was there?"

How could she tell her father that she didn't know a thing about Nick's life now? "We haven't kept in touch." She clasped her hands tightly together in front of her. "I guess he's in Mexico City to . . . to race or something. He's off on another . . . challenge. Something exciting."

"How about you? Did you have enough excitement down there?" he asked.

Kate nodded, unable to lie about what she was quite certain would be the high point of her life. "I have to see to something," she mumbled and half ran out of the room.

Her father watched her go before flipping on the television again. Nick was still talking. " . . . to start a school near the valley to replace the one that had to close down a few years back. A school there will mean a lot to everyone involved." He smiled. "Money can't buy happiness, but it can expedite what has to be done . . . what should be done."

The fog came silently, touching the objects in its path, then swallowing them up in a soft blanket of gray. Kate walked aimlessly around the empty campus, her footsteps soundless on the cobbled walkway.

She pushed her hands into her jacket pockets, hunched her shoulders into the chill and kept her eyes down. She passed the new construction, scuffed at the damp clumps of dirt that had been scattered on the sidewalk and kept going. There was no one around. Even her father had left for San Francisco to visit friends. Kate had stayed behind, but tonight she had found herself unable to stay in the empty house alone. As she walked on, the fog seemed almost friendly, surrounding her, cushioning her from the outside world.

She stopped at the old lecture hall and looked up at the softly lit entrance. Someone had hand-lettered a sign by the locked door: *For a real adventure, go see our new classrooms across the campus.* Kate blinked rapidly. A real adventure? She doubted that the writer knew what he was talking about.

She huddled in her coat, cold despite the heavy corduroy jacket and beige wool slacks. Whistling tunelessly under her breath as she turned toward home, she kept her eyes down. She never even saw the shadowy man coming in her direction from the house.

He stopped on the path, bracing himself for the inevitable collision and doing nothing to stop it. His hands stayed in the pockets of the black trench coat he wore, his long legs spread for balance as he waited. Kate ran right into his chest, the force of the impact thrusting her backward.

The scream on her lips died when she looked up into the shadowed face over her. Nick. For a second she hoped that he was an illusion, a figment of her overactive imagination, but it was no illusion standing in front of her, solid and silent, blocking the path to her front door—and safety.

Chapter 15

Kate had deliberately refused to think about meeting Nick again. She hadn't planned on it, so she was far from prepared for the shock and the overwhelming feelings of love and fear that filled her at that moment. The fear she could deal with, but the love was something else again. It hadn't lessened even a little bit.

"Katherine," Nick said, the sound of her name as deep, smooth and painfully familiar as the foggy night air.

While she stared at him, her voice came out as a tight imitation of her normal tone. "What are you doing here?"

"Trying to find you."

She moved back half a pace, trying to achieve safety through distance. "Why?"

"I'm trying to sort out my life, to tie up loose ends." His presence overwhelmed her, even out in the open. "That meant coming to see you."

Her stomach knotted painfully. "Why?" she repeated.

He didn't answer, only motioned toward the house. "I'm not used to the cold and fog. Can we go inside?"

That was the last thing Kate wanted—to be alone with him in the confines of the house. At least out here she could move; she could use the shadows for protection. "I was out for a walk. I don't want to go in just yet."

He didn't mention that she had obviously been on her way back. "All right. Can I walk with you?"

"If you like," she said, turning to head back to the broad path around the quadrangle. Nick fell into step at her side, but he didn't talk. She walked quickly, but Nick stayed with her. Let him go away, please, she prayed with feeling.

When they reached the lighted entry of the science hall, she stopped and turned toward him. For a moment, in the soft glow from the security lights, it was as if time was being kind, freezing its progress for a moment so she could memorize the image of the man in front of her. His face seemed thinner, more intense in some way, his black hair long enough to curl where it met the turned-up collar of his well-cut trench coat. This could have been that first night when Nick came to see her—but it wasn't. Time didn't go backward.

Nick was talking, saying words Kate didn't hear at all. "Pardon me?" she had to ask.

"Haven't you had enough walking for one evening?"

She had to keep going. "No, I enjoy it."

"All right, have it your way, but can we keep it down to a slow jog?"

Kate looked at him, momentarily overcome with gratitude that he was there and in one piece. She wouldn't think about the nights when she'd barely slept waiting for word that he was all right. Turning, she set off at a slower pace. Her nerves began to ease a bit, and her breathing steadied. The shock of Nick's appearance seemed to be lessening.

"Why did you leave the valley like that?" he asked abruptly, breaking the silence.

Kate kept going. "It was time for me to go—to get back to the real world."

"You didn't stay for the end, for the victory."

She pushed her hands deeper in her pockets and shrugged without missing a step. "For me, victory was when I figured out the last clue." Her eyes darted to Nick, his profile a blur in the fog. Her victory had been her ability to walk away and come back here. "What loose ends are you tying up?"

He didn't answer the question but instead said something that threw her off balance. "Your father invited me here for a visit."

That stopped her, and she turned to face him. With the lights at his back, his expression was hidden. "He knew you were coming tonight?" she asked in a tight voice.

"No, he didn't. I didn't know when I could get away. He said to come any time I could."

"You should have called first to make sure he was here to see you," she said bluntly.

"It wasn't your father I needed to see. It was you," he said softly. "I needed to find out why you came home without waiting to talk things over with me."

Her nails dug into the palms of her hands, hidden in her pockets. "I . . . I thought you would understand."

"Well, I didn't," he said, moving closer and reaching out. Afraid he would touch her, Kate moved back awkwardly. His hand fell, and though he kept his voice low, his words echoed in the fog-shrouded night. "I couldn't do what you asked, not then. I had to do it . . . alone. I had to."

Kate recognized the truth of that statement, and sadness made her voice flat. "I know that. That's why I had to leave, why I had to come back here . . . where I belong."

He turned away from her and crossed to a stone bench set on the cobbles by the edge of the grass. He dropped down facing Kate, his shadowy eyes still on her. He didn't speak. He made no attempt to bridge the awkward silence.

Kate kept the distance between them intact, shifting from foot to foot and feeling sick from confusion. She'd been stupid to think time and space would heal her, would make things right again. "The Indians," Kate managed, filling the void with the sound of her voice. "Did the money from the treasure bring them everything they needed?"

Nick sat straighter, raked his fingers through his hair and sighed. "It will—eventually. That's part of the reason I've been so tied up. There's been so much to do." His gaze pinned her. "Does all this matter to you?"

"Of course. I love Sorrella and Alfredo...and the others, too. I wanted so badly to help them."

"If that's true—why did you run?" He shook his head. "You could have been completely wrong in your translation."

She couldn't admit to him that she had lived with that uncertainty until she heard about his success. "I wasn't, though," she said flatly.

"No, you weren't. Everything was the way you said it would be." His broad shoulders moved sharply under the dark coat. "You were right. You did a wonderful job."

"And you...?" Kate asked, trying to keep her voice even. "Did you get what you were looking for?"

"I got a great deal more," he responded in a low voice.

"How are Sorrella and Alfredo?"

"Very happy, very thankful."

"I'm glad. They're special to me. I thought of writing, but I know Sorrella wouldn't be able to read it very well. And Rosa..." How often had she thought of the girl and of the child she had been carrying? "I've thought so much about her. How is she doing with the baby?"

Even through the darkness, Kate could make out the frown on Nick's face. "There was no way you could know that Rosa would go into labor while Valdez was gone, flying you to Manaus."

Shock tingled through Kate, and she ran to Nick. All she'd thought of that morning was herself and getting away. Now she stood stiffly in front of him and had to swallow twice before being able to speak. "No, she...she's all right, isn't she? I never even thought...I never thought about anything happening. Oh, God, if anything..."

Nick held up a hand. "She's fine, but she had a hard time."

"Nick ... the baby?"

"A healthy little girl." Nick stood to face Kate. "Valdez wanted a boy, but I think he's thrilled with the baby. They called her Katherine."

Tears welled up in her eyes, and she wiped them away quickly. Emotion blurred her voice. "Katherine?"

"Katherine for you, and Sorrella for a second name, because Sorrella was midwife."

There had been no tears since she left the valley, but now they came silently. "Thank goodness they're all right," Kate said. "I've wanted to see them, to talk to them again, to..." She stopped on a gulp when Nick lifted his hand and brushed his knuckles across her cheek, the touch warm on her damp skin.

"I knew that you cared about them very much." No sarcasm, no teasing tainted his words. He motioned to one of the lamps that framed the silent quadrangle. "Come into the light for a moment."

"Why?"

"I have something for you." He reached into an inside coat pocket and held out a tiny box. "An early Christmas present, if you like, or a bonus for a job well done."

"I don't want anything, Nick," Kate said, staring at the box that was dwarfed by his hand.

"It's a remembrance."

"No, I ..."

"A remembrance, Katherine. Take it."

When she didn't move, he lifted her hand, turned it over and set the box on her palm. Its weight was nothing. He let her go, and she lifted the lid, saw something catch the light and looked down at a tiny silver cross inset with diamonds. "It's beautiful," she said.

Nick came closer, his voice near her ear. "I wanted you to have something from the treasure."

Kate lifted the chain, felt the cool metal under her fingertips and studied the cross as it twirled back and forth in the still air. The stones caught the light, shooting fleeting flashes of brilliance in the dark. "I can't take it," she finally said with real regret.

"It's yours. I found it in a box at the man's feet. Coins, jewels, statues—and this."

Kate lowered the cross onto her palm and closed her fingers over it. "If it's part of the treasure, why did the government let you keep it?"

"It's of no special value as an antique, so I bought it from them at fair market value. Money does come in handy at times. And I owe you a great deal more than a simple bauble."

"You don't owe me anything," she said softly. "I got your check. That completed our deal."

"The deal didn't include you changing my life."

"I suppose that finding a treasure would change anyone's life," she said, putting the pendant back in the box. "But I can't take it." She held the box out to Nick.

He didn't move to take it back. "Keep it." He turned to scan the fog-shrouded grounds. "This is a long way from the valley, isn't it?"

"Yes," she said, stuffing the box into her pocket with the intention of giving it back before he left. "A very long way."

"Being here seems like a dream," he said softly.

Kate turned her back to him and closed her eyes.

"Thanks for not following me to the north."

"I didn't have a choice," she muttered. "Alfredo would never have taken me."

"I didn't want you there," he said bluntly.

She spun to face him. "You didn't want me there?" she demanded. "I spent all that time working on your project, and you didn't want me there?"

He shook his head. "That's not it. It was never a question of not sharing success with you. You were too important to me to let you go. That end of the valley is twenty times worse than the south. No wonder the men who stumbled down there fled. It probably scared them to death.

There's more light, more fertility, more insects, and more sickness.''

A lump settled heavily in Kate's chest. How could she go through the rest of her life never knowing if Nick was sick or well, happy or sad—dead or alive? "I'm glad I didn't go," she lied. "And I'm glad that everything turned out so well for you." That statement, at least, was the truth.

Nick touched her shoulder. "Katherine," he said softly, "it seems that every time I come to talk to you, I get off the track completely. That first night we spoke I couldn't keep my thoughts straight. I can't now, either."

Hesitantly, Kate reached to touch his chest, the heavy material of his coat damp under her fingertips. "Why are you here?"

"Did you miss me?" he asked softly.

Kate felt her legs weaken. Miss him? Her life was flat and empty without him. "Oh, yes, I missed you," she admitted.

"Come here," he said softly, and drew her against him.

She pressed her face into the heat at the hollow of his shoulder and stood very still against him. Every place where his body touched hers ached with remembrance. The memories would never be lost to her. She knew that now. There would always be nights when she would awaken from a dream she couldn't remember and reach out for Nick, thinking for that moment that she was back at the compound, sharing his bed.

He slowly made gentle circles on her back. "They're building a school near the valley," he said softly. "I thought you'd like that."

She stepped back, looking up at him, almost afraid to see him this close. "I don't know what to say... how to thank you for what you're doing."

He cradled her face in his hands. "I don't need any more thanks than the look on your face right now."

His touch was warm, and when he bent to touch her lips with his, she didn't dare breathe. The contact could hardly be called a kiss, it was so fleeting, but that didn't stop Kate from experiencing a sudden, swift response that knotted her insides. Nick drew back, his hands slowly dropping to his sides, but she couldn't bear to break the contact, not just yet, and she tentatively touched his chest again.

"I've missed you so much," he murmured unsteadily. "I found the treasure, finished what I had to do, but you weren't there. It was lonely, Katherine, very lonely."

She knew about loneliness. Her hands rose, as if they had a life of their own. She touched his chin and felt the bristling of a new beard along his jawline, then trailed her fingers to his throat, across his racing pulse, then down to the buttons of his coat. Slowly, awkwardly, she fumbled with them and parted the coat to push her hands under the heavy material. Her fingers spread over the soft wool of his pullover, feeling his heat and racing heart. "But you got what you wanted." She shivered. "Everything you wanted."

He bent to bring his face within inches of hers. "No, I didn't," he whispered in a voice rough with intensity.

She trembled and then drew back, deliberately breaking the tenuous connection and clasping her hands tightly behind her back. "What do you want, Nick?"

He was very still, and when he spoke, his voice was low and tight. "I couldn't tell you in the clearing that I loved you. But I did. I loved you then, and I love you now."

Kate shook her head sharply. "No, don't say that." She fought the urge to cover her ears with her hands by hugging her arms tightly around her body. "I . . . I have to go."

"No."

"Don't you understand at all?" she gasped.

"I understand everything...finally." The intensity of his gaze kept her rooted to the spot without the need of any physical restraint. "Stay and hear me out, then go if you still want to."

She didn't have any more energy to fight. Defeat was defeat in any form. "All right."

"One question, and I need the truth."

She nodded mutely.

"Do you love me?"

"Oh, Nick . . ."

"Do you love me?" he repeated without giving an inch.

What could she say? Only the truth. "Yes," she said so softly that she barely heard it herself. "I love you."

Her admission was the final piece of the puzzle to his life. He had come here almost holding his breath, afraid it had been too long, that it would be too late and too much to ask that Katherine could love him. He looked at her, at the tears glistening on her cheeks, and he knew exactly what it had cost her to admit to loving him. His heart swelled in his chest, and he felt vaguely giddy.

It took all his strength to keep from reaching out to touch her. First the words had to be said. "When I came here, when we first met, I was convinced that my life seemed like some crazy cosmic mistake. I had lived instead of Torga. I had beaten the odds. And I had to find the treasure. It was the biggest challenge of my life, the most meaningful."

He had trouble finding the words, but he needed to explain everything to Katherine. "When I met you, it irritated me that you seemed to thrive in this place. I couldn't understand how you could be happy here. I've always seen things in contrasts, blacks and whites, boring and exciting." He paused as something came to him out of nowhere. "My mother always said that gray was created because black and white couldn't be the only shades in this world." Strange that he should remember that now.

"Why are you saying all this?" she asked in an unsteady voice.

Because I finally realized how much I must have hurt you, he almost said. But he stopped himself. "Listen, please," he said simply.

Silence fell between them, until Katherine sighed. "I'm listening," she whispered.

"You walked into my life, and you turned it upside down. You questioned my reasons. You examined my motives. You were there all the time. You understood. You helped. You became a friend, and I'd never had a woman friend before in my life. And it scared me. You weren't the only one who was afraid. I wanted you, I needed you, but I didn't want to do anything to ruin that friendship.''

He gave away his nervousness with an unsteady chuckle. ''I wasn't too good at that, I have to admit. Then you got so sick from the vines, and I was afraid, really afraid, that I'd lose you before I had really known you. And in the bottomland, with Santeen, fear was eating me alive. What if the old man took you? It terrified me.'' The words came, but the cost was enormous. He'd never admitted to fear before—to anyone. ''That was when I began to understand. Oh, I didn't really know right then what was going on, but it was the start.''

Katherine stiffened and withdrew another step, and Nick didn't try to stop her. ''The start of what?'' she asked in an unsteady whisper.

He plunged on. ''There's more before I can explain. I found the treasure. It was right in front of me, and do you know what I was thinking about, the only thing I could think about?''

She shook her head, her eyes wide and questioning.

''You. Were you all right? I wondered. Had you gotten back to the top safely? I left the treasure there and traveled until I finally had to stop. When I got back to the top the next day, you were gone.''

''I don't . . .''

''That's when I understood. If you love someone, you care, you care like hell, and the last thing you want to do is give them pain. I know what you were talking about. When I didn't know what had happened to you, it was like I was dying.'' Words caught in his throat, and his eyes stung. ''God, it was all I could do to get to the village. When Valdez flew back, when I knew you were safely on the flight out of Manaus, it felt as if I could breathe.''

He swallowed against a resurgence of that pain. ''Right then I knew what I was going to do. I went back, brought out the treasure, got everything settled so that it could all be put behind me, and then I came here.''

He'd rehearsed these words over and over again, but they seemed jumbled to him. It was so important to say the right thing, to explain everything, yet he wondered if Katherine understood him at all. She was simply staring at him.

"Katherine, realizing that I loved you enough to change, to put that part of my life behind me, seemed like a real miracle. I'll make a life anywhere, anyway you want to, but it has to be with you. I have to see you every day and know that you're all right. That you're with me. Do you understand?" His words grew rough, yet his emotions were freer than they had ever been in his life.

Kate watched him, listened to his voice growing lower and lower and edged with a wonder that stunned her. "Wh-what do you mean?"

"Katherine, I don't want any other challenge in my life except the challenge of making you happy. I've been such a fool, and the answer was simple. I need you. It's that simple. I need you."

Her breath caught in her throat as her heart leapt. Hesitantly, she reached for him. She had to be sure he was really speaking, really saying those words. "Nick?"

He cradled her damp face in his hands. "Katherine, I finally know where I'm going, what my life is all about and who I am. Will you have me, defects and all? I promise to try to make you happy."

"Oh, Nick," Kate gasped as the full reality of his words hit her. She reached to hold him in her trembling embrace, and she sobbed in relief against his overcoat, "I've changed, too. You aren't the only one, not at all."

He held her back from him, and his face tightened. "What do you mean? You said you love me. You said . . ."

"Oh, I do. I do," she said. "But I've been thinking about leaving here."

He didn't move.

"I was thinking about moving south." Pure joy filled Kate as her world became complete. "To Brazil."

The kiss that came was deep and binding, the sealing of a bond between two people that had been growing since the foggy June night when they had met for the first time.

Nick gently moved her back a bit, but his hands never left her shoulders. "Brazil?" He trembled. "Katherine, I know about this valley and . . ."

"A hole in the ground?" she asked, working at getting her hands under his coat until he gathered her inside with him.

"A regular hole in the ground," he said in a rumbling voice against her cheek. "Will you come there with me? You might find that you like it, and the people. I know they want you back. One of them in particular. It's rumored around the region that a crazy American down there loves you."

Kate looked up to smile at him, and he kissed her fiercely and quickly, then drew back. "Most importantly, Katherine, he wants to make a life with you."

"Do I have to go all the way to Brazil to tell that man that I love him desperately and would follow him to the ends of the earth?" she teased softly.

"I'll get the message to him," he said, his breath catching as Kate continued pushing at his clothes until her hands were under his sweater and on his chest. He shuddered when she found his nipple. "D-do you know what?"

"What?" she asked, delighted at the response she felt under the tips of her fingers.

"Can we be married immediately, then head back to the valley together? You can teach . . ." His voice trailed off as he shuddered.

"Yes," she said. "But what about later, after everything is done down there?"

He drew her to his side to lead the way back to the house. The fog was thicker now, but the chill was completely gone.

"Let's just think about now, about tonight. Where did you say your father was?"

"San Francisco," she said, increasing her pace to keep up with his.

"How long?"

"Until tomorrow."

His hold tightened as his pace grew even faster. "Good."

"Then what?" she pressed, a bit breathless as they approached the house.

"Then I'll buy you a new pair of sandals, and we'll take the first flight out."

Kate fumbled in her pocket for the key, but Nick took it from her and slipped it into the lock. "Valdez will be pleased," he said, his smile flashing as he urged her into the silent house.

"How's that?" she asked as she turned to face him in the small foyer.

Nick looked right, then left. "The bedroom?"

She motioned to the right. "Down the hall, on the left."

He shrugged out of his coat, tossing it onto a chair by the door, then reached for her jacket. At the same time that it landed on top of the overcoat, Nick moved. In one swift movement he had Kate high in his arms and pressed to his heart. "Valdez told me to come after my female. 'Make love to her, and she'll be happy to come back to you.'" He strode purposefully down the dimly lit hall. "Which door?"

"The last one on the left," Kate breathed as Nick carried her into her bedroom. "You can tell Valdez that this female would willingly go anywhere with you... with her impetuous, hot-blooded man."

Nick stopped, pushed the door shut with his foot, then kissed Kate quickly. "All I want right now is for this female to make love with me."

"Such a simple request," she murmured, her lips pressed to his throat.

Nick looked around the small blue-and-white bedroom, then crossed to the twin-sized bed under the windows on the far wall. As he gently set Kate on the blue quilt and lay down by her, he smiled. "Did I ever tell you about this dream I had?"

In the softness of the bed, with Nick at her side, Kate shook her head. "What dream?"

He brushed back the fringe of her hair from her cheek, and she could feel the unsteadiness of his touch. "We were on the beach, on some island, all alone." His hand trailed to her throat, then lower to the V of her white cotton blouse. Slowly, each button slid open as he went on. "We were by the water, under the moon."

Kate felt her breath catch when the blouse parted and Nick's hand found her breast. The lacy covering of her bra did nothing to lessen the effect his touch had on her. "By... by the water?" she managed unsteadily.

"Waves, the night, sand, a full moon," he whispered as his lips trailed fire from her ear to her throat, and his hands pushed her blouse off her shoulders. He tossed the soft material behind him, uncaring where it landed.

Kate quickly helped with the fastener of her bra, sending the piece of lace sailing in the general direction of her blouse. "But there are no waves and no sand here," she whispered. Then she shuddered when Nick began working on the buttons of her jeans. "But it is night," she managed.

Nick chuckled roughly, helping her out of her jeans and panties. "One out of five isn't too bad," he murmured, then stopped, his eyes caressing her with vibrant hunger from head to foot. Every nerve in her body tightened in anticipation, and all her senses were heightened when Nick circled the rosy peak of one nipple with his fingers. "More importantly, I have the woman I want right here with me. No dreams. No make-believe."

His hands kneaded and caressed, until Kate's head lolled back against the pillows and soft moans rippled from her throat.

Nick dipped to taste her breast, and in that moment, when her scent filled every pore of his being and her skin was like hot silk under his lips, he realized what had been denied him since the last time he had lain with Katherine in the jungle bottomland. He couldn't ever get back that lost time, but being with her now, knowing that she loved him the way he loved her, more than compensated for it.

And he wanted all of her. Quickly, he pushed himself back from her, then discarded his clothes. His lips covered her moan of protest at the separation, and his body pressed against hers. "About that dream, Katherine?"

"Mmm?" she moaned as his lips trailed down along her breastbone to her stomach.

"Forget all about it," he said. With no more barriers between them, Nick covered her eager body with his, and knew, for the first time in his life, what it meant to be completely committed to one person.

There was no loss of freedom, no diminishing of himself. Katherine only added to him, only enhanced his world. For a moment he thought of how easy it would have been never to have met her, never to have asked her to go to the valley with him. So many times in his life he could have died and never known there had been a Katherine in this world.

His whole being ached for one fleeting moment as he thought of what might have been; then Katherine reached up for him, drawing him down to her. As she murmured her love for him, he silently offered a prayer of thanks, then loved her.

Epilogue

"Katherine!"

Kate turned, squinting into the glare of the Brazilian sun. Her eyes adjusted, and she could make out Nick striding across the runway, Joshua on his shoulders. The eighteen-month-old toddler held tightly to his father, his tiny hands under Nick's chin to steady himself, his large gray eyes dancing with laughter. Kate stood very still in the doorway of the old airplane hangar, the noise of the schoolchildren at her back, but her son and her husband drawing all her attention.

She smiled, so happy that she wondered how one person could hold so much joy and not burst with it. Turning to look back into the building divided into classrooms by six-foot-high dividers, she spotted Sorrella talking to one of the new teachers by the lower-grade cubicle. "Nick and Joshua are coming. I'll be right back," she said to them, then turned to the brilliance of the day outside.

"Hello, you two," she called, hurrying to meet them halfway between the building and the gates to the play yard. She held out her hands to Joshua, and he fell forward into her arms with complete trust. Kate held him to her in a heartfelt hug.

"Nough, nough," Joshua protested until she finally positioned him securely on her hip. She brushed back his silky auburn hair and smiled at him.

"How are you doing, sweetheart?"

He nodded enthusiastically, pointing with one tiny finger to the hangar. "Cool, cool." He wiggled, trying to get down. "Cool!"

Kate set him on the ground and watched as he ran on chubby legs toward the open doors of the school, his diaper his only covering, except for tiny leather sandals. Sorrella stood at the open doors, watching and waiting until the child got to her; then she swept him up in her arms. With a wave to Kate and Nick, she disappeared into the cool shadows of the interior.

Kate reached for her husband and circled his waist with her arm. "How did it go?" she asked, looking up into his tanned face.

"Santeen still refuses to come up," he said with a shake of his head.

For the more than two years they had lived at the compound, the old chieftain had remained firm. He didn't want to be in the top land. He wanted to stay in his home. "Not even for a while? Not even just long enough for the older ones to see that it's safe to come up?"

"Alfredo and I talked to him for hours, but he's standing firm." Nick stooped to kiss the tip of her nose. "But he did make one concession."

"What's that?" she asked, intrigued that the wily old man would give even a fraction of an inch.

"If you'll come with me to visit him, he'll let you read to him."

Kate pressed her cheek to Nick's chest. "That old schemer." She smiled. "I told him I'd read to him if he came up to the compound. He knows how to make a deal, doesn't he?"

A bell sounded, marking the end of the school day, and Kate watched as the Indian children filed outside, bright papers clutched in their hands. At the door, they fanned out, running off in different directions. Behind them came the older children, teenagers just learning to read and write. She watched a boy who was almost nineteen, one of the few Indians from the bottomland, clutch the same colored paper as the tiny six-year-olds.

"I'll go," Kate said. "If I read to him, he might want to know more."

Nick kissed the top of her head. "Dear heart, if you read to him, he'll listen, he'll be quiet and sit still, but if he takes anything in..."

"Who knows." She sighed. "Miracles have happened before."

"That they have," Nick agreed.

At that moment Kate heard a squeal of delight as Joshua burst out of the building with Alfredo at his heels. Alfredo looked up to smile at Kate and Nick, and when he saw the baby toddling toward them, he waved and ducked back inside.

"What's Joshua going to do when we go to visit Dad next month?" Kate asked. She watched her son stop and drop to his haunches to inspect a piece of string that skittered along the ground, pushed by the slight breeze.

"My firstborn will run around in diapers with mud smeared on his tummy," Nick said with mock disgust.

Kate laughed. "I hope Dad makes concessions for him." The little boy discarded the string and headed toward his parents, his diapered bottom swinging back and forth with each step he took. "What few words he says could come out in English or in dialect. He doesn't seem to sense the difference at all."

"He's like his mother, isn't he?" Nick teased. "We stopped at Rosa's on the way back, and he was listening to little Katherine talk. He kept nodding as if he understood every word. Valdez laughed about it, then took me in to see the new baby."

"He finally got his son. Nicholas. What a lovely name."
Kate grinned. "Good taste."

"I'm flattered," Nick admitted, and she could tell by his
voice that he truly was pleased.

"How was the drive down?"

"The new road makes it seem so easy. It's hard to believe
what it was like before."

"You know, the first time out it scared me," she admitted, watching Joshua stop to inspect one of the tiny trees she
and Sorrella had planted earlier in the week. "Everything
seemed so strange, so alien, yet now it seems like home."

Nick stooped to touch his lips to hers, and Kate savored
the contact until he drew back when Sorrella came out of the
school and walked over to them.

"Sorrella will take Joshua to Rosa's?"

Nick nodded. "Sure." He scooped up his son and handed
him to Sorrella. "See you there later," he said.

The baby giggled and pointed to the old jeep near the
gate; Alfredo was starting the engine. "Go, go," he said as
he bounced in Sorrella's arms.

"Senhor Nicholas?" Sorrella asked, nodding toward the
jeep.

Nick shook his head. "We'll walk back to Rosa's."

Kate waved to her son as he left with Sorrella, then looked
up at Nick, who pulled her to his side. "Now what, husband? You've just talked us into a hot walk back to the village."

"The school. Is it empty?"

Kate nodded. "Yes, everyone's gone." And at that moment the day darkened. With a rushing of wind, the heavens broke and the rain came. Nick and Katherine stood in
the middle of the playground, the dirt rapidly changing to
mud.

"How about making a bet?" Kate asked Nick as the rain
flattened his hair and dripped off his lashes.

"You know I don't bet...."

"I bet I can beat you to the school," she said and broke away from him. With a burst of laughter, she ran through the rain toward the building.

Nick got to her just as she tugged back the door and stepped into the silence. She turned, laughing, as he closed and locked the door behind them, but her humor faltered when she saw the look in his eyes. "You...lost the bet," she said as he pulled her to him.

"And?"

"And you...have to pay." Her voice was getting rougher and more unsteady as Nick calmly began to unbutton her blouse. She held her breath as he peeled the wet material back and dropped it on the nearest desk.

He gently lifted the delicate cross at her neck, then let it drift back against her damp skin. "No, my love, you have to pay." His head lowered, and Kate felt every nerve in her body draw up in the most pleasurable way.

She stared at his bent head. "What kind of bet is that?" she asked.

"My kind. The winner pays."

"How?" she managed, certain that she'd never get used to what Nick could do to her with just a touch.

He looked up at her, his hands cradling the weight of her full breasts, sending a shiver through her in spite of the warmth of the building. "You and I both know that we managed to get a couch for the office, a rarity in this place, and it's got cushions that are relatively soft. I'll make it easy on you...very easy."

Even after all this time with Nick, Kate still felt her face warm at the picture his words suggested. His hands never stilled, and she gasped. "Here?"

"Do you want to wait until we get back to the compound?" he asked in an emotion-roughened voice.

She began to fumble with the buttons on his soaked shirt. "Are you sure the couch is adequate for what you want to do?"

He pulled her to him, capturing her hands between her breasts and his chest. "Is that a challenge?" he asked. "Because you know I thrive on challenges."

*   *   *   *   *

HEATHER GRAHAM POZZESSERE

Shadows on the Nile

CHAPTER 6

Jillian," Alex repeated. "I love you."

He *loved* her. She didn't know which meant more, which touched her more deeply: the husky timbre of his declaration, or the sweet and passionate hunger of his kiss, which was drawing her more and more deeply into a musk-scented world of ecstasy.

She tasted his lips, and his fingers played along the length of her spine, swift and erotic. He breathed in the fragrance of her hair and held her very close to him, and then, when he touched her, it was to remove what remained of her rumpled clothing. He whispered to her as he went, breathing soft fire against every inch of exposed flesh. "Jillian, I love you."

She locked her arms around him, smiling and causing him to stop in his sensual assault. Her eyes were as blue as a clear sky, as honest, and as warm. "Alex, I haven't felt like this since... I've *never* felt like this. Never."

"You've never felt like you're going to, either," he promised her, then proceeded to prove it. His lips fell against the pulse at her throat, while his hands stroked over her breasts, soft and provocative. Then he cupped the full weight of one breast and teased her nipple with his thumb, before circling it with his tongue, the pressure growing hotter and harder. His body shifted against hers, a caress in itself. Her fingers curled into his hair, then into the muscles

of his shoulders, and she began to writhe beneath him, alive
and explosive with sweet sensation.

"Alex..."

He fell to his knees and stripped away the dark bur-
noose, then his shirt, and she smiled, awaiting his return. In
seconds he cast away his trousers, and when he returned to
her, she whispered to him that *he* was the beautiful one. He
laughed raggedly; then his laughter caught in his throat as
she tasted the flesh of his shoulders and chest with fevered
kisses.

The scent of roses surrounded her, along with the sleek
feel of the silken sheets. Soft pillows cosseted her head, but
all she knew was Alex. He made a promise, and he kept it.
She was loved exotically from head to toe, kissed and caressed until she could barely breathe, throbbing and alive
with wanting him. Then she was part of him, or he was part
of her. It made no real difference; they were simply fused
together. She felt that she rode the wind, that she touched
the sun, and she burned with the greatest splendor, reaching to the sky for the stars. And when ecstasy burst through
her, it was the most shattering moment of her life, deep and
erotic, and as magical as the ancient mysteries she had come
to see.

Perhaps, she thought idly later, as he held her close and
stroked her hair, she had discovered the true secret of the
ancients. Love itself was ancient, and a mystery. It could not
be forced, yet it could bloom and grow in the driest desert.

They held each other in silence for a long time; then Jillian touched his cheek and murmured, "You have to admit, you aren't the average Egyptologist."

He exhaled slowly. "I never lied to you about that. I *do*
work for the museum. I was in the special services in the
Marines for several years, and I did some intelligence
work." He hesitated. "John is an agent with a special
branch of the Department of State. Our relations with the
Egyptians are very important."

He rose on one elbow, watching her with a rueful smile.
Drawing a line down her cheek with his finger, he contin-

ued it to the valley between her breasts, and she trembled.
"It's not the best start in the world, is it?" he murmured
wistfully. "The lies. But this is the greatest truth, Jillian.
Every minute meant more than the one before. Falling in
love is so strange. I'm not sure what kind of a bargain I am,
but I'd like to give us a chance, Jillian."

"Alex—"

"Don't!" He pressed a finger against her lips. She felt the
heat and passion in his gaze. "Don't answer me now. Give
me tonight. Please, give me tonight."

She had no power to deny him. He touched her again, and
she marveled at the magic.

He was awake and dressed when she woke up the next
morning. She smiled, drawing the covers around her. He
came over to her, then bent to kiss her on the forehead.
"You'd better get dressed. Achmed Jabbar is coming to see
you."

"Alex?" The call came from outside the tent. Alex responded, asking for a few moments. Jillian flushed and
quickly scrambled into her clothing. When she was dressed,
Alex went to the entrance to invite Achmed in. He wasn't
alone; John was with him.

"We just wanted to let you know that Ali Saud is in cus-
tody and the government will be taking over now. Last night
we went back out and brought him in. It's over, Miss Jacoby, and we're very grateful."

"I'm glad that everything worked out all right," she
murmured, casting Alex a glance that was only slightly re-
proachful.

Achmed cleared his throat, bowed and spoke to her with
dramatic appeal. "Miss Jacoby, you are a fair rose in our
desert. Please, stay with us a while." He reached out a hand
to her. "Please? I will see that you eat well, that you enjoy
fine music, and—"

"And a bath? Please? I'd really love a good bath."

"Ah, surely! With the finest rose oil!" he promised her.
"We shall make a very fine day of it, I assure you."

It was indeed a fascinating day. Jillian drank rich Arabic coffee and sampled goat cheese, as well as delicious breads, dates and fruits. She watched a display of horsemanship and applauded for the men. She laughed with Achmed and John—and with Alex, whom she watched covertly with her heart hammering against her chest. Could it really be forever? For a lifetime?

After a late luncheon of delicious marinated lamb, she had her bath in a steaming tub of hot water, perfumed with attar of roses. She washed away the dirt and sand of the desert, luxuriating in the cleansing steam.

Achmed gave her a stunning emerald silk caftan, softly embroidered in gold, and a pair of jeweled sandals. Once she had dressed in her new clothes, she was anxious to see Alex again.

He was in his tent, lying on the bed, his fingers laced behind his head, staring at the canopy overhead.

He noticed her quickly, though, and rose on one elbow. "Jillian...?"

She walked over to the bed very slowly, and when she reached him, she smiled.

And then she let the caftan fall to the floor.

Night came, and shadows fell. Alex held her close, and Jillian felt her heart take flight again.

"We barely know each other," she reminded him.

"I thought we were fast becoming intimate friends," he protested, his eyes glittering in the dimness. He curled his fingers around hers and grazed his tongue over her flesh. His touch sent a swift river of yearning sweeping through her.

"Alex," she whispered breathlessly.

"Jillian."

"You said not to answer you before. I'm not—I'm not sure what you were asking me. I..."

He released her fingers and pulled her against him, then smiled down at her. "I want you to marry me."

"How can you be so sure?" she asked huskily. "We haven't had much time together."

He kissed her. "My time is your time, love. Whatever time you wish." He smiled, running his palm sensually over the silk sheets beneath him. "Do you like the feel of silk?"

She laughed, smiling curiously, warily. "I love the feel of silk."

"Then let's stay right here for a while. Let's take the time to get to know each other."

She hesitated for a moment. Then she slipped her arms around his neck and pulled him down to her. "I do so love the feel of silk," she assured him solemnly.

Two weeks later they were married. Achmed found them a small church near the Nile. He was there for the wedding, as was John. It was small, but it was very beautiful. Achmed had arranged for wonderful flowers, as well as a champagne reception on a colorful barge out on the river.

Jillian studied the dusky currents, and she shivered. She had longed to come to Egypt, and now she wondered if some instinct had promised her that she might find a modern treasure, as well as the masterpieces of the ancient world. Shadows on the Nile had haunted her; she had been threatened with violence and death.

But the Nile, she thought whimsically, had always been known as the river of life. And, in the end, she had indeed been given life. A new life, with Alex.

A warm, strong arm slipped around her waist. Alex smoothed away the tiny wrinkle in her forehead. "What were you thinking, love?" he asked her softly.

She shook her head, her eyes sparkling and kissed him. "I'm just glad I came to Egypt," she said, smiling.

Then she kissed him again, and they both forgot the conversation entirely as they sailed down the river to their new life—together.

* * * * *

Silhouette Romance™
Legendary Lovers Trilogy

BY DEBBIE MACOMBER....

ONCE UPON A TIME, in a land not so far away, there lived a girl, Debbie Macomber, who grew up dreaming of castles, white knights and princes on fiery steeds. Her family was an ordinary one with a mother and father and one wicked brother, who sold copies of her diary to all the boys in her junior high class.

One day, when Debbie was only nineteen, a handsome electrician drove by in a shiny black convertible. Now Debbie knew a prince when she saw one, and before long they lived in a two-bedroom cottage surrounded by a white picket fence.

As often happens when a damsel fair meets her prince charming, children followed, and soon the two-bedroom cottage became a four-bedroom castle. The kingdom flourished and prospered, and between soccer games and car pools, ballet classes and clarinet lessons, Debbie thought about love and enchantment and the magic of romance.

One day Debbie said, "What this country needs is a good fairy tale." She remembered how well her diary had sold and she dreamed again of castles, white knights and princes on fiery steeds. And so the stories of Cinderella, Beauty and the Beast, and Snow White were reborn....

Look for Debbie Macomber's *Legendary Lovers* trilogy from Silhouette Romance: *Cindy and the Prince* (January, 1988); *Some Kind of Wonderful* (March, 1988); *Almost Paradise* (May, 1988). Don't miss them!

SRT-1

Silhouette Intimate Moments

COMING NEXT MONTH

#233 GUILT BY ASSOCIATION—Marilyn Pappano

When Christopher's brother was arrested for espionage, Christopher lost his friends, his company and his reputation. He left town to straighten out his life, but reporter Shelley Evans tracked him down. Christopher didn't trust Shelley at first, but his quest to prove his innocence gave her time to prove her love.

#234 DÉJÀ VU—Patricia Carro

When Ben disappeared from Lake Cumberland, he left unsolved robberies and a heartbroken Carrie Landrum behind. When he returned, nothing had changed, not the passion—nor the uncertainty. Another crime wave hit town when he arrived, and Carrie was afraid that, once again, she couldn't trust the man she loved.

#235 NOTHING TO HIDE—Irene LeRoy

Anne returned to Noble's Run to keep a promise to her father and found the unexpected: land disputes, mysterious threats—and Rob MacKenzie. He'd been her childhood hero, and now she needed him again—to rescue her from danger and make all her dreams come true.

#236 CONFLICT OF INTEREST—Maura Seger

They were the perfect couple, except for one small thing. David was a reporter, investigating a senator's presidential campaign, and Jo was the candidate's top aide. Even then their growing love might have worked, until David discovered the truth about the senator and the battle lines were drawn.

AVAILABLE THIS MONTH:

ATTRACTIVE, SPACE SAVING BOOK RACK

Display your most prized novels on this handsome and sturdy book rack. The hand-rubbed walnut finish will blend into your library decor with quiet elegance, providing a practical organizer for your favorite hard-or soft-covered books.

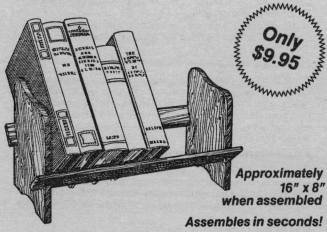

Only $9.95

Approximately 16" x 8" when assembled

Assembles in seconds!

To order, rush your name, address and zip code, along with a check or money order for $10.70* ($9.95 plus 75¢ postage and handling) payable to *Silhouette Books.*

Silhouette Books
Book Rack Offer
901 Fuhrmann Blvd.
P.O. Box 1396
Buffalo, NY 14269-1396

Offer not available in Canada.

BKR-2A

*New York and Iowa residents add appropriate sales tax.

Silhouette Intimate Moments

THIS MONTH
CHECK IN TO
DODD MEMORIAL HOSPITAL!

Not feeling sick, you say? That's all right, because Dodd Memorial isn't your average hospital. At Dodd Memorial you don't need to be a patient—or even a doctor yourself!—to examine the private lives of the doctors and nurses who spend as much time healing broken hearts as they do healing broken bones.

In UNDER SUSPICION (Intimate Moments #229) intern Allison Schuyler and Chief Resident Cruz Gallego strike sparks from the moment they meet, but they end up with a lot more than love on their minds when someone starts stealing drugs—and Allison becomes the main suspect.

In May look for AFTER MIDNIGHT (Intimate Moments #237) and finish the trilogy in July with HEARTBEATS (Intimate Moments #245).

Author Lucy Hamilton is a former medical librarian whose husband is a doctor. Let her check you in to Dodd Memorial—you won't want to check out!

IM229-1R